EIGHT LETTERS IN BETRAYAL

A CROSSWORD PUZZLE COZY MYSTERY

LOUISE FOSTER

OWL CAFE PRESS LLC

ISBN 978-1-955458-20-7

Eight Letters in Betrayal: A Crossword Puzzle Cozy Mystery

Book Cover by Steven Novak

ALL I WANTED WAS SOME CANDY…

What I got was an unidentified murder victim.

No one knew who she was, how she got into the locked storage room, or who killed her.

Though I've solved a few murders in my first year in the field, I usually have a clue to start with. However, within a day, I have multiple missing women with ties to the neighborhood, including my neighbor's granddaughter, who could either be a killer on the lam or the dead woman.

With my precocious twelve-year-old son, a wannabee Sherlock Holmes, and my geriatric landlady rousing the neighborhood to help solve the case, my brain is on overload. The last thing I need is to hear from the overly perky blonde who follows my cases. Unfortunately, she may hold the key that will lead me to the killer.

CONTENTS

1

2 Across; 5 Letters;
Clue: Induce by gift or money.
Answer: Bribe.

"Stop her!" Fear echoed in the woman's scream. "Stop her, now!"

With credit card in hand, my whole body seized. My son, Marcus, and I were in the Miner's Mercantile. As the most complete general store for well over a mile, the place usually had a steady stream of locals.

Two other shoppers froze as I had. Alarmed, I looked for an escaping thief. No one came running through the aisles. Even the coffee klatch tables sat empty.

The next thing I knew a large, callused hand clamped itself over the card reader.

"Hey!" I yelled in the face of the dark-haired man standing at the cash register. Otis Berenger, a co-owner with his wife, Elena, was a husky man who could look straight into my eyes. I'd known him for years.

Elena Berenger ran toward us. Her long, black braid swung behind the medium sized frame. Double doors leading to the back hall where the office was situated, swung wildly behind her. "I *told* you. Stop her!"

Otis looked at me with an apologetic expression. "Sorry, Tracy. I forgot."

Quick witted soul that I am, that's when I realized Elena's cry of alarm was aimed at me. My guilt reflex kicked in for a second then I realized I hadn't done anything.

Marcus, my twelve-year-old son, poked my arm. His straight, black hair hung over his forehead. The dusky skin of his Korean heritage had a soft glow. "Did you steal something?"

My annoyance shot to the red zone. I shook the plastic sack full of candy at the boy. "You picked out the candy to sneak into the movie."

Marcus had indulged in a ten-minute debate to ensure we chose the correct items. Otis snatched the bag out of my hand.

Elena, out of breath, ran up to us. She scowled at her husband, swatting his arm. "I told you!"

"I forgot!" Otis threw his arms out. My sack, held in his fist, would have hit me in the face if I hadn't jerked back.

The Miner's Mercantile reminded me of the general store in my hometown in Kentucky. The store boasted a handful of wooden barrels brimming with candy, a gleaming wooden counter for the soda fountain lined with stools, and walls decorated with memorabilia related to the town's heyday during the 19th century silver strike. At the moment, the nostalgic admiration to a bygone era was lost on me.

Tracy Rae Belden here. Five-nine with gray eyes and short brown hair. A thirty-five-year-old transplant to Langsdale, the resort town three hours north of Las Vegas. The town's population of twenty-five thousand is constantly supplemented with tourists drawn by gourmet restaurants, a world class golf course, and an endless number of boutiques, art galleries, and auction houses.

None of which I could afford even working three jobs: PI, co-owner of a handyman company, and crossword puzzle creator. At the moment, I'd be happy if I could get out of here with four boxes of movie candy.

Marcus had been my foster son for four years. He'd survived on the streets before I caught him stealing my wallet and ran him to ground. His adoption had finally gone through several weeks ago, shortly after my marriage.

Considering my son's attitude, I'd have tossed the boy into a body of water had one been handy. Thankfully, living in the desert made that impossible.

What I needed was Kevin Tanner, my bestie for ten years and my husband of three months to detach himself from the old couple who'd waylaid him on the street.

When the couple asked about a caller who swore they'd won a prize, Kevin waved me onward. My hubby, several years younger than me at twenty-eight, is rumored to be a financial expert. In fact, he's the dis-owned son of an internationally renowned clan of grifters, the Feilens. He parted ways with them ten years ago when his conscience overrode his loyalty. Now, he considered it his duty to help others avoid scam artists.

I didn't think we had a problem with our credit, however, Kevin usually carried cash. All I had was a lone credit card. I'd thrown my purse in the trunk so I wouldn't have to mess with it in the movie.

The bells over the door jingled. Kevin walked in.

A smile spread across my face. The tension left me. My white knight had arrived. All six-foot-one of him. With tousled, black hair and eyes the color of sapphires, the man could be a mistaken for a Greek god. His solid build was the result of clean living and a decade of working construction.

Why he stuck it out with me I'll never know. I met his gaze in a silent plea.

"Tracy Belden." Elena whispered my name in an enigmatic tone. "You're a detective."

The unexpected comment replaced my irritation with wariness. Everyone in the neighborhood knew I worked as a PI for Crawford Investigations. However, an underlying note of fear in her eyes pricked my curiosity.

"Maybe you don't have to pay." Elena's smile reminded me of a snake. She leaned closer. "You like puzzles."

Otis snatched a crossword puzzle book off of a shelf and handed it to her. She waved it in front of my face.

The book was new. I'd been admiring it the day before, especially its boast of puzzles based on countries and cultures around the world. I felt like a fish watching a hook as the bag and the puzzle book danced in front of my eyes.

Elena smiled. "You get the candy and the book free."

Otis cringed. He didn't part with his goods lightly.

The part of me that had spent my adult life scrambling to get by urged caution. Too bad puzzles were my catnip.

Kevin leaned against the counter that ran along the front of the store. With his arms crossed over his well-muscled chest, he glanced at Marcus, who now stood at his father's side. "These two know their audience."

Our son's fist bumped Kevin's. "Word."

I heaved a sigh. Even knowing I was going to regret asking, I couldn't stop myself. "What's your problem?"

Rather than victory, Elena's eyes were filled with worry, which was far more unsettling. "Come with me."

In a quick flurry of movements, Otis thrust the book into the bag and canceled the sale. He and Elena exchanged a look of silent communication. She yelled at Sammy, their teenage employee, who was tending the fruit and vegetable display outside the front of the store. Then, they walked toward the back office.

I favored my two guys with an apologetic look. "We'll miss the movie."

"Movie. Shmovie," Marcus said as he ran after the pair. "This is an adventure."

I watched the boy go with a sense of trepidation. "I'd rather go to a movie."

Kevin put his arm around my shoulders and urged me forward. "Wasn't stopping here your idea?"

"Don't remind me." Kevin and I found Elena, Otis, and Marcus in the back hall. They stood by an office big enough to be a closet in a former life.

Elena stood next to a small wooden desk. Hope mixed with worry in her hazel eyes. Her long black braid lay over her shoulder. "You'll fix this for us."

Her hard tone couldn't hide the fear beneath the stern command.

I squashed my rising curiosity with a hard blow. I was *not* going to be dragged into some sordid mess. Putting out my hands, I fought to forestall an info dump. "If this is a legal issue, I advise you to call the police."

Otis's expression crumpled. His thick lower lip stuck out as if he were about to cry. "There's something in the basement."

He delivered the words in a whisper worthy of a b-grade creature feature. I made a show of looking around at the floor. "What is this, the beginning of a horror movie?"

"The Case of the Monster in the Moat." Marcus added his movie voice over to the mini-drama.

Otis's jaw tightened, but his eyes were pleading. "It stinks. The smell is in the storage room. We don't use it. Too small. Water damage in the back."

"Give her cash." His wife's strident command was accompanied by a hard jab to her husband's arm.

Horror etched itself on his face. The man pulled away as if she had a knife. "I'm not giving her money."

His outraged tone roused my sympathies. I found myself rooting for him. Try to get cold, hard cash out of my hand. See what happens. I caught myself nodding and stopped. I should have walked away. I still could.

With the pit opening at my feet, I tried to withdraw. "Kevin can pay for the candy. We have a movie to go to. I promised our son."

The boy child in question snorted. "Don't drag me into your lame excuses. I want to go monster hunting."

Otis and Elena exchanged a hopeful look. They sensed weakness. The scales were tipping in their favor.

I crossed my arms over my chest. If I was getting roped into this mess, I was upping the ante. "Throw in the latest issue of the graphic novel with the warrior rat and our son will look in your basement."

"I'll go!" Marcus pushed away from the counter. "If you come with me."

Otis scowled. "I don't want the boy."

Kevin's laughter sounded behind me. "Marcus isn't going anywhere."

Elena slapped her hands together. "It's a deal."

Before I could blink, she pushed Kevin aside with a force that belied her smaller stature and disappeared through the swinging doors. She returned in a heartbeat, carrying not one but two issues of the talking rat's adventures. She grabbed the bag from Otis and shoved the comic books inside. The plastic bag swayed back and forth as she thrust it toward me then instantly pulled it away.

Her gaze lit on Marcus. She held the bag full of prizes out to him. "You hold it and wait for your mama here."

Marcus grabbed it, then danced backward. He waved the bag at me.

Elena's clasped hands wound around each other. "There was no smell two days ago."

Her trembling whisper drilled the hook in tighter. She stepped back, evidently trying to distance herself from the whole affair.

Her desperation sent a jolt through my bones. Though my rational side grappled with the siren call, the allure of solving a puzzle intrigued me. "Elena, you need to call the police."

Her jaw tightened and her gaze turned hard. "No police."

"They'll search the place again." Otis's harsh tone mixed with his wife's. "They'll find a reason to close us down."

Breath hissed through my teeth. A visit from a drug-dealing friend two years ago had led to several visits from the narcotics squad. The episode had left a deep distrust of the authorities with the couple.

A feeling of hopelessness swept through me. They'd never willingly call the police.

Otis patted me on the shoulder, subtly pushing me toward the exit sign at the other end of the hallway. "It's probably spoiled food or a dead rat."

Then why don't you go check?

Because we all knew it was neither of those things.

"Bring back a full report." Marcus pointed at me. Then, he shook his head. "We better go with her, Kevin."

"Go watch the store, honey." Elena grabbed my arm and pulled me along at a brisk pace. "There's a small storage room in the basement we don't use."

Despite my better judgment, I took a deep breath. Was there a stench or was it my imagination?

"Go to the back corner of the store. The storeroom door is tucked into the wall. There's a staircase." Elena pushed a key into my hand. She glanced over her shoulder. Otis was gone. "It's Monkey. Tiffie's cat from the hardware store. He sneaks in the corner window. I don't want Tiffie to blame me. I'll pay you a hundred dollars to move the body down the alley."

By the time I deciphered her rapid-fire whisper, she'd spun on her heel and vanished into the store. My heart sank at the thought of Tiffie's cat being dead. The teenager lived on the block and doted on the tabby. Even less did I want to move the body.

Looking over my shoulder, I met Kevin's knowing gaze. The man thinks I have a penchant for adopting strays whether human or animal. Considering the pair of twenty-pound cats we'd *rescued* during a case two months ago he might be right.

Marcus darted around him and snatched the key out of my hand. "Let's go hunt monsters."

"Marcus." Kevin's level tone held a note of warning that couldn't be ignored.

"I won't go in." The boy's high-pitched voice bounced off the walls in the narrow hall. A mischievous grin danced in his eyes. "But she'll need back-up when the monster snatches her and drags her down to oblivion."

Kevin smacked his forehead. "Of course, a witness to her moment of doom. What was I thinking?"

"Thanks, guys." Who needed a movie when Marcus could create his own world-ending scenario? "Be sure to stand back so no blood splatters on you when the monster grabs me."

Marcus ran ahead on the balls of his feet. "Come on. We have to hurry."

"Whatever smells that bad isn't going anywhere." I cringed at the image that produced. I didn't want it to be a dead cat.

Perhaps it was a prank. Except no one in the neighborhood had a grudge against Otis or Elena. Maybe it was a rat. How big did a creature have to be to give off a noticeable stench? A sense of dread skittered up my spine.

A moment later, my hand traced the white smooth wall as I rounded the back corner. The door to the main basement was in the middle of the building. Pallets stacked with boxes of supplies sat within easy reach. Beyond that the alley dead-ended at a six-foot tall privacy fence.

Walking on a few feet, I spun around to face a locked door. Tucked away like this few people would know it was here.

"Our journey begins on the wicked streets of the harsh inner city." Marcus's narration sounded like a noir movie.

I rolled my eyes at his hyperbole.

"The trip to the neighborhood grocer had started innocently enough." The boy continued.

That much was true. How had stocking up on movie candy gone so wrong? I raised my gaze to the scorching blue sky above. Sweat trickled down my spine. Why did I let myself get mixed up in these situations? I held out my hand for the key.

Now that the moment had come, the implications struck me full force. A horrible smell that wasn't there two days ago? I shied away from the worst-case scenario.

What if I walked away? I might be able to convince Kevin, but Marcus would rat me out. Him and his adventures. "You two stay here. I'll handle this."

With all the harsh language and stern looks at my command.

Without giving myself a chance to back down, I opened the door and hurried down the stairs to a landing. A second door, flush with the back wall, greeted me. I jiggled the knob. Locked.

My hand stopped short of inserting the key. This was madness. Before I could back out, my curious brain, which is not my wiser half, unlocked the door and pushed it open to reveal a long, narrow space.

A gag inducing stench swept over me. My overwhelmed brain forced out one thought: this was not a dead cat. Was a noxious smell enough to call 9-1-1?

I gasped as the overhead light hit my eyes. I looked over and saw my hand on the switch. "Anyone here?"

That was stupid. Did I expect an answer? My muscles knotted with tension. Weathered wood covered the walls. Thick dust sat on shelves along the wall. A few decrepit cardboard boxes were stacked along the wall.

A dry wind swept through the open door, hitting me with unexpected power. Climbing up and over my back, the hot, desert air ruffled my hair. Clouds of dust and a horde of flies swirled like small tornadoes. The rancid stench, previously contained, roused like a living beast.

I grimaced and put a hand over my mouth. My eyes watered.

The smart thing would be to leave and call 9-1-1.

That's when my brain told my feet to go forward.

No one ever accused me of being smart.

My gut and I both knew my brain would say anything to find out the truth. That's the way it's wired. It had to know the answer.

When I reached the last set of shelves, I stopped. Last chance to call 9-1-1. But what if the smell *was* a dead cat?

Two small windows high on the wall let in squares of sun. Light shining through a crack showed one latch undone. An animal might have pushed their way in then become trapped.

My hand was still over my mouth. My breath hissed between my fingers. I didn't want to move but I couldn't *not* look. Stepping forward, I faced the corner.

A body lay on the concrete floor. A set of shelves with dented metal boxes on them faced the wall behind the body. The plaster in the corner crumbled with age. Pity filled me at the sight of the figure on the hard floor.

The dark skirt on the figure was stretched tight. Her bare legs were akimbo. One foot was bare. A low-heeled pump sat nearby, perfectly upright. Her jacket sleeve was pulled back showing her discolored forearm.

I grimaced at the swollen purple flesh of the arm lying across the face of the victim. Whether she'd tried to protect herself or if she'd fallen that way, there was no telling. She was on her side, slightly curled.

Dark, dried stains colored the cement floor beneath her head. The hair, pulled back in a chignon, looked dark but with the shadows and the blood it may have been lighter in life.

"Oh, my God." I breathed the heartfelt words into the heavy silence. Then, my mind stepped back from the tragedy. My narrowed gaze scanned the walls and the boxes lining the shelves. No splatter.

One arm covered most of the victim's face. The blood under her skull indicated she'd been struck here. Were the marks on her arm the result of a beating or the passage of time? I reached for my phone to take pictures only to come up empty. My phone was in my purse which I'd thrown in the trunk of the car. What a day not to have my phone. Marcus would never forgive me. I was disappointed in me, too.

The high windows looked too small for someone to squeeze through. So, who locked the door after the woman died?

I crept forward on cat-like feet. Crazy, I know. It was me and a dead woman. And she was definitely dead. I wasn't about to check her pulse. I had to breathe through my mouth. After the first lungful, that wasn't hard to remember.

"TR!" Marcus's high-pitched, impatient bellow almost unbalanced me.

My arms flailed as I fought to stay upright rather than pitch face-first into the body. With a grimace, I gained my feet. "Time to call the police."

I addressed the words to the dead woman. I felt like I should apologize. Though for what I couldn't say. Disturbing her, perhaps? I retreated around the corner.

The doorway leading to the stairs showed a rectangle of bright light. I fought to ignore the invisible thread of obligation that already bound me to the dead woman. Striding forward, I swept the room. Nothing looked out of place.

Don't ask me how I knew since I'd never been in the room before. It was more of an impression. A few seconds later, I blinked as I stepped into the brightly burning heat of the sun.

"It's a body, isn't it?" Marcus straightened. His lip curled. "We smelled it."

I met his gaze and nodded. Then, I met Kevin's somber expression. "I need to call the police."

2

—·—

1 Down; 7 Letters;
Clue: Unveil secrets.
Answer: Divulge.

Fifty-five minutes after discovering the body, Marcus, Kevin, and I were loitering in front of the Mercantile. Marcus had noted the details of the crime in his phone. At least as much as I could tell him.

The homicide detectives and the crime scene techs arrived in short order. Crime scene tape marked off the alley and the back door. Police personnel had taken over the store.

Marcus had spent the last hour talking to several officers he knew. He accosted the ones he didn't know. A few uniformed officers returned him, rather forcibly, to Kevin and me several times with an admonition to constrain the boy.

I've been trying to do that for the last few years to no avail. I told them as much. They were police. Weren't they trained in crowd control? They accused me of not taking the matter seriously. Can you imagine?

Kevin considered the affair a good opportunity for Marcus to work on his people skills. He also knew Marcus was more a force of nature than a twelve-year-old boy. It had taken me years to... well, not tame, but at least wrangle him into cooperating.

When I felt like it.

I just didn't feel like it.

As I studied the growing crowd of gawkers, our boy child darted around the corner of the building on the right. Moving with a deceptive speed, he skittered across the front of the store until he ducked around the far corner.

Before I could blink, an out-of-breath uniformed officer rushed into view. The stocky, white guy had his arms in front of him as if he were about to grab someone.

If Marcus was this man's prey, the guy was sadly outmatched. My peripheral vision caught Kevin's raised brow at the failed effort. I bit my lip against an outburst of laughter.

The officer looked around as if Marcus might appear out of thin air, ready to surrender. His eyes were wide with an almost comical expression of surprise. He looked at me and Kevin. "Did you see that kid? He's yours, right? Do you have him?"

With my hand over my mouth to mask my smile, I fought to look sympathetic and left it to Kevin to answer. He had better control than I did.

Kevin spread out his hands. "He's not with us right now, but he's safe."

The officer's expression darkened and his fists shook.

Evidently, he wasn't concerned with Marcus's safety.

That's our boy.

The man stalked back the way he came. He was barely out of sight before my laughter escaped from behind my hand. I muffled my amusement in Kevin's shoulder. I hope the guy didn't hear me. My laugh isn't a polite ladylike giggle, it's closer to a donkey's bray.

In my defense, a number of uniform officers are familiar with our little rascal. Impressed by his passion to learn their job, they treat him as a younger brother or a mascot. However, some do take offense at his rampant curiosity.

I straightened and wiped the tears away. "Dealing with Marcus will build their character. It's not like we can leave. Detective Wilson insisted he wanted to question us again."

That sounded better than admitting I found Marcus's antics a diversion from thinking about the dead woman. Any distraction was welcome.

"Uh-huh." Kevin eyed me with a knowing look.

He'd known me too long and too well. My hubby could have taken the boy in hand. He'd helped me track down the street urchin after the wallet stealing incident. He'd also helped us find mysteries at used book stores and libraries. Marcus and I had devoured and dissected every novel and short story we could find, looking for and criticizing plot flaws.

With the sun beating down and sweat dripping between my shoulder blades, the air-conditioning in the car would be a paradise, but neither Kevin nor I were about to waste the gas it would take. Besides, that would be a barrier between me and the crime scene.

The store was off limits. However, the neighborhood denizens had caught wind of the drama. Familiar faces ringed the crowd behind the police cordon. I waved to a few.

More than one pair of eyes looked at me with a hint of accusation. My reputation as a magnet for trouble had followed me to Langsdale. I don't know how that happens. I'm sure it's not me.

I studied the crowd. The old cliché about the criminal revisiting the scene of the crime ran through my mind. I subtly nudged Kevin. "You keeping track of faces?"

He didn't deign to answer. Kevin had spent the first eighteen years of his life separating people from their money. Thanks to his family of internationally renowned grifters, Kevin's skills were numerous and varied.

Memorization techniques for license plates, recreating a scene he'd barely viewed, mentally tracking time. The list goes on and on. Early on in our acquaintance, I'd been constantly stunned at the things he could do.

Selling sand in the desert or ice in the arctic was child's play for him. Once Kevin locked his sapphire eyes on someone, his target would walk off a cliff without knowing they'd left solid ground. If not for his morals, and possibly mine, we could have made a fortune.

Of course, if not for his conscience, we never would have met. His family had planned to scam a company I worked for out of several million dollars. When he'd balked, his reward had been a frame for murder. His family is not the forgiving kind. That was my first murder, but not my last, which is where Kevin's talents come in handy.

Among his skills is facial recognition. Grifters have to know who they've met before. It wouldn't look good to be confused when you're trying to convince the mark to hand over millions of dollars. The upshot was that Kevin could track who was in the crowd, including strangers.

With that matter taken care of, I reached for the sack of candy that had cost us our movie and wondered when I could talk to Otis and Elena. "I better fortify myself."

Kevin held out the bag on his fingertips. "Elena and Otis will be the chief suspects."

Being on the same wavelength is why my bud and I were besties for ten years. I felt bad for the couple, but I was on the sidelines. So far.

I should have listened to myself and left when I had the chance, but wanting answers is my curse. Creating crossword puzzles barely pays for my flavored coffee, but I've loved puzzles for as long as I can remember. Once I start one, my brain won't disconnect until the puzzle is solved.

As the questions about the body in the basement multiplied, I was in serious danger of being hooked.

Could I walk away from the dead woman? Would she and the unanswered questions haunt me? "Do you think it's-"

"Yes, it's too late." Kevin spaced his words, deepening his voice. "You're doomed."

His dark tone brought to mind Marcus's imitation of movie voice overs.

I chuckled, though he was probably spot on. An added complication to being involved was knowing the owners. The room had been locked. A quick check when I left the basement showed no overt signs of forced entry. Not that I had my magnifying glass to check for scrapes.

Marcus deplored my lack of planning. Detectives, he told me, should always have the tools of their profession. He was especially upset about the lack of crime scene photos.

What could I say? Unlike my boy child, I didn't seek out cases. Especially not ones without a promise of payment. Which made this situation quite the dilemma.

"Did you hear that?" Kevin grabbed my arm. His voice held a note of mock panic. "I know that yoo-hoo."

Pulled from my thoughts, I heard sing-song notes on the hot air. It reminded me of the call of hunters riding to the hounds. The voice came complete with a British accent.

"Luvs, I'm famished, I am." Mrs. C's lilting voice spoke between puffs for air from the rear of the crowd. "'Tis too hot to walk. Good thing I have an acquaintance who happens to be a cabbie, eh?"

Despite the circumstances, a chuckle escaped my lips. I may have given an unladylike snort. Good thing my mom wasn't around to hear me.

Kevin saluted me with his chocolate candy star before catching it in his mouth. "Marcus's back-up has arrived. Mrs. C is on the job."

Mrs. Alice Colchester, alias Mrs. C, is my landlady. She's also been my self-proclaimed maid for the past nine months. Don't ask me why. I didn't hire her. Therefore, I feel no obligation to pay her.

Her only duties seem to be letting herself into the apartment and making breakfast. She doesn't clean, but honestly, neither do I. The amazing thing is she likes to do laundry.

Her other noteworthy skill is that she has more contacts than MI-6. No matter what profession might be useful in my cases, she has an acquaintance she can contact. The internet has nothing on this woman.

The milling crowd on the left parted like a stream giving way before a rock. Mrs. C's slight, five-foot-six-inch figure appeared in the opening. Her bright blue muumuu, covered with yellow flowers flowed around her. She marched between the battle lines like a general at the scene of battle.

A general wearing gray slippers with cat heads bobbing up and down. Shoes are too confining. However, her collection of slippers rivals most department stores.

On reaching the police barricade, she paused. Cue the trumpets, the queen has arrived. Mrs. C is, in fact, British. She left the isle over fifty years ago to escape a murder accusation. Her past came to light a few months ago when a copycat tried to frame her for another murder.

When she caught sight of me and Kevin, she raised a hand in greeting. "Hello, ducks. So nice to see you here."

As if she hadn't known exactly where we were or what had occurred. This neighborhood was like a small town. News travels fast and Mrs. C is in the thick of it. What she can't spy with her binoculars, her book club and her contacts keeps her apprised of.

Tossing a smile and a wave to the gawkers, she walked around the barricade while the officer looked for guidance.

Kevin and I watched her performance in silence.

When the older woman reached the Great White Beast, she put a hand over her heart. She stopped at Kevin's side and patted the beads of sweat on her upper lip with a white hanky.

"Rather warm, innit?" Her pale green eyes looked completely innocent for showing up. Despite the fact that she'd been too comfortable to drive to the movies with us. "Bit of a do, eh? Any on dit I should know of?"

Kevin took her arrival in stride. He jerked his head at me. "Belden discovered another body."

Mrs. C flipped her hanky. "Of course, she did. Dear girl has a talent for it."

She sounded a bit pleased. I would have protested, but I have found a few bodies over the past several months. "I was dragged into it. Maybe not against my will, but I was set up."

Mrs. C's eyes widened at Kevin's confirming nod. "Otis and Elena? What have they gotten themselves into?"

My antenna went on high alert. "Anything shady in their backgrounds? They've been here... ten, twelve years?"

I moved into my current apartment and met Mrs. C eight years ago.

Mrs. C looked thoughtful. "Eleven years. Married fourteen years. Elena was a widow of three months when she wed Otis. Her husband left her several years before that. There was some talk of the two running from money issues in their previous life."

Leave it to Mrs. C to have the history at her fingertips. "Maybe someone found them."

The older woman clicked her tongue. "Their assailant can't have been looking a'tall. Far as I know, their names are real."

I was disappointed, but I had to scratch the hidden identity path. Mrs. C had successfully kept her name under wraps for decades. She knows how to ferret out a lie in that area.

Mrs. C slid a narrowed glance at the door. "I've always been more interested in how they acquired the shop. Harvey Lester owned the place for twenty years. Married to Monica Sutton for... oh, a decade or more. She wasn't around much, stayed in their apartment above the store, or in the stockroom. Rumor had it that she would tell the children wild tales. Their daughter... his stepdaughter left for college when she turned eighteen. He showed no signs of selling. A few years later, his wife died. Then it's tally-ho and he rode for the hills."

That raised a flag. I looked at her across Kevin. "Did you see him after the sale?"

She paused in thought. Then nodded, not without a hint of disappointment. "A few days before he left. He was going through his wife's possessions. Said he was ready to move on. The daughter, Savannah, was helping him. He got sick and the girl closed the place up after he left town."

I settled back, still leaning against Kevin. "Did you hear from him after that?"

Her vigorous nod sent the wide rim of her straw hat bobbing up and down. "He settled in Seattle. Savannah lives there. He sent me Christmas cards for a few years."

"It sounds legit." I crossed my arms over my chest, unable to hide my disappointment. "He still alive?"

"Died three years later." From her musing tone, she obviously wondered if she'd missed out on a clue. "Savannah sent a card to the store. That's the last anyone heard from her. I'll put out feelers. The book club meets this afternoon, don't you know?"

The six women who formed Mrs. C's spy brigade were unstoppable in their quest to stay on top of neighborhood news. I'm not even sure they read books. However, the police department's loss was the neighborhood's gain.

I settled against the car. My mind replayed the morning, up to finding the body, broken and forgotten in a dark corner. I grimaced. What had brought the woman to such an end? I hoped the purple marks on her arm were due to decay rather than a beating while she was alive.

Either way, someone had deliberately left her there. They'd walked away, locked the door, and never returned.

Why didn't Otis or Elena go into that store room? Who had a key? What was in the boxes? I put the brakes on my ruminations.

I couldn't afford to indulge my curiosity if I wasn't on the case. In addition to being a PI and creating crossword puzzles, Kevin and I own a growing handyman business. Combining our households after marriage has allowed us to crawl out of poverty onto the lowest rung of the middle class.

We have money in the bank. We're hundredaires.

Despite our upward mobility, I didn't have the luxury of indulging my curiosity. I ignored a pang of disappointment.

Raised voices and clanging metal of overturned garbage cans set my heart racing. What now?

3

— • —

3 Down; 10 Letters;
Clue: Pertaining to the rudimentary; Basic;
Answer: Elementary.

A black-haired rocket flew around the corner of the building. Marcus barreled toward us full tilt before he skidded to a stop and forcefully wedged himself between me and Kevin. Taking a deep breath, the boy put an angelic expression on his face. "Act casual."

He'd barely settled when two police officers skidded around the same corner. They looked up and down the sidewalk. Then the dark-haired, white guy from earlier swatted the young, Hispanic woman on her arm. Taking matching breaths, they squared off and walked forward. Their eyes were lasered in on Marcus.

"Hey, officers." The boy went on the offense immediately. "How's your morning going? A murder scene is always so sad."

From his anguished expression and the strain in his voice, anyone would conclude he'd known the victim personally, possibly a relative.

The woman faltered. The man strode forward.

"Green. Moreno." The call came from a man in plain clothes who resembled a walking scarecrow. His name was Lawrence Wilson, a homicide detective. "Help canvas the alley. Examine everything, Dumpsters, weeds, litter. We have no purse, no ID, no phone."

The two officers exchanged disgruntled looks. With one final glare at the boy, they turned away, inches from their prey.

Wilson's long stride brought him before us in seconds. His gaze swept over the four of us. He slowly shook his head. "This reminds me of the mug shot of Butch Cassidy and his gang."

Marcus wagged a finger at the detective. "That wasn't a mug shot. It was a joke, hubris: that means a show of arrogance. The picture eventually brought them down."

Wilson raised a brow. His mouth formed a stiff line, probably trying not to smile at the boy's hubris. "It still applies. What are you doing here? Why do you find bodies everywhere you turn?"

While the first question could have been directed at any of us, including the universe, the last was aimed at me. I've asked myself the same thing several times. I went with my usual response. "It's a gift."

"From an evil genie?" Wilson snorted in laughter. His raucous guffaw startled the bystanders.

Marcus pointed at the detective. "Maybe she was visited on you for something you did that upset the karma wheel."

The detective heaved a sigh. A look of resignation settled over his irregular features. "That's very likely."

"Belden is not a curse or a punishment." Kevin, whose arm was looped over my shoulders, came to my defense. That's what hubbies and besties are for. "She's a force of justice and we are her trusted soldiers."

Marcus rubbed his hands together. An unsettling light seemed to beam from his eyes. "Soldiers of fortune loosed on the world."

Mrs. C straightened her shoulders. "I rather like the idea of being a soldier. Never been one before, have I?"

I raised my eyebrow at the lot of them and focused on Wilson. "I and my family came to buy candy. A friend asked me for a favor. Urged on by my son, whose fingerprints are all over my back, I agreed."

Wilson eyed the child in question. "That I believe."

Marcus, not shy in the least, met the man's gaze squarely. "You're lucky I don't have your desk."

The detective returned the look. "Most of the detectives on the force are grateful for the age restriction on the police force."

I didn't doubt that one bit. "You know the rest. You can take the lead now."

A dark flush suffused Wilson's face. "How many times do I have to tell you and the rest of the neighborhood, you're *not* on the force? You're a civilian, an annoying one at that. You had no business going into that basement."

I pushed away from the car.

"Uh-oh," Marcus muttered. "He's in trouble."

Putting my hands on my hips, I stepped up to the detective. "No one knew what was in the basement. It could have been an injured animal. Besides, I had an obligation to my friends."

"They paid us in candy and graphic novels." The plastic bag rustled behind me. No need to say who spoke. "Technically, they're our clients."

A triumphant zing shot through my body. I smiled at having an arrow in my arsenal. "What he said. They were my clients."

"Puh-leeze." Wilson got in my face. The smell of the dark roast coffee he preferred hung heavy on his breath. "Now you're just making stuff up."

"And lastly," I raised my voice and leaned forward until we were nose to nose. "I was curious."

The man wagged a finger under my nose. "Finally, the truth. The whole truth and the only truth. You're nosy."

"Oh, guvner," Mrs. C's British amused trill lanced between our tense voices. "We already knew that, didn't we? The whole neighborhood knows."

"Definitely." Kevin spoke amidst other murmurs.

Wilson's sharp eyes gave no indication he'd heard. "What do you know about the dead woman?"

"Nothing." Though I had little more to say, I refused to retreat. Arguing with Wilson is a kind of therapy for both of us. Other people get upset if you yell at them. Wilson and I shrug it off, walk away, then meet later for coffee.

"You claim you didn't know about the body in advance?"

A glint I didn't like appeared in his eye. I was honestly confused. Except, of course, advance knowledge would implicate Elena and Otis. "Why would you think that?"

"Why is your other confederate on the scene?" He flung a long arm out to his left, away from our apartment. So, not Mrs. C. "Him being here is a little convenient for an unexpected death, isn't it?"

I looked where he pointed. Standing behind the barricades and gawkers on the other side of the alley stood Jack Rabi.

A black man in his late fifties, he has ashen colored skin draped over a skeletal frame. His shiny, shoulder length hair fell in perfect waves, as always. The somber look on his thin face had nothing to do with the murder. He looks serious ninety percent of the time. For any sign of emotion, watch his eyes.

Surprised at Rabi's presence, I waved. Then, I saw his girlfriend by his side. A tall, dusky skinned woman with short hair. "Hi, Rabi. Hey, Tasha's here, too."

Neither will admit to being a couple, so, don't spread that around. But they've been keeping company for several weeks as my grandparents and their cronies would say.

Kevin and Marcus sent their greetings. Mrs. C's accent overrode the others. "Oh, ducks, you're a welcome sight, you are. I've got the lemon bars for you and the recipe."

"Oh, good grief." Wilson rolled his eyes. His triumphant expression melted to a frown. He glared at me. "This is your fault."

Why do people always blame me? "If you didn't want this to be a free-for-all, you shouldn't have pointed at Rabi. And to answer your question, I have no idea why he's here."

The detective clicked his tongue in patent disbelief.

I swept on. "Maybe he and Tasha were walking over to see us. Perhaps Mrs. C called Tasha to get the lemon bars. And I hope I get one as well. For that matter, word travels fast in this neighborhood. He may have heard there was a gathering and wanted to be part of it."

That last possibility was a stretch considering the man was basically a loner except for the local VFW and our little adopted family.

"I texted him." Marcus's small, familiar voice sounded behind me.

"Or that." I jerked a thumb over my shoulder. "I should have seen that coming."

"Neither of you knew that would happen?" Kevin's derogatory tone left little doubt what he thought of our oversight. "And you call your-selves detectives."

"Ye-ah." Marcus's voice was full of pre-teenage attitude. "We got paid. We're on the job. I'm not giving these books back. So, you two start sharing information. It's a two-way street, Detective Wilson. You tell us what you know and we'll tell you what we find out."

The detective shook his head. "Give him ten years, the kid's going to outrank me. Hopefully, I'll retire before then."

I chuckled, in sympathy. "He already outranks me. Maybe we should band together."

Wilson met my gaze.

I decided to take pity on him. "I can't tell you anything about the woman. Except she was evidently an executive. She was in a hurry when she was attacked and she almost certainly knew her attacker. I'm assuming she was familiar with the neighborhood, possibly from years ago."

The man's expression cleared. His narrowed eyes watched me closely. When I paused, he remained silent.

I returned his gaze. "She should have been reported missing by her company if she had no family. Maybe she was supposed to be on a trip. If not, I'd look at the rest of the executives and personnel in her business."

Wilson cocked his head to one side. "You looked at the body for less than a minute. How could you come up with that much detail if you have no prior knowledge of this crime?"

"It's obvious, Watson." Again, my helpful sidekick, a wannabe Sherlock Holmes, kicked in his two cents. "Go ahead, tell him."

As if Marcus wasn't hanging on every word, wanting to hear the on dit, as Mrs. C had said.

"The boy is going to be the death of me." I shared the whisper and a look of resignation with Wilson. With my hands before me, I started on my bullet points. "Executive. The woman was dressed in a skirt suit. Good quality from what I could see. I might not own top notch outfits, but I recognize them."

I usually see them when getting thrown out of high-end establishments.

"The great percentage of those going into the office are upper echelon. As for her being in a hurry, one of her shoes fell off. The toe was ripped on the top. The side of the shoe might have been damaged on the cement in a struggle or when she fell. For the top to tear, she had to catch it on something when she was upright. A car door, the edge of a screen door, maybe a gate."

Behind his sharp gaze, Wilson's mind was recording the points. He'd probably noticed them. Maybe not all, but though he resembled a scarecrow, Wilson was not someone I underestimated.

He folded his arms across his chest. "She knew her attacker?"

"That's the easiest." I was at my most confident on this point. "This is a busy neighborhood. It took me a few minutes to walk from the car to the store because people kept stopping us to talk."

"Mostly to me and Kevin." Marcus piped up with this little tidbit.

Sure, drive the point home. They're the charming ones. I don't need to talk everyone I meet. I have other fine qualities. "People are always walking around this neighborhood. There's the Mercantile. Silvered Sweets's pastry is to die for. The flower shop. The butcher shop. The victim's scream could have brought several people to her rescue. At the very least, someone would have called the police."

The detective gave a short nod.

The next part was actually the most puzzling to me. "That feeds into her knowing this area. I've been coming to this store for years. I didn't know there were two separate basement rooms. The smaller alcove isn't obvious. The dead woman or her attacker had to know it was walled off from the main basement."

Wilson's eyes narrowed. "Otherwise, she'd have been found much sooner. Otis and Elena get stock from the main basement every day."

"Exactly." I stabbed a finger at him. "The blood stain under her head shows she died where she fell. She wouldn't have gone down there with a stranger or an enemy. It was someone she knew, trusted, or thought she could control. And, how did they get into a locked room? It didn't look like the lock was picked."

When Wilson started to shake his head then stopped himself, I knew I was correct. That didn't bode well for Elena and Otis.

"See?" Marcus spoke with a note of triumph. "It's obvious. Right, Rabi?"

Surprised, I noted Rabi's former position was empty. Looking behind me, I saw the tall, lean man standing ramrod straight next to Mrs. C.

Rabi had an amazing ability to disappear in plain sight or move without anyone seeing him. A skill he'd no doubt fostered during his twenty-two-years in Special Ops. He used to be a delivery man, picking up packages for my now defunct job for an on-line mail order company. We'd spoken in passing. I'd give him coffee while he waited for me to finish. That changed when Marcus came into my life.

The boy broke through the stoic man's defenses. Rabi changed his route to stop by before Marcus went to school. Within the first week, the boy knew about the man's military history. Now, he was a firm fixture of our adopted family. He'd recently left his delivery job to work for my and Kevin's six-month-old handyman business.

Now, his black eyes shifted to Marcus. He had a half-smile on his lips. "I wouldn't have seen any of that."

Marcus sent a lighthearted laugh into the air. "It's obvious when TR explains it. Now, we need to know who the dead woman is or was."

His exclamation ended on a somber note.

As intriguing as the puzzle might be, it all came back to the victim who'd been struck down before her time. I refocused on Wilson. "Any ideas?"

He shook his head. "Looks like someone beat her face in. Between the damage to her skull and the delay in finding her, it'll take time to ID her. ME estimates it's been three to five days."

"Hmmm, business trip?" Mrs. C floated the suggestion. "The office doesn't expect her and she's no one at home. Divorced or separated I'd wager."

I raised a brow. There was no basis for her guesses. "How do you figure?"

The older woman waved a handful of fingers tipped with bright orange. "I've not got your crystal ball. I'm playing the odds. Sometimes it pays off."

Kevin nodded. "Good bet."

"More suspects." Marcus's whisper to Rabi, loud enough to carry across Kevin, was heard by all.

A twelve-year-old can only be somber for so long.

Wilson nodded to a crime scene tech calling to the detective. He pointed at me. "Come to the station, this afternoon, better yet first thing tomorrow and give your statement."

I groaned.

The detective looked pleased with himself as he marched away. "The station. In the morning. Be there."

Distance and his long legs gave him the last word. Marcus couldn't escape so easily. I pointed my finger at his nose. "We're not on this case. I like Elena and Otis, but I am not investigating a murder for some candy and a couple of comic books."

"Graphic novels, TR." The boy looked unperturbed. "Of course, we're not taking the case for a bunch of candy. That was for walking into the basement. We're done... for now."

I straightened. The boy child had given up far too easily. I decided to go on offense. "Otis and Elena have nothing to worry about if they're innocent."

Nobody believed that. It was a locked room mystery and the owners had the key. If no other leads came to light, it would be all too easy to find a connection, arrest them, and close the case.

I felt bad. However, proving them innocent in the woman's death was not my problem. They couldn't afford to hire Crawford Investigations, which was the PI company I work for.

"Tracy." A loud clap accompanied the excited exclamation. "Thank goodness, you're still here. Elena and I need to speak with you. Come. You, too, Marcus. Kevin?"

My hubby waved the offer away. "I'm good. You go ahead."

He was speaking to me and Otis, since the steak of lightning that was our son had disappeared through the front.

Mrs. C had shuffled off to join the spectators, plumbing them for news, no doubt. The cat heads on her slippers stared at our neighbors, innocently sharing confidences with the Brit.

Rabi leaned against Kevin's pearly white nineteen-sixty-seven Cadillac. My hubby was buying it on payments from his mechanic. No one listened to me when I told them it was stolen and would soon be recovered.

The Great White Beast as I called the vehicle was useless as a stakeout car. The thing had a garish red leather interior. It was also a gas hog. However, the car had the smoothest ride on the planet. Something I refused to admit to my husband or my son, who both loved the Beast almost as much as they loved me.

I heaved a sigh. "We're on the case, aren't we?"

Kevin took a position next to Rabi. "The troops are in the field, general. You better catch up."

4

— • —

4 Down; 7 Letters;
Clue: Have an idea of the truth without proof.
Answer: Suspect.

I was on the case of the Body in the Basement; as Marcus dubbed the murder, ala Perry Mason. On re-entering the store, Otis pulled me to one side. Marcus was already in the back hall.

Elena sat at the tiny desk in their puny office. The woman had a death grip on a pencil. She tapped the eraser against a spreadsheet in a mindless rhythm. Her expression was stiff and tight. Her hazel eyes stared straight ahead.

My heart went out to her. She and Otis were in the eye of a hurricane. Until the police found out who killed the victim, their store, their past, and their family would be torn apart. To solve a murder, the police leave no stone unturned.

Marcus squeezed between me and Otis in the doorway. His small frame topped Elena's by only inches as he stood next to her chair. He patted her shoulder. "TR will get the goods. She'll find out why the woman was down there and who killed her. TR never quits until she solves the puzzle."

Elena slowly turned her head to meet the boy's sympathetic gaze. No glimmer of life or hope sparked in her eyes.

"Did one of you kill that lady?" He pointed at Elena. "If you did, 'fess up now."

The other woman's eyes sparked fire. "Neither of us touched that poor woman. We don't know who she is, how she got in the extra room, or who killed her."

At least, Marcus had broken through her despair. It's hard to deal with someone who won't talk.

I opened my mouth to share my sympathy when Otis put a hand on my shoulder.

His expression held none of the usual jovial nature. His gaze met mine. "We want to hire you. Mrs. Colchester and Marcus brag about your agency all the time. You can solve this."

The Belden Tanner Agency only existed in Marcus's mind.

Before I could speak, the boy slid between me and the store owner. "We can solve the case. We have the inside track. We know everyone."

If the woman or her killer left the area years ago, what brought them back? I steeled myself against the puzzle's siren call. "Hold it, boy child. You're not agreeing to anything."

"Of course, not." Otis held up both hands to stop us both. "This would be an official contract with Crawford."

Elena popped up. "I like Crawford. He's a good man."

Otis gave a quick nod. "We'll pay the fee. I'll throw in graphic novels if the matter is settled quickly."

The boy's face lit up. "Deal. You and Crawford iron out the details. The Belden Tanner Detective Agency will start on the background."

What background? Not even the cops knew who the victim was, how she'd died, or when. I frowned at the boy.

He scrunched his face up in a weird, artificial smile. If he was trying to freak me out, it was working.

Otis smacked his hands together in an ear-splitting clap that made me jump and distracted me from Marcus's bizarre smile.

"I have your boss's office on the line." Elena said, waggling her cell phone. "We'll get this straightened out. Once we hire a PI, the police will know we're innocent."

I painted on a false smile. The police didn't eliminate suspects in a murder because they hired a PI. Only alibis or hard evidence counted. However, I couldn't dash her hopes.

"Yes," Elena spoke breathlessly. "I'm calling about a murder. I want to hire one of your investigators."

Roxie, Crawford's assistant, must have answered.

If they wanted to pay Crawford, who would pay me, I was happy to check out the woman's death. My crossword grid already had items of interest.

Otis and Elena throwing money at the case might not mean anything to the authorities, but I was impressed. Otis's stiff jaw and thin lips were evidence of the pain at parting with his hard-earned money.

I put a hand toward him, glancing at Elena as well. "Detective Wilson is honest and thorough. He'll get to bottom of this. You don't have to worry about him railroading you."

Elena jumped up. She thrust her body forward, impinging on my personal space. Ignoring my frown, she shook her finger under my nose. "No backing out. We're paying the money. You find the truth."

Marcus broke into a happy dance. Wiggling his hips, he waved both arms in the air. "We're on a case. We're on a case. Murder is way more fun than stupid divorces."

"Marcus!" My sharp tone didn't cause the boy to lose a beat.

"Is this a daily charge?" Otis tapped my shoulder. "Could you wrap this up in say, a day? Maybe two?"

My scowl moved to my new client. I was happy to note Otis's over-blown expectations earned him equally harsh stares from his wife and Marcus, who'd stopped his jig in mid-step.

The boy shook his head slowly.

Elena gave her husband's arm a light slap. "She's good. She's not *magic*."

I couldn't have put it better myself. "I'll do my best, but unless you have information on the victim's identity, I'll have to wait until the police identify her."

I paused. For several seconds. And then, a dozen more.

Otis and Elena stared at me with gazes unmarred by any hint of hidden knowledge regarding the victim.

Where was Kevin when I needed him? The man could measure breathing rates, eye dilation, any flinch. All I had was my gut, which I hoped wasn't colored by the fact that I liked Otis and Elena. However, I didn't like clients who lied to me. I kept eye contact with my erstwhile friends.

"Don't lie." Anyone who knew my son's penchant for drama wouldn't be surprised that Marcus's voice was edged with warning. He stared at them both. "TR doesn't like who clients keep secrets. If you want to keep her on your side, talk. If we're implicated in a murder, I could go to jail."

His voice broke on the last word. He stuck out a lip and put on the sad puppy eyes as if he were about to cry.

I drew in a breath to intercede before the melodrama reached epic proportions.

"Okay!" Elena's shrill scream echoed off the low ceiling and walls of the narrow hall and office. "I admit it."

Focused on my son, I nearly jumped out of my skin at her ear-piercing screech. Fighting to still my revved-up heart, I stared at her. Was my case over before it began?

The only thing that salvaged my pride was seeing Marcus and Otis both jerk like puppets who'd had their strings pulled.

Otis's eyes bugged out of his head. "Elena! What are you saying?"

"You killed that lady?" Astonishment rang in my son's voice. His eyes bulged out of their sockets. Planting himself solidly against my side, he kept his gaze on Elena. "The cops are outside. You watch these two. Want me to get Rabi? He can take 'em both."

Rabi could handle these two, me, and the police officer outside singlehandedly. "I don't think that's necessary."

Elena, whose attention had faltered between her husband's outburst and Marcus's accusation, found her voice again. "I didn't kill her."

Her hands reached out to Otis in a pleading gesture. When she pivoted to Marcus, her expression darkened.

Though I put her behavior down to shock, I shifted my body between them. Too stunned to protest, Marcus stared at the woman he'd accused of murder.

Elena reacted to my changed stance by pulling her gaze from my son. She looked me in the face, her hands still clenched into fists. "I didn't hurt her. Nobody. Anybody. Tell them."

"Enough." I raised my voice to a decibel certain to override the woman and my child.

Solving and creating puzzles are my addictions. Knowing there is a solution helps me believe I'm in control of some miniscule corner of the world. I realize it's an illusion, but logic is my warm blanket. What I don't do well is screaming and gnashing of teeth. I wanted answers. For a heartbeat, I reveled in the silence.

"Elena." I pegged my tone low and slow to calm the woman down. A lesson learned from watching Kevin deal with people. "I don't think you killed the dead woman."

Relief showed in her eyes. She leaned against her husband who tightened his hold as he held her to his side.

Softening my expression, I put a bit of distance between us. "What do you know?"

She slid a glance at Otis. "I knew about the smell two days ago."

Otis's jaw dropped. His face paled. "You saw her?"

"Let Elena finish." I put my hand out. I looked at the woman and spoke quietly. "You smelled the odor two days ago. Today is Saturday. That would be Thursday."

Elena pressed her lips together, forming a ring of fine lines around her mouth. "I went to the paper room."

Marcus, still half-hidden behind my body, thrust his head toward the woman. "You have a room made of paper?"

Seriously? How could he think that?

Otis's shoulders lost some of their tension. He pointed to the end of the hall. "We keep paper products in the storage room at the end of the hall."

Elena nodded, pointing as well. "A vent connects that room to the lower room."

Marcus nodded. "Where the body was found."

The woman's fingers twined around each other. "I smelled an odor as I counted supplies. I knew it came from the storage room."

Her face scrunched up. Her eyes filled with tears. She shook her head, casting her sorrowful eyes at Otis.

He put his arm around her.

"You closed the vent." I finished for her. "What did you think it was?"

"I thought it was Tiffie's cat." She screamed with a desperate intensity. She wiped away tears that threatened to overflow. "A motorcycle hit the poor thing last week. It was limping but no one could catch it. I thought it crawled in the basement and died. I didn't want to tell her the cat was dead."

Otis ribbed his wife's arm. "Monkey showed up days ago. I thought you knew."

Marcus nodded. "Wednesday, I think. Tiffie's been feeding him tuna and milk on his cushion. He's good."

Relief wreathed Elena's face. She clasped her hands. "I'm so relieved. I didn't tell you because you would have insisted on checking. The stairs are too narrow for you."

Otis gave her a gentle frown. "I'd have sent Sammy down."

And the stockboy would have discovered the dead woman and I might not be involved, but here we are. These three acted as if the cat's safety resolved all our problems.

"Good thing the cat's alive." Marcus looked up. His carefree grin faded after one look at my face. "I think TR wants to talk about the dead woman."

"You think?" Injured cat versus dead body. I'm not callous, but I grew up on a horse ranch in Kentucky overrun with felines. People on farms have a completely different view of the cycle of life than city dwellers. I took a calming breath. "Do either of you have any idea who that woman is? Is anyone missing? Has someone from the neighborhood come back for a visit?"

And never made it out of town?

I fixed them both with a level stare. "Otis? You're not in the clear. You knew something was down there, too."

The man pulled a dirty, wrinkled handkerchief from his pocket and wiped the sweat from his brow.

These two better beef up their stories before Wilson got them in an interrogation room. The detective would crack them in seconds.

Otis shrugged his beefy shoulders. "The paper room was stuffy. I opened the vent this morning."

He grimaced, practically gagging.

I found myself cringing in empathy. The blast of air that must have engulfed him would have been putrid.

He looked at me with sad eyes. "I was going to tell Elena, then we got busy."

"Back to my question. Anyone missing?"

The guilt was back in the man's gaze. He nodded.

Elena elbowed him in his substantial gut. "Who's missing?"

Otis reared back, his jaw set. "I told you. You never listen to me. You were watching that young delivery boy."

When Elena pursed her lips, I knew a disclaimer was coming. I couldn't stand it. I have many fine qualities, but patience is not one of my virtues.

"Enough." I swept both hands through the air. "Who. Is. Missing?"

Otis looked at Elena carried an air of "I have to deal with the crazy woman". He faced me. "Phyllis from the flower shop said Amos Gilbert's granddaughter dropped out of sight last week."

The man pulled at his lip. "Or is it his grand-niece?"

Elena tapped his arm. "Granddaughter. His second son adopted her as a baby. Remember? Her birth mother abandoned her."

This reminded me of a conversation between my grandparents tracing lineages in Kentucky. Who cares about semantics? I clenched my fists and counted to ten. I only made it to seven. "The relationship doesn't matter. What happened?"

"Nothing." Otis shrugged. "He hasn't heard from her for days."

"I just remembered." Elena waved her hands, like a first grader wanting to be called on. "That survey lady."

"It wasn't about a survey." Her husband looked at her as if she'd lost her marbles.

I felt like I were losing my sanity, but I gamely struggled to followed the tangled threads of this conversation.

Otis rubbed his chin. "Amos was expecting a call, but not about surveys."

I was growing more confused by the second. Were their stories even related? I smacked my forehead. "Otis. You're talking about Amos who plays chess at Mule Train Park, three blocks away, right?"

He and I both ignored his wife who was smacking him lightly on the arm. Otis nodded before turning to defend himself.

"Don't confuse me." Elena spoke in an accusing tone.

She'd taken the words right out of my mouth, but I marshalled my little gray cells and carried on. I glanced at Marcus, still hugging my side. "Remember the pointers to Amos."

He nodded, his wide eyes ablaze with interest.

"Elena." I sharpened my tone as I pointed at the other woman. "Is the survey lady and the granddaughter the same person?"

The couple turned to me with matching frowns.

Elena's lip curled. "Of course not. The granddaughter never called. The survey lady came here, to the shop."

"Okay. You're talking about two different women." That answered one question. Did any of this connect to the dead woman? "Did the survey lady tell you her name?"

Elena's blue fingernails wiggled in the air as she thought. "Her name was... Burlington?"

"No-oo." Marcus dragged out the word with an air of disdain. "That's a railroad company in Nebraska."

The woman frowned. "Bradford? Buffington. I think."

My son moved away from my side, phone in hand. As he typed on the keyboard, he muttered. "I'm taking notes."

He made it sound like a threat.

I was grateful to have a record. Perhaps later I could make sense of this conversation. "Did the survey lady ask about Amos or is she missing? Don't elaborate. Just tell me."

Elena, who'd opened her mouth, shut it. She looked disappointed, but after a slight show of pouty lip, she responded. "She's missing. I think."

I bit back a groan. The only fact anyone knew was that an unidentified corpse had appeared in the locked room in their basement. Didn't they realize they were currently the only suspects for her murder?

5

— · —

18 Down; 7 Letters;
Clue: A person who pursues stealthily.
Answer: Stalker.

That's what I got for asking. At least I was getting paid in cash instead of candy. "When was the survey lady here?"

Marcus looked up from his phone. "How do you know she's missing when she was only here to ask questions? And what-"

The boy's rapid-fire delivery reminded me of... me. Nonetheless, I put a hand in front of his nose. "Good questions, but let Elena talk."

The woman's gaze grew distant. "She came into the store Tuesday morning."

That would allow time for the smell of decay if she'd been killed soon after her appearance. "What was she wearing?"

A pucker appeared on Elena's forehead. "A dark skirt with a matching jacket. Expensive cut. Black or blue. A navy top with a slim collar. Walking shoes."

Exactly what the victim had worn.

"What did she say?" When her voice faded, Marcus slipped in the prompt.

I gave him a wink and a nod of approval.

Otis, silent until now, watched his wife. "I didn't see her. Where was I?"

"You went to the bank." Elena answered absently, still focused on the past. "She came right after you left, late afternoon. Sammy was on break. I was alone."

The store was rarely that deserted. Had catching Elena alone been part of the woman's plan?

"Tuesday." Otis spoke in a quiet tone. "I stopped at the bakery for the jelly and cream rolls on the way back."

Marcus groaned. "Those are the best."

An image of the succulent treats filled my brain. Everyone in a ten-mile radius knew the schedule. The queue to buy one started before dawn. There was a limit on purchases. When the delicacies sold out, they were gone for another seven days. No exceptions.

With an effort of will, I pulled my attention back to the moment. "Tuesday. A woman came in with a clipboard."

Marcus frowned at me. "Old school, TR. Probably a tablet."

Elena frowned. "She was empty-handed. I remember her nails tapping on the customer service counter out front."

The customer service counter is a polite name for the corner where Otis sits on a tall stool. He does work on a shelf that juts out from the wall. From this vantage point, he can see most of the store via strategically placed mirrors. He also has a view of the boxes of fruit and produce on the sidewalk.

There are a few tables with chairs nearby that serve as a gathering place for regulars. They come, grab a cup of coffee from the pot, then sit and gab. It's the neighborhood's version of a smalltown café. Mrs. C has spent many a morning catching up on the news and dispensing her share of information.

A survey taker with no way to record information sent up a flurry of red flags. "What did this woman ask about? Try to remember exactly what she said."

"Burlington." Elena muttered the name of the Midwest railroad again. She closed her eyes. "She was visiting small, independently owned shops. The tourist board is looking for ways to promote small businesses."

Good story, on the surface. However, the five-star eateries, boutiques, and specially designed golf courses that bring in the big money are far removed from this low rent neighborhood. The tourist board isn't going to renovate a corner grocer in a borderline area such as ours.

Otis stiffened. His worried gaze mirrored my own. "What did she ask about?"

Elena's eyes opened to slits. "How long we'd owned the store. Had we renovated the building? How was business? Did we plan to expand?"

My antenna for suspicious activity quivered with each question. Those topics weren't tourist related, more like a takeover or a buyout.

"Her lanyard!" Elena's eyes popped open. Her raised voice echoed off the ceiling. "That's why I thought of Burlington Railroads. I grew up by a train yard. I got tired of answering her questions and asked her for ID."

"A little late," muttered Marcus, my resident cynic. Like mother, like son.

Privately agreeing, I kept my gaze on Elena. "What did she say?"

Elena's hazel eyes hardened to stones. Her lips tightened at the memory. "She made a show of looking in her bag. A Gucci, no knockoff either. When she pulled out some items, her lanyard was in her hand. She dropped it right away, but I saw it."

"Out of sight." The words popped out of my mouth without thought.

"The nametag had a ghost image of a train. There was printing, but I couldn't read it." Her voice rang with anger. "She lied about the whole thing. When she turned to leave, I tried to follow, but several customers came in. The survey lady slipped away."

I cocked my head to one side. "Did you ask the other store owners if she stopped in?"

Elena stabbed the air. "None of them spoke with her."

"She targeted this place." Marcus's voice quivered with excitement. He had his fingers on the keyboard of his phone. "What did she look like?"

Elena faced the boy. "Five-eight in low heels. Shoulder length blonde hair, straight, with bangs. Not a good look for her thin face. Hard, wide jaw. Oversized sunglasses. Medium build. She looked a little familiar, but certainly no one I'd seen around here."

Marcus finished typing then looked at me through his thick lashes.

"A different hairstyle, but it could be the victim." I answered the question in his eyes. Considering the state of the body, the dead woman's build was hard to pin down. "How do you know your lady's missing?"

Elena chewed her lip. Long seconds stretched into a notable silence.

This shouldn't have been a hard question. I was running out of patience when she gasped.

"I wasn't here." She looked at Otis. "You said a man came into the store asking about his missing niece."

Otis nodded. His round cheeks were uncharacteristically tight. "Wednesday afternoon. His shirt was soaked with sweat. He had his coat slung over his arm. Heavy material for this time of year."

Not from this area, was my first thought. A PI was my second. "Did he identify himself? Or the missing woman?"

Looking abashed, Otis shook his head.

"Why was he looking for her here?" Marcus asked. "He must have given some reason."

The timeline worked for the decomposition. My brain pinned the days on the calendar.

Otis scratched his head. "He said he was looking for his long-lost niece. His sister-in-law ran off with the girl twenty-five years ago. His wife recently got an anonymous e-mail saying the girl lived in Langsdale for several years and they'd find her here."

I considered my own methods for finding missing people. "Did he give you their names? Did he have a picture?"

Otis eyed the door to the shop with an impatient air. "He had a twenty-five-year-old picture of a woman and a young girl about nine or ten. It was taken right before they left. The woman was Cathy Stanton and her daughter Erica."

Marcus nudged me. "You think he's a PI?"

Something didn't add up. "Did you tell him the woman was here?"

Elena's expression brightened. "I called him when Otis told me about the man later. I couldn't say for sure if the survey lady was his niece. It was an old picture and she didn't leave a card or contact information."

The picture was getting muddier by the minute. The woman had acted suspiciously, but why target a neighborhood grocer?

Mrs. C had mentioned Harvey Lester's stepdaughter, but would she return and not give her name and why now? I didn't think I'd get more usable information. Might as well see about the other lead.

"Go back to Amos's granddaughter." I made a rolling gesture with my hand. "What else do you know about that?"

"Nothing." Elena looked apologetic. "Neighborhood talk."

"That's about it." Otis looped an arm over his wife's shoulders. "Nattie said Amos was worried because Lily hadn't called him on his birthday. She calls every year. It's a tradition."

Elena pointed to the back of the building. "You can ask him. He's at the park."

"When is Amos not at the park?" I asked in a teasing voice.

The man's over eighty. He plays chess at one of the stone boards set up in the shade. When he doesn't have another player, he feeds the birds or watches people. He can usually be found in his favorite spot seven days a week. Every once in a while he goes for a walk or grabs a snack or coffee at a local shop. Wait ten minutes and Amos will return.

The others grinned.

Questions popped up in my brain like wild flowers after a rain. I put them on hold, not wanting to lose the thread of the conversation. "When was she supposed to call?"

Elena looked up, searching for the answer. "Ten days ago?"

Otis frowned. "Tuesday."

"Amos must have tried to call her." I noted out loud.

"I never heard." Otis glanced at Elena who shook her head. His gaze strayed toward the store. "You should talk to Amos."

Weariness coupled with frustration dragged down his tone. Elena's eyes were starting to glaze over. Wilson and the crime scene team had left. The basement storage room was cordoned off with crime scene tape. The detective had given permission for them to re-open the store. The longer they spoke to me, the more money it cost them. They had a long day ahead of them.

"We're done for now." I noted their looks of hope mixed with desperation. "I'll be in touch. If you think of anything, let me know right away."

Marcus slipped his phone in his pocket. He patted Elena's arm. "The Belden Tanner Agency always solves the case. TR's the best, with our help of course."

I wasn't sure my boss man, Crawford, would appreciate our gang taking the credit. On the other hand, like me, if Crawford got paid, he wouldn't care.

A moment later, we walked from the cool store onto the burning concrete. Stifling heat settled around me, adding to my bad mood. Not a whiff of a breeze stirred my hair. The crowd had cleared except a few diehard gossip junkies.

Kevin and Rabi were still leaning against Kevin's Caddy, side-by-side. They looked disgustingly cool and collected.

No sign of my septuagenarian landlady, maid, friend. In spite of her small stature, a white-haired woman wearing a muumuu and slippers stands out. "Where's Mrs. C? Don't tell me she retired from the field."

Kevin jerked a thumb to his left. "I drove her to the park. She dug up a lead."

"That's where *we're* headed." After a covert glance around the street, Marcus lowered his voice. "Two women, possibly missing. Amos's granddaughter is overdue for a birthday call."

Rabi, still as a statue, listened to the boy's delivery. "Good work."

Kevin tapped a few beats on the car. "Want a ride to the park, little lady? Or would you rather walk and get in your steps?"

As if I counted my steps. I grunted, throwing in a scathing look for good measure. "The street doesn't come with AC."

A moment later, I wilted against the creamy red leather in the Great White Beast.

Kevin shot me a sideways glance at my long sigh. "How about we take the long way?"

A rapid pounding shook the seat. Marcus thumped his fists on Kevin's side of the seat. "We could go through the drive-in at the Silver Sluice and get flavored sodas. It's our duty to support locally owned shops."

I chuckled at his justification. "You are the master at rationalizing your treats."

He flopped against the back seat. "I learned from the best."

Kevin and I exchanged glances. My hubby shook his head. "He is not talking about me."

I waved a languid hand. The diversion would give me a few more minutes in the deliciously cool air.

"My treat." Rabi's low drawl added his vote. "I just got a raise."

I chuckled as I closed my eyes.

A few weeks ago, Rabi quit his job as a delivery driver to work at B&T Inc. Kevin's and my fledgling painting and handyman business. We don't pay well and can't afford a retirement plan, but as Marcus promised, we're way more fun and far more flexible when he needs time off for one of my cases.

Considering the heat, the line at the Silver Sluice wasn't bad. Besides, I was in air-conditioned comfort. Marcus passed the time telling the guys what we'd learned.

Kevin eyed our son in the rearview mirror. "Otis and Elena heard of rumors and had a run-in with two unknown women in the past two weeks?"

"Maybe his granddaughter called and he forgot." Marcus suggested. "Or she'd e-mail instead and he didn't check his account. Amos is old."

I frowned without turning around. Considering the child has called me old more than once, his view of age couldn't be trusted. "Old people have e-mail, too. But you're right, this might be nothing. We need to follow every lead until the body is identified."

"Why did Mrs. C go to the park?" Marcus's tone would have been suited to an interrogation room. "Did she hear about Amos's granddaughter or is she looking for info?"

The park was at a crossroads of five intersecting streets. With numerous hotels in walking distance plus a playground and a handful of stone chessboards, the tree lined area drew people from a radius of several blocks.

The boy child's rapid delivery continued without pause. "You think the police know about these leads?"

I gasped and smacked my forehead. "Elena and Otis didn't tell Wilson about either woman. They were too scared to think. They need to set the record straight."

"They're in trouble." Marcus's voice was laced with doom. "Police don't like to be lied to or have information withheld."

I scowled at him over my shoulder as I pulled out my phone. "No one lied. He should thank me for getting it out of them with my skilled, friendly methods."

Feeling self-righteous, I dialed the store. I didn't expect an answer, but a gruff male voice greeted me after the third ring.

I frowned at the unfamiliar voice. A cop? Why had they returned? "This is Tracy. Is Otis or Elena there?"

"Tracy?" The lighter tone sounded instantly familiar. Sammy, their sixteen-year-old stockboy, was tall and lanky. A string bean topped with blond curls any woman would envy. His hair contrasted with his dusky skin and bright brown eyes. "I thought it was the cops or a reporter."

I relaxed against the seat. "Hey, Sammy. I didn't think you'd be in today."

"Yeah, no." The teen answered with a confusing disclaimer. "I heard what happened and decided to see if they needed help. I'm cleaning. We've got the back doors and a few windows open. Airing out, you know."

"Ugh." I did know. I grunted as the boy's rapid-fire delivery continued.

"Elena's lighting candles." The boy whispered, either he was worried about being overheard or the religious connotation. "Cleansing the air, she said. Anything will help. They don't really need me. I think they want the company."

I should have asked for Otis or Elena, but curiosity got the better of me. "Why did you answer the phone?"

"If it wasn't the cops, I was going to yell at the reporter." Anger made his voice harsh. "They've been calling constantly and the voicemail is full."

I gave in to an edgy response. "Don't answer the phone. Write down the callers and give them to Detective Wilson. Then delete the messages."

He clicked his tongue, evidently disappointed. "O-kay."

I perked up as it came time to order. After nodding to Kevin's silent question of "the usual", I focused on my call. "Did you work the past few days?"

"Yeah, the cops grilled me." His voice rose in excitement. "When was I here? Did I see anything? Smell anything odd? Did I go to the basement?"

His interview would get quite a bit of play over the next few days between his family and friends and the customers.

"Did you?" I asked. "Notice anything? Inside? Outside? People?"

"Nothing." He sounded disappointed. "We got fresh produce delivered and I stocked the display on the sidewalk."

The Mercantile had an array of baskets full of fruits and vegetables across the store front. The colorful offerings tempted many customers into their store.

"I like being outside," Sammy spoke against the clanking sound of cans. "Wait. There was a guy. He kept glancing at me from the flower shop. It was odd because he didn't look like a flowery kind of guy. You know what I mean?"

Marcus, on the edge of the seat, eyed me like a vulture ready to pounce.

My interest meter shot up a few pegs. I faced Kevin, who had money in hand. We were one car back from the pay window. "Tell me about the guy."

My son's hands gyrated wildly toward my phone. "Put it on speaker. Do it!"

I pointed at the window. Kevin was handing over the money. Within seconds the exchange had taken place. With my gaze locked on my raspberry flavored iced soda, I put Sammy on speaker.

"... notice him at first." The teen's voice broke into the silent car in mid-sentence. "I was taking my time stocking the fruits and veggies. I never hurry when I'm outside."

"Yeah," I murmured agreement.

"The guy wiped his forehead like five times." The teen sounded defensive. "I kept wondering why he didn't go inside the flower shop, you know?"

"Uh-hunh." Marcus chimed in.

I cast the boy a warning glance. I hadn't told Sammy he was on speaker, but the teen either didn't notice or didn't care.

"And he had his suitcoat over his arm."

The comment drew a wide-eyed exchange between me and my son. Marcus handed his soda to Rabi with a pleading look and grabbed his phone. His quick fingers flew over the keyboard.

Gripping my phone, I sipped my soda. The icy tang of the raspberry slid across my tongue. I raised my glass in salute to Rabi as I concentrated on Sammy's news. "When did you see this guy? What day? What time?"

"Today's Saturday." The boy's voice softened then died. "I was off yesterday. My friends and I went to the old mine. The renovation is so cool."

I bared my teeth at the phone. "When did you see the man across the street?"

"Thursday, late morning." Sammy continued. "The truck dropped off the fruit early. I'd been at it awhile, stocking and watching people go by. He messed with the flowers a long time, but the guy never bought anything."

The mystery stalker was no PI. No one had seen his license. He knew nothing about stakeouts. The target isn't supposed to spot you, let alone some teenager. "What did he look like?"

"Hmmm, five-ten, pudgy." He repeated for good measure. "Short, light-colored hair. Older, mid-fifties."

"That's good." It would give me an idea if I saw him. I took the phone off speaker. "When you get off the phone, call Detective Wilson and tell him about this man. Every detail.

"Are Otis or Elena around? I forgot to tell them something."

Sammy's whoop almost took out my eardrum. "I get to give another statement. Wait 'til I tell the gang."

Elena and Otis weren't nearly as excited as Sammy at the prospect of calling Wilson. They complained about the wasted time. The store was busy, thronged with gawkers and neighbors. I had no doubt Otis and Elena were giving every visitor the hard sell to buy something as a price for their curiosity. If they had to have a body in the basement, they might as well cash in. The last thing they wanted was to stop and call the police.

I finally used my mom voice to order them to dial the detective as soon as we hung up. "This is a murder investigation. He will find out about those women. It won't look good if you don't come clean now. Call him or I will tell him."

That drew groans followed by a reluctant promise to comply. I hung up. "It's like having two more children. Okay. We have a survey lady asking weird questions, a missing granddaughter, and an inept stalker masquerading as a PI. Something's in the wind, but are these people connected?"

A long drink of soda brought cool sparkling flavors dancing over my tongue. I rested a hand on Kevin's shoulder. "How'd the job go yesterday? You never told me if you finished it after Finn took off without warning."

"That left us short, but..." Kevin looked smug as he turned into the park. "New guy's working out. I did good when I hired him."

"I told you to hire Rabi years ago." Marcus piped up. "I get credit."

Kevin's laughter mixed with Rabi's chuckle. "Job's done. Carlos is a great worker, too. He's wiry and he's got a solid work ethic."

"Calendar's clear if you need help." Kevin parked under a shady tree. He pointed the car keys at me. "You're up, Belden."

Marcus opened his door. "We have to find out what Mrs. C learned. That way we can beat the police to the killer."

A shiver ran down my spine. A murderer on the loose in my neighborhood didn't sound exciting to me. We'd all be better off once the killer was caught.

6

—•—

13 Down; 7 Letters;
Clue: Not in its expected place.
Answer: Missing.

I scowled at my boy child. "I'm in no hurry to find the murderer. I still get paid if the cops nab the killer first."

Marcus scoffed and rolled his eyes.

Obviously, he didn't believe me. That was okay. I didn't believe me. Despite my cavalier tone, acting indifferent was a hard sell. Puzzles intrigue me. Though I only had a few pieces to this mystery, the hunger to find the solution already had its hooks in me.

Without a word, Marcus jumped out of the car and sauntered toward a stand of trees. The boy flashed a cheeky grin, wiggled his eyebrows, and mouthed: "Reconnaissance."

"Good grief." I scanned the area. Sure enough, Mrs. C was chatting up passers-by from a carved stone bench within sight of the chess players. With her upright posture and knitting bag, she might have been a queen at her court.

Had the Amos connection brought her here? Or was she using the location as a clearing house for information? Many paths led to the park.

Literally, six sidewalks and two bike lanes wound through the circle of greenery.

Raucous yells and childish laughter from the playground provided a carefree backdrop. Picnic tables and the covered pavilion between the plaza and the play area provided a noise break. Six stone tables bearing engraved chessboards each had a seat on all four sides.

The ring of benches embraced a cobblestone circle lined by a shaded sidewalk. Amos sat at his usual table which was in full shade most of the day. Mrs. C had positioned herself within a few feet of the man.

Rabi opened his door and stepped outside. "I'll join recon."

"Well?" Kevin cast me a sideways invitation from his gorgeous blue eyes. As he and I walked toward the chess boards, the playground noise faded. Conversations from the benches were subdued. Three tables were occupied. Two had on-going games. The third had a lone occupant.

Amos had wide shoulders. His gray hair was short. Neighborhood debate put his heritage as a mix of African American and Hispanic. He had laugh lines around his alert brown eyes, but the rest of his skin was wrinkle free.

His weathered hands rested on a carved walking stick held loosely in his grasp as it leaned against his chest. Though his eyes looked like they were closed, no one ever caught Amos unaware. He watched his kingdom through narrow slits of his eye lids.

He'd been a carpenter and handyman for many years before he retired. While not wealthy, Amos seemed to live comfortably. He and Harvey Lester were of the same generation. Amos had done jobs in the Mercantile. Could that old connection possibly pertain to the current case?

He'd grown up in town, but he rarely spoke of himself, preferring to ask questions. However, under the laser focus of a certain twelve-year-old boy's engaging smile and never-say-die questioning, Amos, like so many before him, gave in to Marcus's friendly interest.

However, Marcus confined his questions to whether Amos had ridden into battle with Teddy Roosevelt. My son's perception of dates and people's ages left a bit to be desired.

Amos cackled and launched into several stories about cavalry charges. Since Mexican and Civil War battle sites were intermixed, I didn't count on the veracity of the tales. Marcus left happy, which is all that mattered.

I scanned the area. The usual mix of locals and tourists sauntered by. A few people watched the games. Most moved on.

Mrs. C exchanged significant looks with Marcus and Rabi. Their subtle greetings reminded me of *The Sting* which we'd watched a month ago. What good was subtlety? Did anyone in a ten-mile radius *not* know the five of us were a collective?

I rested a hand on the stone table. "Hey, Amos, got a few minutes?"

"Been expecting you." Sitting up, he opened his eyes, alert at the promise of a game. He waved a slim hand at the chair facing him. "White moves first."

I'd dreaded this turn of events. "Kevin's a better player."

My hubby and Rabi were both skilled at chess and had played against the older man. Mrs. C had tried her hand, winning on at least one occasion. Though I knew the moves of the pieces, my play was erratic.

Amos shifted his walking stick. "Kevin going to ask the questions?"

I bit back a sigh. I'd rather concentrate on my case than the board. At the moment, I wasn't sure I had the mental capacity for both. However, we all knew the answer. I sat and reached for a pawn.

When Amos moved his king's knight forward, I got worried. I had to make this game last long enough to ask my questions. I gave Kevin a pleading look.

He crossed his arms over his chest. "Play your game."

"Fine." Annoyed at being thwarted, I slid my queen's bishop into a position to assault one of the squares the opposing knight could move to. "Amos, you've heard about the dead woman at the Mercantile."

It wasn't a question. The only thing that flies faster than rumors in this corner of Langsdale is news. Like Mrs. C with her spiderweb of contacts and her binoculars, Amos knew what happened before the police.

The older man gave me a look of admiration, evidently my bishop's aggressive advance had been the correct move. He answered by moving a pawn at the edge of the board. "Desperation fuels brilliance. So does fear."

"Which is it with you?" I watched his eyes while my hand randomly moved a pawn.

Amos raised a brow. "You should play distracted more often."

I drew a breath for a comeback, but his gaze was on the board. Breaking the rules of the game might earn me too many demerits to recover from. Glancing at the pieces, I realized my bishop coupled with the pawn covered a large part of the area between our lines.

"I didn't know I had that in me," I admitted softly.

Amos slid the queen's rook halfway up the side. "I heard about the dead woman. Locked room. No ID. Rumors my granddaughter's overdue. You want to know if it's her."

My jaw dropped open at his casual tone. "Don't you?"

Amos scanned the board with a slow, methodical gaze.

Only on a continued, intense study did I note the stiff facial muscles; the clenched jaw; a pulse throbbing in the base of his throat. My muscles stiffened as well. My heart hung like a lead weight in my chest.

This wasn't going to be good.

A moment passed. Then another. Amos exhaled, a long, slow breath. A bleak look settled in his eyes. He pushed a pawn forward. "My family's gone. My sisters, my two boys, daughter-in-law. Buried 'em all."

The air around me thickened at his hoarse, strained voice. The chess board lost all meaning. I stared at the man.

His head remained bowed. His empty gaze was on the board. "Nobody left but me and Lily. Thirty-three. Visited me two weeks ago."

His soft tone sliced through the quiet air like a knife.

His granddaughter was the right age for the dead woman.

Was the victim of mixed heritage? My gut said no, but with the bruising and the passage of time, I couldn't be certain.

The older man seemed frozen in time. "Lily has called me on my birthday for thirty years. She didn't call this year."

Amos had moved his piece. I knew because he looked at me. That was my cue. However, chess wasn't my game. Puzzles were. Playing them. Creating them. Solving them. In a crossword grid or, sometimes, a murder. I hated to ask my next question because I feared the answer. "Have you called her?"

His eyes met mine. A dark abyss of pain threatened to erupt. "Just goes to voice mail."

The strain in his voice was almost unbearable.

A whoosh of air escaped my lips. My chest hurt as if I'd been punched. That would be the timeline for the murder. This kept getting worse. I didn't want his granddaughter to be the victim, but if not, where was she?

The question of his granddaughter's fate settled around me like a pall on a coffin. The timing made a connection to the murder all too credible.

I made no move to analyze what Amos had done or to answer with my own unthinking response. I was here to play my own game. Time passed. I couldn't say how long.

After a few seconds, perhaps minutes, he looked at me. Pain burned in his gaze. Without shifting his eyes, he pointed at the board. His movements stiff.

Feeling shellshocked, I stared at the pieces. Hopefully my brain was taking in what it saw. Not to save my life, could I have tracked Amos's move.

My hand grasped my second bishop and pushed him across the board. Normally, I'd question if this was too early to put it into the fray, but the thinking part of my mind was stacking clues.

Profit and loss. Passion and fear. That's what most crimes come down to in the end. "Where does she live? What does she look like?"

"San Diego. I called the local cops. Gave a report. Then, nothing." He swallowed hard. "She's five-five. Brown hair."

Again, spot on for the victim. Drat. I fought to keep my expression neutral. "Picture?"

Amos made a show of studying the board.

I doubt he saw anything.

"I can't identify the victim from a picture." I clarified quickly, putting a hand partway across the board. In addition to the bruises and the decay, the dead woman's arm had covered most of her face. Fortunately, I kept those details to myself. "The picture would help my investigation. I'll need her address, phone number, and place of business. Where did she work?"

"Loan officer at a bank. Dressed well."

That might explain the clothes, though Gucci was high-end.

The strain in Amos's shoulders relaxed. He could hope for a while longer that his granddaughter was alive. Somehow. Somewhere.

When he didn't move, I wasn't certain he'd heard me. Then, his shoulders rose and fell with a deep breath. His hand moved quickly to snatch his phone out of his shirt pocket. Without looking, he slid it toward Kevin. "In my contacts."

Kevin, with an understanding look at the older man, picked up the phone and swiped the screen to open it. Evidently, no lock code. As Kevin searched for a picture of the granddaughter, Amos moved a piece.

My hubby stopped. He shifted the phone to Amos.

The older man's gaze lingered on the picture with a pained expression, then he nodded.

"I'll forward it." Kevin turned the phone toward me.

A white woman in her mid-thirties smiled at me. Her light brown hair curled around her face. Was her hair long enough to be in a chignon, like the dead woman's? Maybe. With my questions multiplying, I schooled my expression to reveal nothing. I faced Amos with a questioning look.

"Lily was adopted." He explained. From one moment to the next, life returned to the old man's seemingly hollow frame. His eyes met mine with an impatient look. He gestured toward the board.

Where to go from here? The question floated through my mind as my hand shifted my second bishop across the board to take a knight. Now, it was my turn to sit back. He studied the board while I studied him. "Was her visit a social call?"

Admiration gleamed in the old man's eyes. "Logical progression in battle. Fall back and survey the field."

He sounded like Marcus. The boy viewed life in military terms. Amos viewed the world through a chess board. But who am I to judge? I make up crossword puzzles in my head to solve cases.

Everyone finds their own method of dealing with the hand they're dealt. It's not like anyone gets instructions to get through life. We make it up as we go.

"Her fifteen-year high school reunion is this year. The school's combining the ten, fifteen, and twenty-year class reunions with the Fall Festival in September." Amos reached toward the board. "Lily was on the planning committee. She asked me about the town's history and the local neighborhood."

I searched for a pattern, on the board, in the puzzle, in the case. Amos worked at the Mercantile years ago. Could his old stories connect with the dead woman? "Did the Mercantile come up?"

The man's gaze was locked on the board. "She found maps of the original town layout, plus blueprints of local stores. Owners and miners used to build hidey-holes for their silver. Several of the original buildings on Main Street have the hidey-holes, including the Mercantile."

"Did you mention her visit to anyone?" I asked.

Amos gave me a flat, hard stare. "She talked to several people. I didn't."

I believed that. Take away chess and local history and Amos makes Rabi look like a chatterbox. "What did you two talk about?"

"She was mostly here for research and to see me. She talked about her plans for the reunion. She was so excited." A glimmer sparked in Amos's gaze. His features softened when he grinned. "She wanted to do a treasure hunt using fool's gold. She planned to contact businesses and make it a big event during the festival. She was going to get prizes donated for the children."

"Did she visit old friends while she was here?" I asked. "The other people on the planning committee? Did she mention names?"

Amos's clenched fist on the side of the chess board relaxed. He met my gaze. "She had a couple of friends in high school. Neither one lives in town, and they couldn't get away to see her during her visit. She e-mailed them about her plans and getting together for the reunion."

A solid lead. Yearbooks from the local high school would give me pictures and background. "What were the names of her friends?"

Amos's brow furrowed in thought. "She talked about Savannah and... Audrey. She mentioned Paige once, then she stopped and changed the subject real quick. She mentioned a boy who hung around with Audrey's younger brother. I didn't meet him, but I remember they joked he was named after a famous lawyer. Lily called him a shyster, said he could talk his way out of trouble."

"Sounds like he had a lot of practice. This is great, Amos. It's more than I had." I'd spent eight years hunting down people who didn't want to be found for Crawford Investigations. Audrey, and the others were bound to be in their high-school yearbook. "I'll find them."

My detecting meter went into overdrive. Threads were fitting together. Sort of. Maybe.

I considered my next move. Attack? Defend? Whether applied to the game or the case, there were only so many options once the pieces were in play. I had no chance of winning the chess game, but I didn't plan to go quietly.

When in doubt: attack. It doesn't guarantee success, but it makes me feel better. If I can't grab the win, I'm satisfied with being an irritation.

In a flurry of moves, I took several of Amos's pieces before he cornered my king. When I tipped the poor little dude over, I eyed Amos with a mischievous grin. "Thanks for the game, and the info."

Amos studied the pieces still standing. He only had a few more on the board than I did. "You make sense of it?"

"Not yet." I folded my arms on the table, leaning forward. "But I will."

The older man put my fallen soldiers back on the board. "If you work your cases the way you play chess, you're going to leave a trail of scorched earth."

Kevin snorted. "You got that right."

I bunched my legs to stand.

Amos's long fingers reset the pieces. He scanned the circle of benches around the cobblestones.

People came and went. The afternoon had faded away. Waiting for the police and talking to Wilson had gobbled up hours before the game. I stared at my king, then stood him upright.

Amos watched me with a somber gaze. "Tracy."

Hearing an edge in his tone, I looked up. "Yeah?"

When our eyes met, his guarded gaze revealed nothing, not even a glimmer of hope. "You play a mean game when you're riled."

I cocked my head to one side, wondering where he was headed. "I've heard that before."

"I need to know." For a few seconds, silence reigned. Then, he swallowed hard. "Either way. You hear?"

Our gazes locked. Another lesson I'd learned, in high school, in marriage to my loser first husband, after taking in Marcus: Never make a threat or a promise you don't intend to keep. I put my fingers on the table. Light as a breeze, solid as stone. "I'll find her. I promise."

Either way. I ignored the voice telling me the statistics of people who disappeared with no trace. People who left and were never seen again. It's a heartbreaking fact that some questions cannot be answered. Some battles cannot be won.

None of that lessened my resolve.

The weight of the burden thickened the air around me. Though it would make my job easier, I didn't want the dead woman to be Amos's granddaughter. I cringed at the thought. The victim had been someone's daughter, wife, sister. Finding her name would bring sorrow to some family.

With a final nod, I walked away as clues lined up in my mind. Whoever had killed the dead woman had brought my private life and my PI job crashing together. I didn't like it.

Kevin and I strolled to the sidewalk. A long sigh hissed between my teeth. I'd been on this case for a few hours and all I had were more problems.

"What's wrong with her?" Marcus, who'd been working the crowd in between playing pirate on the jungle gym, sidled up.

Rabi and Mrs. C joined us on the walk to the Caddy.

Kevin jerked a thumb at me. "She promised Amos she'd find his missing granddaughter."

Marcus's dark eyes searched mine. "Is she the victim?"

"I don't know." My dark tone betrayed my feelings. She might be. Odds were looking that way. I kept that part to myself. "I have to check her out background. Find the facts. Find her friends."

The air seemed to have grown heavier. The day had started on a lark. Now I was on the hunt for the person who'd had brought death to my neighborhood. And I was going to find them. But first, I had to find a clue.

7

— • —

O nce in the car, everyone wilted. Except the boy child, who apparently worked on solar power. The day in the hot sun had amped up his energy. That or the investigation.

I was in no mood to cook. Not that I would have done the actual work anyway. That path led to a scorched stove and burnt food. I suggested eating out.

Marcus pounded on the back of the front seat. "We have to eat at home so we can solve the case."

The boy was confident if nothing else.

He continued without pause. "I can search the internet for missing women. The victim's been dead for days. Maybe a week? I'll have to check the rate of decomposition."

This heat was enervating. Now, even eating at a restaurant seemed too much work. "Hey, we still have that pan of broccoli lasagna in the freezer. Mrs. Pelton brought it over last month when we got back from Kentucky."

Kevin's expression turned suspicious. "How did lasagna survive a month in our freezer?"

I painted on an innocent smile. "I may have hidden it behind the frozen vegetables to save for a rainy day."

"Yes." Marcus threw himself against the back seat. "This is that rainy day."

Mrs. C snorted. "I'd give me left knitting needle for rain today."

The last I heard knitting needles didn't come in left and right pairs, but I shared her sentiment.

The older woman continued. "There are the makings of a salad in the fridge, plus raspberries, walnuts, and feta. I can throw together a nice treat."

I tapped Kevin's shoulder as the Desert Rose Dough bakery came in sight. "Stop here. I'll grab a couple loaves. One for bruschetta. One for garlic bread."

He parked before I finished speaking.

I'd planned a quick in and out, but having grabbed the bread I got stuck behind a trio of talkers. Discussing? The mysterious corpse. My gaze roamed over the delectable mounds of rolls and breads. The heavenly aroma of baking bread calmed some of my impatience. Although I was mentally urging the gossiping men and women to complete the sale and get out of my way.

Evidently, no one else shared my attitude. From the snippets of conversation, everyone around me was raking up their own version of the crime. The one who stood out to me was a young woman standing at a small table, ignoring the coffee and cinnamon roll in front of her. Her brown hair was pulled back in a ponytail. A baseball hat hid part of her face. Her tense posture and narrowed eyes betrayed an avid interest in the conversations around her.

An older woman whose name escaped me stopped near the table. She studied the younger woman's face. "You from around here? You look familiar."

A smile bloomed on the younger face. Convincing, but her eyes were wary. "I just arrived this morning. Sounds like you've had some excitement."

I half-listened to the older woman's answer while I noted the mysterious watcher hadn't actually answered the question. Their exchange ground to a halt as the younger one smiled blankly, clearly wishing to be left alone.

Fortunately for my curiosity, her interrogator had nowhere to go. She plopped her bag of items on the table. Looking around, she met my gaze and inclined her head toward the holdup at the register.

I smiled in acknowledgement then looked away. Outwardly indifferent to the pair. That's how you blend in.

The older woman sighed. "I used to work at the high school in the front office. Retired a few years ago."

A pause in her soliloquy alerted me. I glanced over.

The retired secretary was tapping her chin. "You attended the high school, didn't you? What's your name? Audrey. That's it. You're Jared Houlding's sister. You were listed in the article about his death a few months ago."

A jolt of electricity shot through me at the name. This was Lily's friend. The one who couldn't make time to meet Lily during her visit? Why was the woman here now? Had Amos been wrong? Had she met with Lily? I held myself back from jumping into the fray. I couldn't have done any better on the third degree than the older woman.

A look of sorrow crossed Audrey Houlding's face.

"I'm so sorry for your loss." The older woman continued. "Jared was such a lively soul. We saw him in the office more than a time or two, him and his friend, but he was too young to die."

Unfortunately, no one is too young to die. However, her comments pegged Jared as a troublemaker. I remembered his death. It had happened here in the neighborhood.

"Have you come back to see to his things?" The interrogator asked. "Did they ever find that car of his?"

Pain lanced across Audrey's face. She blinked her eyes and tightened her chin against a fresh wave of sorrow at the reminder of her loss. Her gaze sharpened whether in determination or anger was hard to pinpoint. "Yes, I'm here to settle matters."

That was the first honest response she'd given.

"It's been... what? Fifteen years since you graduated?" the older woman rattled on, oblivious to Audrey's reaction. "Lily was in town a while ago. She said she e-mailed you and Savannah. Did you meet with her?"

"No," Audrey answered through a tense smile. "The timing didn't work then."

The younger woman's gaze drifted to her cup. "She was supposed to return - "

Audrey's voice fell to a whisper. I strained to catch her words. Had she said return? I fought to contain my surprise as the younger woman broke off in midsentence. Amos hadn't spoken of Lily returning to town.

The older woman barely paused long enough to take a breath. "She talked to Amos about local history. She's planning activities for the reunions during the festival. Such fun. I love these events. Will Savannah attend the reunion?"

The same blank smile froze on the younger woman's face. "I'm sorry. I have to meet someone. Nice talking to you."

She flew out the door like a bird taking to flight.

The older woman blinked in surprise. "Well, I never."

I shrugged in response to her puzzled look. If my hands weren't full, I might have applauded. Mrs. C should add this woman to her quiver. Armed with the knowledge that Audrey was in town, I could track her down. A moment later, I plopped into the seat, cradling the fresh bread. "Guess what everyone's talking about?"

"Anything new?" Marcus perked up instantly.

I couldn't hide my excitement. I gave them a rundown of the conversation. The ride home was filled with speculation.

Moments later, we were in the loft apartment the Belden Tanner family called home. I'd lived here for eight years with Mrs. C as the landlady. She had the apartment on the first level. Marcus moved in four years ago as my foster son. After Kevin and I married in April, was it only three months ago? Anyway, Kevin joined us. Honestly, the place seems more like Grand Central Station somedays, especially when I had a case.

My investigations were group efforts. We all did our bit, but only I got the money. That seemed fair, to me. I could have worked the cases by myself, but the others enjoyed it so much. How could I refuse?

As usual we sat around the kitchen table. Marcus insisted we set up the whiteboards to catalogue what we knew. He had long ago anointed himself the king of record keeping.

Taking notes was the least of my concerns. My stomach had taken control while my brain worked in the background. I munched on a slice of Italian bread topped with fresh tomatoes, soft mozzarella, olive oil, and sea salt, crowned with basil. My tastebuds were drowning out my son when a pounding sounded on the door.

I swallowed before speaking. "Who can that be?"

"Belden!" A loud, gruff voice shook the door and echoed off the walls. "What are you doing?"

Crawford, my bossman and owner of Crawford Investigations, had a fog horn voice that had stopped many a brawl during his twenty-five years on various police forces from Kansas to Vegas to Langsdale.

Halfway across the room, the door was flung open. I scowled at Crawford. "Why are you harassing me in my own home? It's after hours. You have no business being here. You'll disturb the neighbors."

"You have no neighbors and PIs work twenty-four-seven!" He stalked past me. "You cause more trouble in less time than anyone I ever met. Hey, Marcus. How's my best operative? Not to mention the best report writer I have on staff."

The last quip was coupled with a hard stare at me.

Marcus returned the greeting with a puffed chest and a proud look.

I snorted at Crawford's jibe with unfeigned indifference. "My teachers couldn't make me turn in reports on time. I don't know why you think you can."

"Because I pay you." He spoke sternly. His attitude softened as he turned to the older woman. "Mrs. C, you're looking lovely, as always. Rabi. Kevin."

He greeted each man with a nod. When his gaze fell on the bruschetta, his eyes lit up. "Italian night."

"I made those," I said proudly.

He sent me a flat look as he sat at the table.

Kevin slapped a bottle in his hand which earned a smile from my garrulous boss and friend of over fifteen years. "What's Belden done now? She's only been on the case a few hours. Other than Wilson and a few neighbors, she hasn't spoken to anyone."

Crawford took a moment to chew and swallow. He reached for another bruschetta and pointed it at me. "Your reputation precedes you."

It usually did. "Deny everything. That's what I do. Who's riding your case?"

"The Langsdale Chief of Police," Crawford bit off each word. "Doesn't want you to interfere, be involved, or speak to anyone regarding the dead woman."

I sat back in surprise. I don't know what I expected, but that wasn't it. "That's going to make it a little hard to solve the case. I've never had dealings with... him? Her?"

No name or face came to mind to match the title.

"Oh, he's new, luv." Mrs. C chimed in.

The woman listens to news channels all day. She indulges in one-sided conversation telling the hosts what's wrong with their delivery. She also solves the world's problems. If only our transplanted Brit were in charge. Chaos would reign supreme, but it would be a lot more fun and have a British flair.

She took a delicate sip of her iced tea. "David Chumley, III, has been in his position for six weeks. No doubt the man wants to make a name for himself. Possibly secure the uptick in salary he was promised for raising the arrest metrics during the first months of his position."

Seeing my boss man's slack jawed look, I chuckled. No need to ask about her accuracy. The woman has a contact in every profession in the city. She especially loves to look behind the scenes in city business, including the police department.

Marcus laughed out loud. "Mrs. C, one. Police dept, zero."

Crawford tossed a rueful grin at the boy. "Don't let the chief hear you say that."

I frowned at the man. "Why does Chief Chumley care if I'm on the case? Wouldn't catching murderers be good for his metrics?"

"Credit." Rabi inserted his opinion in the fewest number of words, as was his want.

Crawford pointed at the other man. "Politics."

I growled in case my frown didn't send the proper message. "Wilson didn't object a few months ago when I helped close one of his homicide investigations. If I never see my name in print again, I'll be perfectly happy."

"Blah. Blah. Blah." Crawford leaned toward Marcus.

Marcus's high-pitched laughter almost drowned out Crawford as the boy joined in the chorus.

Crawford tilted his bottle in my direction. "The chief's talking tough. Mrs. C and Rabi get the picture. I delivered the message."

"And you knew it was dinnertime," I added. Crawford's wife and daughters were in Las Vegas for a shopping spree for an upcoming wedding. I'd heard the plans earlier in the week when I went into the office. "You're tired of takeout."

Marcus slapped Crawford's arm lightly. "That's why she's the detective. Except she still won't share any money with us."

My boss took a slow drink while he eyed me. Then, he turned to Marcus, shaking his head. "That's just wrong. The rest of you do all the work."

I slapped my hands on the table. "They do not. I do my part. I ask questions."

"Oh, su-ure." Marcus added plenty of attitude before he pointed at me, while still looking at Crawford. "She also delegates jobs like a pro."

"She's good at that." Crawford threw back his head and roared with laughter.

Laughter erupted around the table.

"How else will they learn?" Of course, I prefer to do the least I can do. Doesn't everyone? Besides, they volunteer. I sipped my lemonade. "This is going to be a long night."

Crawford had the final word. "At least I get to see the crack team in action."

***

An hour later, dinner had been eaten and cleared away. The whiteboards were in the living room in front of the television.

With Marcus standing next to his display, the rest of us arrayed ourselves on the u-shaped sectional. As the first piece of almost brand-new furniture I'd owned as adult, the sectional was my pride and joy.

Jimbo, a friend of Kevin's, had given it to us as a wedding present. The mural on the back had started as a scribble by the four-year-old child of the first owners. When they returned it to the store, Jimbo agreed to dispose of it. Marcus personalized the picture for us.

I sat in the lefthand corner, curled up next to my hubby. Mrs. C was situated just beyond my feet. Her knitting bag lay on the floor as her needles clicked away.

Crawford claimed the corner opposite me.

Rabi sat on the ottoman facing Mrs. C. He liked to have a wide field of view.

Our two cats, Rookie and Mr. Pickles, who we'd liberated on one of my cases, roamed freely. The two twenty-plus-pound felines looked like gray ghosts as they rubbed against people's legs.

"This is what we know." Marcus slapped an orange marker in one palm. His narrowed gaze scanned the circle facing him.

I clicked my tongue and put my mouth close to Kevin's ear. "Is it too late to ban the child from watching film noir?"

Kevin's shoulders shook with silent laughter.

Marcus pointed the marker at us. "Silence."

Kevin scowled at me. "Great, get me in trouble."

I'd have protested but I couldn't risk more demerits from the little dictator. I gave the boy a narrowed look. Our standoff ended with matching grins.

"Get on with it," I admonished. "Crawford doesn't have all night."

"Meh." My boss didn't point out that with his wife and daughters out of town he had nowhere to go.

"This is the victim!" Raising his voice, Marcus pointed to the board with a dramatic flourish. The picture showed the crumpled body of a woman with blood on her scalp.

Crawford scowled and leaned forward. "Where did you get a crime scene photo?"

"It's a stock picture from my files." Marcus shook his head as if he were addressing a four-year-old.

"Every detective should have fake crime scene photos." I added a note of disdain. "Until they can get the real thing."

Crawford glared at both of us equally, pressing his lips together.

"TR didn't have her camera with her." The boy child gave me a censoring look through his lashes. "Lack of planning."

"I was trying not to gag." I offered in my defense. "And my purse was in the trunk."

"Detective Wilson refused to share his crime scene photos. We'll have to look elsewhere." Marcus cocked his head at Mrs. C.

The older woman responded with a slow wink and a confirmational nod.

"Wait. What?" Crawford looked around. He stopped, seeming to consider his next words. After a heartbeat, his broad-shouldered body eased against the sofa. "I don't want to know."

"I've found that's best." I could have dug up the information on my own. During my friendship with Crawford, I'd met a number of people on the force. I'd also done research for eight years prior to going into the field.

However, Mrs. C would find the information anyway. It'd be a waste of time if we both pursued the same goal. Besides, people might let a few extra details slip with her. Everyone thought she was a harmless old woman.

If they only knew.

A tapping drew my attention back to the moment.

Marcus had written down my earlier guesses concerning the victim. "Do you think the dead woman is Lily?"

I'd thought of little else since speaking with Amos and come to one conclusion. "I don't know. I sent Wilson Lily's picture. The victim's face was badly beaten. Evidently some blows before she died, some after. The ME is going to use facial reconstruction. Until I know for sure, Lily is a missing person."

"You have to be sure." Marcus agreed in a serious tone. "But familiar with the neighborhood could be the most promising. Lily Gilbert grew up in this area."

His words started a ricochet in my brain. "I made a few calls while supper was cooking."

Marcus spun his hand in a circle. "While *we* were working."

I tossed my head. "I was doing my job. I called the loan company where Lily worked. They had her flight information. The airline confirmed Lily checked in for her return flight. Records show the seats were full."

Kevin tapped his leg. "Anyone see Lily after she arrived in San Diego?"

I nodded. "Her co-worker saw Lily in the office last Saturday. Monday, Lily planned to head to Fresno to meet a friend. That's as far as I've gotten. She never returned to San Diego. She didn't call Amos Tuesday on his birthday."

Kevin was now tapping a rhythm on my thigh. "Fresno's a four-hour drive from here. She could've returned."

"It's closer to five hours if you're not on the racing circuit." I patted his shoulder and smiled. "But, yes, she could have driven back to Langsdale."

Marcus's eyes narrowed in thought. He tapped his mouth with the marker. "Maybe she found something on those old maps she found. She came back to dig up the treasure. Somebody found out and didn't want to share."

"Or she had an accident and is in a hospital." Which was a long shot, especially considering the resemblance to the dead woman.

"Plausible." Crawford pointed at Marcus before looking my way. "Both of them."

Unfortunately, he was right. "I'll start calling hospitals and checking police reports first thing in the morning. Also- "

"Oh!" Marcus's exclamation cut me off. Both of his fists were clenched as he pounded his feet. "Lily could be the Survey Lady."

I clenched my jaw and glared at him. "As I was saying, I'll take Lily's photo to the Mercantile. Elena can confirm if it was Lily who came into the store. The timing's a bit off and her co-worker said their logo doesn't have a train on it. Also, Elena must have seen Lily around town when visiting with Amos over the years. She thought the survey lady looked familiar, but I think she would have remembered Lily."

"Good job." Marcus gave me a thumbs up. "Cover the basics."

"I'm glad you approve." My mind sorted through the possibilities. My gaze lit on Rookie, who'd jumped onto the ottoman and gazed at me with her arrogant green eyes. "I called Amos. He has a copy of the old blueprints Lily found."

"Gold and silver." Marcus crowed as he jumped up and down. "If you find buried treasure, you have to tell me first."

"Deal." After promising, I faced Kevin. "You're second in line."

Kevin appeared unconcerned. "I can live with that, as long as I get my cut."

Marcus dutifully made notes. Then he shifted to a blue marker and moved to the clean whiteboard. "Other news?"

"A bit more." The older woman twisted yarn around her fingers and flung out her arm, pulling a long section free. Her thoughtful gaze met Marcus's. "The survey lady visited no one else. One or two remember seeing someone of her description in the covered alley behind the deli last week."

Rabi narrowed his eyes.

Crawford frowned. "There's a covered alley in this area?"

Marcus stretched one arm above his head and pointed at me with the other. "TR is in for the score. She said the victim knew the neighborhood, obviously better than Crawford."

Kevin patted my leg. "It's sandwiched behind the Mercantile and the Crystals and Quartz Shop. The six-foot high wooden fence facing the street is painted with a mural. The lock on the gate looks intact, but it's not. Few people outside the neighborhood know it's there or that it can be accessed."

Crawford grunted and gave me a nod. "The dead woman knew the area. She lived here years ago."

"Including Lily or her mysterious friends." Marcus starred the bullet point he'd written earlier. "Anything else, Mrs. C?"

The older woman, who loved melodrama as much as the boy, worked on a few stitches. The smile quivering on her lips emphasized her wrinkles. "Tracy stole my thunder by finding Audrey Houlding first, but several people have seen her in town."

Marcus's eyes widened. "Maybe she's the Survey Lady."

I'd told them about the conversation overhead in the bread shop. "We know Audrey Houlding isn't the dead woman."

"She has questions about her brother's estate." The older woman pointed a needle at my son as Mr. Pickles rubbed against her legs. "He's the bloke found dead at the bottom of the stairs in his apartment building. Broke his neck, he did."

I noted the woman's suspicious tone. There'd been some questions about his death. "He died in May, two months ago. Something went missing after his death."

"His new car!" Marcus shouted.

"That's the ticket, innit?" Mrs. C cackled with glee, thrilled with the stir she'd made. "His sports car. Convert top. Sped through the streets with no thought for man nor beast, didn't he?"

Rabi smirked. "The blue bullet."

"How could I forget?" I considered if the car or his death tied into the current plotline. "He only had two weeks before he died."

A look of appreciation crossed Kevin's face. "A sweet ride, and pricey."

Rabi met my hubby's gaze and nodded. Then, his expression clouded over. "Vanished."

Without a trace. The neighbors swore the car was in his garage the morning Houlding died. When his family came two days later to claim the body, the garage was empty. I would have thought someone would notice the flashy, blue convertible being driven out of the neighborhood. But no.

Crawford grunted. "Insurance never paid off. Hundred thousand dollars. A buddy on the force said the sister can't find the title. She's pushing to have the case reopened. She thinks that would help get the insurance to pay up."

A chorus of murmurs rewarded the news.

Crawford grunted. "You all have the whole city covered with your sources for information. No wonder Chumley's worried about being beaten to the punch. Just don't give interviews."

Mrs. C continued with a satisfied expression. "The Houlding family moved to Oregon after Audrey graduated high-school. They invested in a fishery."

"Belly up?" I asked, sympathy at the ready for a family-owned business in these risky days.

Mrs. C cast me a sideways look. "On the verge of bankruptcy. Mrs. McLaren's cousin works for them. The sister's back to find the car and the cash."

"Pretty coincidental that she's in town, even ominous." Marcus's tone matched his words.

Ignoring the melodrama, the boy had a point. The family's financial struggles sparked a new idea. "Where did Houlding get a car worth that much money?"

Mrs. C inched up on the sofa cushion. Her pale green eyes sparkled. "He claimed to be a professional poker player. Crowed about winning a tournament."

Marcus tossed a marker in the air. It spun around twice before he caught it. "Maybe his bookie repossessed the car and killed him in the process. There were no witnesses when he fell, right?"

I gasped as a memory surfaced. "Elena found Jared Houlding's body the day he died."

"She didn't report it!" Marcus's high-pitched scream echoed off the ceiling. Mr. Pickles jumped up next to Rabi, looking for comfort. My son snapped his fingers. "She was... late for something."

"The airport." I clenched my fists in excitement. The details of her misstep replayed. "She was flying to her niece's wedding. She ran into the apartment building to pick up a wedding quilt the Stansbury sisters made."

"The cabbie waited out front." Mrs. C pointed a knitting needle at me. We'd discussed Houlding's death more than once. "Elena feared she'd never make the flight and miss the wedding if she reported the young man's death."

I snorted. "She was right, too. Police questioning takes hours."

"If you didn't get into those situations, you wouldn't be caught." Crawford met my accusatory look with a scowl. "Policing is for the greater good of pursing justice. People have to cooperate. But you're going in the right direction."

Rabi stroked Rookie's silky gray fur, but he followed the story. "Who knew she kept quiet?"

Good point. Elena's failure, discovered days after Houlding's death, never hit the local news or the paper. City officials prefer to keep violence and crime out of the public view. They believe it might discourage tourism.

"If one person in the neighborhood knew Elena found the body, the whole place learned of it within the hour." Crawford spoke in a growl a bear would have envied. "Why did she tell anyone?"

Marcus tapped his lip. "The police found out. When the Stansbury sisters left the quilt in the hall, Houlding's body wasn't there. When they came back half-an-hour later, Elena's check was on the table and Houlding was at the bottom of the stairs."

"She wasn't charged with obstruction?" Crawford asked, betraying his police background.

"No crime." Kevin gave a careless shrug. As a member of a grifter family, his attitude to the law was much more laid back. "Several tenants had reported the loose carpet at the top of the stairs. It was torn where he'd caught his foot. A piece of it was in his shoe."

"Death by misadventure." Marcus underlined the words with a deep, dark tone. Then his ominous expression gave way to a sunny grin. "No crime. No foul. Elena got a slap on the wrist. She promised to be good."

I chuckled at his odd choice of words. "The next time she finds a body she'll report it?"

As soon as the words were out of my mouth, my brain hit pause. I gasped. "Like today?"

Crawford eyed me with a skeptical expression. "That puts a new spin on her story about the dead cat."

I reviewed the exchange in the store. "I don't think either one of them knew about the dead woman. They wouldn't have involved me if they had."

"Is Survey Lady Houlding's sister? Lily Gilbert? Or someone new?" Marcus raised his voice to get us back on track. He outlined what Otis and Elena said about their visitor and the man following her. "TR told them to contact Wilson."

I couldn't ID any of the women from what I'd seen of the body. "What about the possible PI? Crawford? Does he sound familiar?"

My boss man frowned and shook his head. "He's not from town. I know them all."

And they knew him. They wouldn't cross his trail once word hit the streets this was his case.

"The guy's not a PI spinning a story. He's an uncle looking for his niece just like he said." Crawford's harsh tone conveyed his opinion of the man's lack of professionalism or maybe the whole affair.

Kevin's expression sharpened, though no one else would have noticed any changes. "Survey Lady could be the missing niece. Or could Savannah Lester might be the missing niece?"

"Way to connect the dots!" Marcus wrote down Kevin's observations. "And who told the aunt and uncle their missing niece was in town now?"

"Good question." One of many I had. I shot the boy an admiring look while patting Kevin on the back.

Marcus preened as Kevin and Rabi rewarded him with looks of congratulations. He added the possible connections to the board. In a swift spin, he jabbed the red marker at Crawford. The boy's narrowed eyes targeted the man in an unprovoked attack. "We need the woman's identity."

My boss, taken aback at the sudden shift, spread out his hands. "I've heard nothing. I'm not even on the case."

Marcus tapped the marker on his lips. "Did Chief Chumley contact you directly to keep TR off the case?"

Crawford's hesitation only lasted a heartbeat. "A quick call."

"I hope you told him to mind his own business." I don't like being told what to do. "And you're paying me even if you give back the money."

Crawford waved a hand at my outrage. "I told him it's a free country, but I was more diplomatic than you."

"Hah." If I didn't trust Crawford to have my back, I wouldn't have stuck with him this long. I've burnt more than one bridge when people left me swinging in the wind. I faced my son. "For the record, I haven't caused trouble. Yet."

My son smirked at me. "It's only a matter of time."

Kevin squeezed my leg. "The man's scared of getting upstaged. He should let you do the work then take credit."

"I have no quarrel with others taking credit. All I want is my paycheck." I admitted. "That works for Wilson."

Crawford smirked. "Wilson wants a collar. Crumley wants to be the only face in front of the cameras. Don't do interviews."

I snorted. "Don't worry."

Marcus's eyes widened as he focused on Crawford. "You and Wilson are buddies. He knows if he tells you stuff, you'll tell TR. Then she can solve the case and Wilson will get the collar."

Crawford answered the boy's suggestion with a stern expression. "I'm not going to be one of your stoolies."

"Fine." Marcus's disgruntled tone spoke volumes as he waved away the man's protest. "I'll talk to Wilson. He knows the score. He loves me."

"It's my case." I warned Marcus. "I'm the PI."

"I am, too." Marcus wagged his head, grinning at me. "Ha-ha. I have a PI license from Crawford Detective Agency. Besides, I'm a little kid. People think it's cute to talk to me."

Like Mrs. C, people underestimated the boy's determination to solve a mystery. They were both cute and sympathetic. What did I have going for me? I was annoying and pushy. I glared at Crawford. "This is your fault."

Crawford folded his hands on his belly. He gave me a flat stare. "He writes clearer reports than you ever did, and I'm not the one using him to do all my work."

"How else will he learn?" I fell back on my earlier defense before sitting back. "Wilson eats breakfast at the Mineral Café every Sunday. I can hit him up there for the latest info."

Marcus threw his hands in the air. "Road trip!"

8

— . —

19 Across; 6 Letters;
Clue: Lie in wait for someone.
Answer: Waylay.

The Sunday ambush turned into a family affair. Marcus refused to be left behind.

Kevin invited himself as well. "I'm not cooking breakfast for myself while you two live high on an expense account."

Marcus, settling into the backseat of the Great White Beast, gave a thumbs up. "Word. She only looks out for herself."

"Be nice or I'll leave you behind." Though I fixed the boy with a stern gaze, I was happy to have them along. Like Marcus, everybody loves Kevin.

As I leaned back, the boy thrust himself forward and rested his chin next to my shoulder. "What's wrong, TR? Are you confused? Depressed? Down hearted? You're grumbly."

Kevin glanced at us. "When is she not grumbly?"

I shook my finger at Kevin's laughing eyes before facing Marcus. "You sound like those commercials for feelgood pills."

The boy's eyes brimmed with sympathy. "You want answers."

"And I have none." I groused. "I spent last night going through my missing person check list for Lily Gilbert."

"Her disappearance fits with the timing for the dead woman." Marcus noted quietly.

The argument that the victim was Lily looked solid, but my brain pushed me to go through my missing person checklist. I think my brain didn't want to face Amos. "I checked hospitals and morgues around Langsdale, Vegas, and San Diego. There was some pushback, but they finally confirmed the three Jane Does aren't a match."

Kevin cast me a quick sympathetic look. "You faxed her picture to them?"

"Yes." I dragged out the word in a hiss of frustration. "No one has a coma victim under a different name from the time in question."

"You check on coma victims with different names?" Astonishment rang in Marcus's voice. "How does that work?"

"I've found people hiding under an alias who got injured. Twice." I looked over my shoulder. "One was admitted under a fake name. One was buried under their false identity. I did this for eight years. I need correct answers for my puzzles to work."

Kevin glanced at Marcus in the rearview mirror. "That's why Crawford pays her. She won't quit."

The boy studied me with a steady gaze from his dark eyes. "You're pretty obsessive, TR, but you're good. I never would've thought of comas and fake names, except Lily's not hiding."

I shifted to look at the boy directly. "How do you know?"

After a few seconds, Marcus nodded, conceding the point. "We're just beginning to investigate. You'll find the answers and you'll clear Elena and Otis. Lily may already have been found."

Kevin's gaze was analytical as he drove down the street. "Belden won't admit that until she eliminates every other option.

The man's ability to hit the bullseye on profiling marks had made him an unbeatable asset to the Feilen family. I couldn't blame them for being furious when he left.

"At least, Elena and Otis are innocent." Marcus spoke with the certainty of youth. "They hired us to find the murderer."

"And that's what I'll do." Feeling satisfied with my decision, I released the breath I'd been holding. "First, I need to fortify myself."

Fifteen minutes later, Marcus led the way into the Mineral Café. The small building made of pink stucco had Spanish tiles on the roof. A wooden lattice shaded a patio from the sun. Large misting fans stirred the air. Fortunately, it was relatively cool compared to the heat of the afternoon.

The weather person promised a cooling afternoon, but I wasn't holding my breath. After all, it was July in the desert.

The Mineral Café was crowded as always. The small diner was a neighborhood hideaway with great food and seventy years tucked under its belt. Thankfully, it wasn't listed as a tourist destination. It was also a distance from most of the police stations. Which was one of the reasons Wilson liked it.

Marcus walked up to the detective's table with a conspiratorial smile. "She sent me in first as a shill."

Wilson chuckled and tapped the place setting to his right. "I got a four-seater with room for expansion. I figured the whole gang would be here."

Marcus's grin widened. "We went low-key so you wouldn't be intimidated. Besides, you don't have the autopsy results and you won't share the crime scene photos."

"I'm hoping I can delay you hacking into my files or bribing someone with one of Mrs. C's coffee cakes." The lanky, scarecrow like detective took a sip of coffee. "But I appreciate the consideration. I also want it on record I won't report you if you bribe me with one of Mrs. Colchester's desserts."

"Noted, and for the record, Rabi's busy." Marcus admitted while taking his seat. "Mrs. C planned to hit up the bakery for a scone and tea with her book club friends. She's working on the crime scene photos. We should have them by tomorrow."

Wilson narrowed his gaze as he acknowledged me and Kevin with a nod. "Keep me updated."

"Quid pro quo." Marcus intoned. "We could invite you to be a guest speaker at one of our meetings."

"Depending how this case breaks, I'll keep it in mind." The man greeted me as I took the seat opposite him. I like to face people head on when I'm questioning them.

Wilson and Kevin exchanged pleasantries.

"I'm just here for the food." Kevin picked up his napkin. "An expense account is serious business with the Belden Tanner Agency."

The server walked up before I could draw breath. She and every other female in the room had watched my hubby walk in. I didn't blame them for being enraptured. It's not every day you see someone who resembled a hero out of Greek mythology.

Kevin, who was the only person she looked at, ordered coffee for the two of us before asking Marcus what he wanted.

Wilson watched the breathless server walk away. "At least, I won't have to wait for anything now."

I studied the menu, lingering over the delectable descriptions. A meal at the Mineral Café must be given due consideration.

"Hey." A mischievous grin crossed Wilson's face. "You could pay for me."

Crawford and I often crossed swords regarding my expense account. I'd won the company award for the most inventive expenses more than once. He'd already reimbursed Mrs. C for multiple pairs of slippers she'd sacrificed to my cases. Boss man knew he'd have to pay for the gang on occasion. If he didn't, I'd turn Marcus loose on him, possibly Mrs. C for good measure.

That was a fight he wouldn't win.

I considered Wilson's request. Putting down my menu, I smiled. "That would depend on how good an informant you are."

"Just my luck." His expression fell. "I can tell you what I *don't* know."

Marcus balanced his chin on his fist. "The woman's name."

The detective stabbed his fork at the boy. "No solid match to anyone missing in three states. Her face is too damaged for a picture to be of any use. I can't check dental records until I have a name."

Good thing no one at the table had a weak stomach.

We paused as our server delivered his meal and our drinks. I thanked her, though I wasn't sure she heard me. I nodded at Kevin who ordered for all of us.

I chose French Toast stuffed with cherries and sweet whipped cream cheese with a side of bacon. Yum! Kevin went with pancakes served with strawberries and lemon curd. Marcus chose waffles with whipped cream and mixed berries.

Once the waitress left, I inhaled the aroma of the dark, roast coffee before focusing on Wilson. "Do you have any leads?"

His features sharpened like a hound on the hunt. "Amos's granddaughter is a strong contender. Elena called regarding the woman supposedly conducting a survey. Sammy was thrilled to describe the suspicious male. Thanks for the photo and pushing them to call."

Marcus was hunched forward, impinging on Wilson's personal space, though the detective didn't complain. "Crawford said the guy isn't a local PI. He probably is looking for his niece, but the timing is very suspicious."

"That saves me time." Wilson spoke in a serious tone. He pulled out his notebook to scribble the detail. "Crawford would know."

He chewed in thoughtful silence for a moment.

"That's it?" At Marcus's outburst, Wilson jumped. The boy's gaze held a stark accusation. "That's not going to get you a free breakfast."

"We..." The man wiped his mouth with a napkin. A disgruntled expression accompanied a harsh look. "*I* caught a break with the autopsy. A visiting coroner jumped at the chance to work with the ME. They're doing the exam this morning and trying a new technique for facial reconstruction. I'll have preliminary autopsy results this afternoon. Facial reconstruction could take a few days."

"Good news." Kevin made it sound like he was congratulating Wilson as if it had been the detective's idea. My hubby had the ability to make people feel like no one else existed.

Wilson's shoulders relaxed.

Everyone tenses up when I talk to them.

In the next heartbeat, Wilson rounded on me. "Do you have anything?"

I weighed my options then decided to come clean. "Jared Houlding's sister, Audrey, is in town. I saw her yesterday trying to stay low key at the local bakery."

The light dawned in Wilson's eyes. "The guy who tripped down his apartment stairs two months ago."

I leaned back as the waitress delivered the rest of our meals with a promise to return with a pot of coffee. "Rumor has it she came back to town with questions about his missing car. The Houlding family owns a fishery on the Oregon coast. I'm sure you have the resources to track down details. Audrey was a friend of Lily's. Lily e-mailed Audrey and Savannah about her plans for the upcoming class reunion."

I updated him on my talk with Amos, including the old blueprints and the planned hunt for fool's gold and fake silver nuggets. I relayed the conversation I'd overheard with Audrey Houlding, including the possibility of Savannah Lester being Elena's visitor.

The detective busily scribbled notes in his omnipresent notepad as I spoke. "Savannah Lester wasn't on my radar. She could be the missing niece."

Marcus pointed his knife at Wilson. "You have to update us on what you find. So, we know whether to pursue the Houlding angle or not."

"I'll let you know." Wilson winked at the boy. He tapped his notepad. "Anything else?"

I shook my head. "If it wasn't for the connection to Elena and the odd timing, I'm not sure I'd give the Houlding connection credence. The family left town years ago."

Wilson's narrowed eyes met mine. Behind his gaze, the wheels were turning. "If she hung out with Savannah Lester, she knows about the store and the covered alleyway."

I took a bite of my stuffed French Toast. The cream cheese filling mixed with cherries and covered with syrup exploded in my mouth. I fought to focus on the case. "Audrey Houlding might be in a management position, CEO or VP. She might be living above her means."

"Dressed as an executive." Wilson's expression grew somber. "You hit the target, Tracy. The victim's business suit was top of the line. I'll contact the Oregon authorities for more information on the family business."

At the first pause in our by-play, Marcus jumped in. "You should also note the make and model of Jared's missing car."

"Thanks." Wilson responded in a dry tone as the boy tapped his notebook. He did make a note, shaking his head as he did so. "I don't remember any mention of the car when Houlding died."

Kevin spoke up. "It disappeared after the fact. Once the coroner declared the death an accident, the police closed the case. No crime. No foul. No report."

I leaned forward. "The family reported the car stolen. The vehicle was insured for a hundred thousand dollars. Crawford says the insurance refused to pay off due to a question about the missing title. So, the family is out that money along with some cash Audrey swore he had."

Wilson threw down his pen with a sharp gesture that spoke of frustration. "I could eliminate some of these threads if I knew the victim's name."

"Maybe Jared had something on him when he died." A slow smiled spread across Marcus's face. His black eyes were aimed at a spot somewhere over Kevin's shoulder. "What if Elena took Jared's keys then stole his car? The sister came back for revenge. They got into a fight and the sister was killed."

The boy ended his story on a triumphant note. Grinning, he ate a bite off his fork and poked the utensil at each of us around the table. "Pretty good, hunh? It may have a few flaws."

"A few?" Wilson asked in an incredulous tone.

"You don't even know who the dead woman is." Marcus argued back.

I took a long drink of my coffee, feeling its warmth running through my veins. "We need more information."

The detective raised a brow. "I believe you have me confused with your gang of miscreants."

Marcus, his mouth full of strawberries and waffles, shook his head as he chewed quickly. "We're legit. I have a license."

Noting that he'd swallowed his food before responding, I flashed a proud mama smile at my hubby. "We did good."

"Besides," Marcus continued. "TR was stating a fact. I'll hit the keyboard when we get home. Mrs. C has feelers out all over the city."

"I'm getting scared." Wilson met Marcus's slow wink with a deepening frown before glancing at me. "Crawford told you the chief wants you to stay away from reporters and their cameras."

Knowing my boss man wouldn't leave me hanging in the wind, I smirked. "I'm a licensed PI investigating a matter for a private citizen. The police have no legal basis to stop me. Besides, your chief will have to take on my boss man if he starts an argument."

Crawford put in twenty-five years, mostly in homicide, before retiring from the Langsdale Police Department. He cleared two murder cases without corpses. He's well known and well respected by the rank and file. Several politicians and wealthy members of the community were indebted to my boss. He'd saved them from the embarrassment of being dragged into a crime when he knew they were innocent.

Chumley would bury me in a mudslinging match, but he wasn't going to win a public battle against Crawford.

Wilson indulged in a soft chuckle. When his phone rang, he checked the readout. A gleam of anticipation lit his eyes. "This is Wilson. What do you have?"

Marcus's gaze slid to me. "Autopsy?"

My heart beat faster. I understood the boy's uncertainty. The ME could barely have finished examining the body. "I think so. They must have found more than they expected."

We'd both whispered, all the while watching the detective.

Wilson had his notebook out. His pen scribbled as he grunted into the phone. Then, he froze, pen, hand, body. His gaze traveled slowly across the table. His eyes locked on a spot in the middle. "Which one killed her?"

My brain searched for the other half of the conversation. I lit on the answer as Kevin's fingers brushed the back of my hand.

Two of his fingers tapped the table. "Two fatal wounds."

He glanced at our son, making sure he'd heard.

I nodded. Wilson's grunt drew my attention.

He drew a long breath. His gaze met mine. "I agree, stabbing someone in the heart after bashing her head against a concrete floor is overkill."

My jaw dropped. I'd seen the blood beneath her head, but not the stab wound. The forensic team should have seen both wounds, but they couldn't confirm both were fatal or which caused the victim's death.

Though in shock, I noted Wilson made a point of repeating the information. He could have kept a poker face even when hearing of the astonishing result.

His revelation made clear where he stood on my involvement in the murder investigation. Not that he could stop me any more than Chumley could.

Like me, Wilson wanted to find the killer, but who had wanted to silence the woman so badly they would strike twice to ensure the victim's silence?

9

---

8 Down; 8 Letters;
Clue: The end of a route; i.e., planes.
Answer: Terminal.

On Sunday afternoon the mercury passed one hundred for the fourth day in a row. So much for the weather people hitting the bullseye. Fortunately, I was sitting at my kitchen table finishing a crossword puzzle in my new book, compliments of Elena and Otis. The theme was Paris.

For once I had the apartment to myself, except for two cats who let me live in their domain. Mr. Pickles was stretched out on my legs as my feet rested on another chair. As I rubbed his back, his purr reverberated into my bones.

Rookie, his sister, patrolled the apartment in a constant circle. She may have been searching for her human brother. I told her Marcus and Kevin had invited Rabi to go to a construction company for supplies even though it was Sunday.

The cat didn't listen to me. She never does.

As I stared at the two letters in the squares for twenty-one down, inspiration struck. My subconscious pulled fragments from different sources and put them together for the answer. That's the way it happened a lot of times with puzzles and cases. Not so far with this case, but I'd just begun.

Mrs. C hadn't made an appearance, which was odd. She knew our plan to waylay Detective Wilson this morning. I'd expected her as soon as I returned.

Hopefully she was following a lead. Glee filled me at the possibility of Chumley going after Mrs. C. Behind her knitting needles, the old woman was a gray-haired shark who could turn public opinion against the man in a flash.

"I could look at the balance sheets for the handyman business." I stroked Mr. Pickles's silky gray fur. "But we'd both have to get up if I did that."

He twitched an ear. A clear vote against movement of any kind. With a last check of my completed crossword puzzle, I relaxed and let my mind drift. It drifted to the case. I couldn't see the whiteboards, but I knew what they said.

After Wilson's stunning revelation, he'd relayed the ME's belief that the head blow and the knife struck almost simultaneously. However, the fractured skull had killed the woman. Based on the damage to her skull, she'd been thrown to the concrete floor. Not fallen or tripped, forcibly thrown.

I had to wonder if she and her attacker had been fighting. The blows to her face had come both before and after death. The momentum of a forceful attack could have propelled her backward and smashed her head against the floor.

At some point during the final seconds, her killer shoved a six-inch blade into her chest, slicing her aorta. Whether due to luck or knowledge was an open question. The angle of the wound and the relatively small amount of blood proved she was stabbed after she was dead.

The detective, who'd finished eating, packed up his notes and left.

I put his meal on my account. I couldn't wait until Crawford saw that entry.

"She walked into that basement with someone she knew. Though I can't figure out why anyone would go into that basement." My soft words in the empty apartment drew a flick of the tail from Mr. Pickles. As I batted it aside, Rookie stared at me from a crouched position in the archway. "Were they looking for something? Did one betray the other? Was the meeting a set up?"

I was under no illusion either feline was paying attention, but hearing the facts out loud gave me a clearer picture of what might have led to the murder.

Footsteps pounded on the stairs interrupted my monologue. The door rattled violently in its frame before a key turned in the lock. Marcus bolted into the apartment, stopping to greet Rookie who loped into the kitchen at his feet.

The boy shot me an accusing scowl. "Why do you lock the door? It slows me down."

"Heaven forbid my safety come before your grand entrance." I laid on a thick slice of sarcasm to absolutely no effect. "Did you get the supplies in order?"

"Yep." Marcus, heading for the refrigerator, threw the answer over his shoulder. "Jim at Consolidated Supply Company delivered the drywall and paint as a favor to Kevin. We all helped unload it."

Mr. Pickles, roused from his nap, jumped off my legs. After a long stretch, he sauntered out of the kitchen. He and Rookie, his tag team partner, exchanged glances as she walked in. "Your turn to watch the humans. I'm off duty."

I smiled at the fanciful exchange.

Kevin walked into the kitchen. "Don't fill up on junk food. Rabi's getting the grill ready on Mrs. C's patio. We popped for burgers and cheddar baked potatoes. Mrs. C wants to watch some show streaming from Down Under."

Our son shut the refrigerator door with more force than necessary. "Mrs. C has news. The book club scored. I'm putting them in my report as the Gray-Haired League. I can't wait to hear what Crawford says when he reads that."

I hadn't moved since their arrival. "I take it the whiteboards are going downstairs?"

"Absolutely." Marcus ran by with a sack full of bottled drinks. "I have to help Rabi. I hope Mrs. C didn't find more women missing. You haven't eliminated the ones we have now."

I winced as the door slammed behind the Marcus whirlwind. The boy took my breath away. I met Kevin's laughing eyes. "Why is it my case when things go south?"

"'Cuz you're the big cheese." He held out his hand. "Play time's over, Belden. Back to work."

I let him pull me to my feet. My stomach growled at the promise of a grilled burger with onions and mushrooms. "Are we watching a soccer match or a royal family event?"

"Mrs. C didn't say." Kevin sounded resigned. "Between her and Marcus, there were several conversations going on."

"Why am I not surprised?"

***

I'll skip over the scrumptious meal. Afterward, I collapsed in Mrs. C's overstuffed chair in a food coma.

"That was delicious." My eyelids drifted shut as all my blood rushed to my stomach. "Thank you, Rabi, for standing over the grill on a day like today."

"TR." Marcus's soft whisper sounded in my ear as his breath fanned my cheek. "Are you in there?"

His finger lifted my eyelid. His almost black iris stared at me from an inch away.

I jumped and put a hand on my racing heart. "Don't do that!"

The boy stared at me. "You can't sleep."

"I could if you'd leave me alone," I retorted. Taking a calming breath, I resettled myself.

He leaned forward. "What about the case? Mrs. C has news. Where's your dedication?"

I frowned up at his determined expression. "What makes you think I was ever dedicated?"

"You're just being funny." My son turned toward the whiteboards. "You really care, deep down inside."

Kevin snorted with laughter. "*Way* down inside."

I burrowed into the British flag printed on my pillow, leaving one eye open. "We can't talk about the case. Mrs. C needs to listen to her show. What is it? Soccer? Royal marriage? Burial?"

"A polo match from Australia." She spoke in excited tones about the team and their record. "The young royals are in a special match with Queensland Polo Association. This is the pre-show. The game won't start for hours. We've time aplenty to discuss the case."

"Oh, goody." Hours? Crickey. Something nudged my leg. I looked down to see Rookie jump on the ottoman. Mr. Pickles put his paws on the wall and stretched. "Why are the cats here?"

"They're part of the team." Marcus grinned at me as he walked by carrying one of the infamous whiteboards. "Mrs. C didn't find another missing woman."

"Good." Kevin spoke with emphasis. "We are full up with unidentified women."

Resigned myself to living without a nap, I struggled to a semi-upright position, putting a pillow under my head.

The telly showed crowds of people filling the sidewalks and green spaces of London. With a miniature Union Jack in the potted plant and pictures of English villages and Trafalgar Square surrounding us, we could have been in a London flat.

The older woman sighed as she gazed at our little circle. "You Yanks have nothing to compare to the pageantry of the royals."

"Nope, we don't." Marcus agreed cheerfully, if a bit hurriedly. "Better get the meeting started so you don't miss the important stuff later on."

My lips twitched at his patently false show of concern.

"That's sweet of you, ducks." Mrs. C crooned. "Thinking of others."

"Absolutely." I shot a narrowed look at my son who studiously ignored me. "What's the news, Mrs. C?"

"It all begins with a single knot." The older woman untangled her knitting project from a skein of yarn. "The ladies in the bridge club and the book club put out feelers. It turns out Berta Hollins's former foster son has a girlfriend working at a car rental agency."

I ignored the string of contacts to grasp the final point. "One of our suspects rented a car?"

"Oh, no, dear." Her crushing tone admonished me for jumping ahead of the story. "The planes arrive and depart directly across from the agency's front window. A six-seater landed Wednesday. She noted the date because air traffic was restricted that morning. No flights in or out."

Please, no one ask why.

"Why did they block flights?" Kevin asked.

No one listens to me. I frowned at the man, who smirked in return.

"A foreign dignitary was flying through the area enroute to a secret meeting." Mrs. C pointed up with her knitting needle, whirling it in a circle. "Eastern Europe trade negotiations for next year's grain crop."

So much for international secrets. The CIA will never know what they lost when Mrs. C decided to stay local.

When Marcus opened his mouth, I leapt into the fray. "What did the... foster son's... girlfriend have to say about the plane? Did she see who was on it?"

Surprisingly, I was able to dredge up the connections.

"Why wasn't the plane shot down?" Marcus asked with ghoulish curiosity.

As if that would happen. I held onto my patience as my attempt to stay on course failed.

"Interesting point." Mrs. C aimed her pale green eyes at my son. Her knitting lay in her lap, not one stitch ahead of where it had been at the beginning of this conversation. "The six-seater came in unannounced."

Kevin raised a brow. "No flight plan?"

"Flew under the radar." The older woman sat back. A triumphant smile curved her lips. "Three people on board. A pilot known to make dodgy flights, probably running drugs, and an older couple. The little girlfriend, Jenny? Julia? Whoever, had gone to the airport canteen. Berta says it's a lovely little diner."

"We could go there for intel." Marcus quivered with excitement. "It'd be a perfect cover."

Gritting my teeth, I ignored the boy child and pointed at Mrs. C. "What did Jenny Julia have to say?"

The older woman glanced at the television before picking up her needles. Thankfully, she could knit without looking. Once she found her place, her fingers did the rest. "The older couple were impatient, saying they dare not lose the trail. They mentioned ties to Langsdale."

"Interesting." Kevin kept his keen gaze on Mrs. C. "Was his companion the murdered woman?"

"No, dear." Mrs. C shot down the idea immediately. "The woman at the airport was close to sixty. Short, sandy brown hair mixed with gray. Close to six-feet tall and rather plump. However, the man fits the description of the stalker watching the Mercantile. No names. No saying where the flight originated. Small planes can fly up to one thousand miles."

"Good deal, Mrs. C." Marcus, who'd hung on every word, added the facts to the board. The descriptions were listed under a new entry of Airport Woman and the current one of Uncle.

I'd give my son's markers for a real name.

"The airport has security cameras. Local businesses, too." Kevin's brow furrowed. He looked at Rabi. "That temp last month, he went back to work at the airport. He could provide intel."

He winked at Marcus, obviously pleased with himself at the military reference. If our gang went to military protocol, I'd be kicked out. The temp worker might be a useful connection. However, few people would have access to the security footage.

The lean man nodded. "Janitor. Keys to everything. His brother works security."

I stared at the man in disbelief. Why did the pieces fall into our hands? Were we looking at another breaking and entering gambit? I started to object, but Mrs. C cut me off.

"Isn't that lovely?" Mrs. C looked like a cat with a bowl of cream in front of her. Of course, she'd dive in to a B&E. "I have an acquaintance at the airport as well. Perhaps we could run out together. I'm sure Marcus would love a behind the scenes look at the operations."

"Perfect." Marcus fisted both hands in the air. A sly expression covered his face. "I'll say it's a project for school. People love to talk about their jobs. I can ask about security or distract them."

I stared at them with my mouth hanging open. This is how I lose control of these situations. "What school? It's July."

"I could be in summer school." Marcus's raised eyebrows disappeared under his straight black hair. His wide eyes were full of innocence. "One of my teachers is bound to assign a project like this eventually. You want me to do well on my schoolwork, don't you?"

On non-existent assignments? What child makes up their own projects? Only our boy.

Marcus turned to me with shining eyes. "You two want to come, TR? Kevin?"

I didn't see a way to derail this plan, but I didn't intend to be part of it. "I'll leave this with the professionals."

Better deniability.

"I'll sit out, too." Kevin sounded disappointed. "I need to keep an eye on Belden."

I gave him a flat stare before facing Marcus. Since I couldn't stop them, I might as well support them. "I have no doubt the three of you will make this work."

Kevin jerked upright. The grin on his face bordered on crazed. "If the plan goes south and you get arrested, we have money to pay your bail."

"Whoo-hoo!" Marcus jumped up and down howling at the ceiling. "We're rich!"

Mrs. C stopped knitting. Her eyes widened. "Let's not go that far, luv."

For once, I agreed wholeheartedly with the older woman. "Let's hope for the best."

Marcus snorted in laughter. "With the three of us running this scam, the airport won't know what hit 'em."

That's what worried me. "It's a good lead, Mrs. C. If it pans out, we might get names. That would be a huge help. So far, we're flying blind on suspects and the victim."

"Cops, too." Rabi clicked his tongue as his long fingers stroked Mr. Pickles's soft, gray fur. The purring cat raised a white paw and spread out his toes, six on each paw. A legacy of his and Rookie's polydactyl heritage. "No matches."

The tidbit diverted me from the cat's antics. I'd expected the police to gain a few leads. Someone had to be unaccounted for.

Kevin showed no surprise. "Too many tourists and day trippers. If she stayed under the radar, no one knows she's missing."

Disappointed, I raked my fingers through my short hair. "I'll dig into the pasts of the Houlding family and Harvey Lester. The yearbooks for the high school might be on-line. If not, I'll get one tomorrow for Lily's graduating class."

"In the meantime..." Marcus drew himself up to his full height. His eyes gleamed like searchlights. "We have a lead on the woman."

I smiled at his showmanship. "How do you have a lead when no one else does?"

The boy's grin widened. "I received an e-mail in response to the Belden Tanner Agency's emergency alert."

My brain came to a full stop. The boy had built my cases into his own empire, but... "We have an emergency alert e-mail?"

"You're on the e-mail, TR." Marcus's shoulders slumped. He slapped his forehead. "This is why you never made it in the corporate world."

Kevin burst out laughing. "That and her inability to listen to authority."

I slapped the arm of the overstuffed chair. "Hey! I lost a cushy corporate job saving you from a murder charge. I'd just received a promotion I'll have you know."

"And I'll — " Kevin was laughing so hard he could barely get the words out, "always be grateful for your sacrifice."

My righteous indignation crumbled as honesty rose up. "Although I didn't like my job or my jerk of a boss."

"Don't sympathize with her." Marcus ungiving attitude left no room for argument. "She'd have cracked under the pressure and jumped somebody for stealing her flavored coffee. She'd be in the clink causing all kinds of trouble."

I started to object, but his scenario was all too likely. "I could see that happening."

"Now," Marcus continued as he waved the marker with each word, "she's cleaning up the violent streets of Langsdale."

Kevin eyed him with a wary look. "Violent streets? Are you trying to inspire us or are you running for office?"

"With *our* help, she's putting away criminals and killers." The boy swept the marker through the air. At the high point of the arc, Rookie launched herself from the arm of the sofa. She wrapped her seven toed front paws around the boy's arm and clamped her teeth on the marker.

Marcus, staggering under the big cat's unexpected attack, let go without a fight. As Rookie ran off, the boy yelled at her. "Rookie! I need red for our murder victim."

The cat pinned the marker with her oversized paws. She stared at Marcus, daring him to reclaim her prize.

With a final glare, Marcus turned away. "TR can be bossy, but she's a better PI than a paper pusher. I excel at both 'cuz my e-mail blast brought a lead that could blow everything wide open."

He spread out his arms to underline his claim.

"What is the news?" Kevin slapped the sofa with each word.

Marcus crossed his arms over his chest. "Holly answered my e-mail."

The others looked surprised. I was confused. "Holly who?"

They turned to me in one move.

Marcus rolled his eyes. "Your number one fan. A consulting member of the Belden Tanner Detective Agency. The head of public relations at the Silver Swan Resort. *That* Holly."

My number one fan? More like my *only* fan. The news left me breathless in shock. "Oy."

The woman had been involved, I'm not sure I can say helpful, in a previous case. My parents won a free weekend at the Silver Swan and got caught up in a murder case from Mrs. C's past. Holly was their contact. Turned out, she follows my cases when they hit the local news. I never give interviews, but I have been mentioned a few times.

"Holly?" I wilted at the thought of facing her again. Honestly, the woman's perkiness could outshine the sun. "What would she have to say about this case?"

"Hello?" Marcus wagged his head back-and-forth. "Hotel? Out of town woman? She has to be somewhere. The clues flow together to form the answers."

He was parroting me regarding crossword puzzles.

How could I shoot down my own logic? Despite my reservations about the flighty, frothy, over-the-top woman, I was desperate for a clue. Heaving a sigh, I girded myself. "So, Holly recognized your description of the victim?"

"Sort of." A smile danced on Marcus's lips. "A woman matching the description is registered there. Alive and well. She thinks."

A round of exclamations echoed through the room.

I felt like I was eleven, when my brother Zach hit me in the gut with a stick. Could this be Lily? Audrey? Savannah? And what about the mysterious Paige Amos mentioned? "Alive?"

With everyone's attention on him, Marcus grew serious. "Holly heard about the woman's body in the Mercantile, but the police haven't released a description. They're keeping it on the down low until they find a name."

I'd only found the victim twenty-four hours ago.

"Then, Holly read my e-mail alert." The boy sucked in a breath. "I listed TR's guesses as facts."

"Wait a minute." My brain circled back to the message. "Who got this e-mail? Our family and friends in Kentucky?"

Marcus looked at me like I was crazy. "Of course. I had to spread a wide net. We don't know where the woman's from."

Okay, in theory she *could* be from anywhere, but *Kentucky*?

"Yeah... I guess." Yep, that was my best comeback.

"Anyway." He shot me a harsh glare for interrupting. "Holly says a woman at the Silver Swan is a possible match. She was overheard asking about the Mercantile."

"Ooohh." Mrs. C tapped her knitting needles together. "A tie-in to the case, clear as day, innit?"

The trail might be clear, but the picture was getting muddy.

"Who's the mystery woman, you ask?" Marcus filled in the silence with the timing of a game show host. "That's what we have to find out."

I gave the boy a flat stare. "Are you done with the drama?"

He gave me a cocky grin. "For now."

Kevin pointed at me. "You and I could head out- "

"No!" Marcus waved both hands at Kevin. "Holly has a plan."

"Oh, no." My exclamation was involuntary. My trepidation was real. "This can't be good."

"It's perfect." Marcus's grin widened. "Holly arranged a meeting tonight."

Mrs. C mewed in disappointment. Her sorrowful gaze strayed to the TV. Two commentators were discussing the teams and their respective pedigrees. "What about me game?"

"Got you covered, Mrs. C." Marcus snapped his fingers. "Holly is organizing two international weddings. She's having a taste test for the menus and cakes."

"Seriously?" Again, I couldn't help myself. "I mean, party planning is Holly's strength."

Kevin snickered at my back pedaling.

Marcus continued blithely on. "We get to test the food and wedding cakes. A seventy-five-inch tv will show the match."

"Oh, ducks!" A clap sounded as Mrs. C clasped her hands. A rapturous smile covered her face. "That sounds grand."

"And you still get the royals." I had to smile as the stars aligned for Mrs. C, even if it meant facing Holly. "Who could ask for more?"

Kevin's serious expression contrasted with Mrs. C's. "This could either eliminate or confirm the Houlding connection."

"Either would be progress." At least we had a plan. "Between this and the visit to the airport, we might identify the victim and a possible suspect."

I hoped neither would be Lily.

10

—·—

12 Down; 5 Letters;
Clue: Bubbly and Lively;
Answer: Perky.

Several hours later, I entered the palatial entrance of the Silver Swan. After two valets opened the car doors, an escort greeted us at the entrance with a bow.

Kevin nodded then walked on with an air of savoir faire.

Awestruck, I gave them the royal wave I'd seen on the telly earlier. What can I say? No one's ever bowed to me. On my previous visit, I'd been obsessed with keeping Mrs. C out of jail and my family safe. This time it was like seeing the four-star resort with fresh eyes.

The two-story atrium had crown molding with swirling designs outlined in silver. Gleaming silver decorations and crystal chandeliers were offset by pale yellow, pastel aqua, and soft reds.

If Holly thought pulling out all the stops would cement her place as the lead consultant of Marcus's imaginary detective agency, she was on the right path. I want it on record that my opinion of the woman has nothing to do with her intelligence or her drive. It's her perkiness that astounds me. I can't sustain that level of enthusiasm.

After a confusing series of turns, our party stopped before a set of double doors. Two uniformed employees, a black guy and an Asian woman, opened the doors in unison.

Our escort walked to the doorway. His solemn stare reminded me of an English butler at a stately mansion. "The Belden Tanner party has arrived."

Marcus laughed out loud. "We're a party wherever we go."

His joke prompted him to laugh all the more.

I groaned at his weird humor. He never failed to amuse himself. The boy hurried forward to enter at Kevin's side. As the three of us stepped through the door, petals cascaded down from a flowered arch. I felt like I'd entered a fairytale. Not even my cynical side could come up with a snide comment.

In a few steps, all five of us progressed through the confetti petal parade. A click sounded behind us, signaling the doors had been closed.

A petite blonde stood on the left. Her golden hair was twisted in a professional knot. Her big blue eyes shone like headlights. With her clasped hands trembling and her lips pressed together, I worried she might explode.

For a moment, she simply stared. Then her fists pounded her legs. Her mouth opened in a silent scream. At least it started out silent. The sound slowly built from a thin, screech to a full-throated yell.

Over-the-top, am I right?

"We're not this exciting." My whispered comment was lost in Holly's borderline hysteria.

"You're here!" She threw up her hands as if someone scored a touchdown. "I can't believe the gang is together again."

She stilled suddenly and put her hands on her cheeks until only her shining eyes showed. "I'm an official consulting member of the Belden Tanner Detective Agency, and we're on a case. I'm so excited."

"I see that." Since she was staring at me, I figured a response was required. She reminded me of Marcus when he'd gotten his junior PI license from Crawford's office. "We're happy to be here."

I tried to add zest to my tone. I'm not sure it worked. I spoke for everyone. Mrs. C and Marcus were a given regarding enthusiasm. As for Kevin and Rabi, I put their presence under the offer of free food. Maybe that was me. Either way, we were here.

The woman threw out her arms and rushed toward me. Not being a touchy-feely person, I braced myself only to jostled aside.

Mrs. C brushed against me in a headlong flight forward.

I think Holly was more surprised than I was when Mrs. C embraced her. "I don't know whether I'm coming or going. I'm that excited to be here."

"Everything worked out perfectly." Holly's grin grew wider as her voice shot up an octave. She pulled back and looked at Mrs. C. "With my planning two weddings coupled with a royal wedding, it was meant to be."

Holly swept a hand toward a large television mounted on the wall. An old-style carriage gleaming with polish and drawn by six matching horses proceeded at a stately pace down a wide dirt track. A guy in a red uniform rode one of the horses drawing the coach. You don't see *that* in Kentucky. I don't believe Australia usually goes in for that kind of thing either.

Table settings of gleaming china and sparkling crystal glasses faced the television on one side.

Mrs. C took the center seat. Rabi, with what looked to be a smirk in his dark eyes, threw me to the wolves and aimed toward the chair on the far right. Kevin went with the other man. Cowards.

I found myself next to Holly, who eyed me like a starving shark would a minnow. Panic built in my throat. I wasn't sure I'd survive hours of direct exposure.

Marcus, my little hero, slithered between us. He gently, but firmly, nudged me to the right. "When does the match start? We have to discuss the case if it takes all night."

"I feel like the queen, I do." Mrs. C's lilting British accent seemed right at home with the backdrop of the polo watching throng straining at the barricades. The fancy dress and outlandish hats showed in the background. The locals must be going all out for their British royals playing.

Feeling like I was in a game of musical chairs, I took the seat next to Mrs. C before my boy child could change his mind.

The older woman, in the spirit of the evening, gave a royal wave. "Not to worry, duckling. I can watch and listen. I'll do my bit for the cause."

I had no doubt she could attend to both the polo match and the case. She's a crafty old gal.

"Good." Marcus, on my left, faced Holly. "We need to be next to each other so I can get the facts straight. TR is a horrible note taker. Good thing she doesn't work in an office."

"Heavens, no." Holly looked horrified as she took the final seat. "It would be a terrible waste of her talents. She's needed to fight crime."

I tossed my head and looked at Kevin. "I'm like a super hero crime-fighter."

The man shot me a skeptical look before he aimed his charming smile at our hostess. "Thank you for arranging this, Holly. What's on the menu?"

Now that I was sitting, I realized the table was curved. The semi-circle made it easier to see and talk with each other.

Holly picked up two cards from her plate. "The dishes on the peach menu will be served first. There are four courses plus two desserts. Since we have two taste tests, the servings will be small. You can vote on those choices. The listing on the mint green card will be brought out second."

The menus contained a dizzying number of dishes with elaborate descriptions. I felt like the pauper who'd been transplanted to the royal court.

"Oh, these are lovely," Mrs. C murmured.

Figures the woman would recognize the dishes.

Marcus tapped a card. "Steak and 'tatoes. Can't go wrong."

So much for the boy being intimidated.

I gestured at Holly, with the cards in my hand. "This should be fun and any leads would be a huge help."

"I'm thrilled to be part of a case." Her cultured, professional tone and demeanor evaporated before a wide, blinding grin. Her fists pounded on the table. "I've always wanted to be a Scooby."

Marcus's smile matched hers.

"Now, to business." Her professional mask returned, but the shining eyes betrayed her real feelings. "Once the servers bring out the first entrée, we can discuss the investigation. They'll return when we're ready for the next course."

I was relieved we'd be alone. My stomach growled as the plates were brought out and placed before us.

Two appetizers, rolls with flavored butter, and a salad came and went before the entrée. Beef Wellington, small new potatoes with a lemon-flavored sauce accompanied by asparagus. The servings were tiny but appropriate if we were expected to get through four plates and multiple desserts.

Marcus frowned at his plate. "These are teeny. Good thing there's a lot of stuff to eat."

Several moments later, my tastebuds were dancing. I was ready to vote then and there. Not that the Silver Swan's gourmet chefs would ever create anything but perfection.

On the screen, one team rode across a polo field with measured lines. Their slow strides drew out the moment the onlookers had waited hours to see.

Having laid my utensils on my plate and dabbed my mouth with the cloth napkin, the case returned to my brain with full force. "That was delicious."

Leaning forward, Holly brushed aside the compliment. "Now we can discuss the case."

I was in mid-nod when her blue eyes narrowed and shifted from side-to-side in the empty room. I almost matched her movement, but other than the now absent servers, we'd been alone from the first moment.

Holly took a deep breath. She looked at Marcus with a serious expression. "The description in the emergency alert sounded familiar. We're booked, of course, but I make it a point to familiarize myself with all the guests."

Like I said, Holly's skill was never in question. Well, except for a few minutes when we'd been kidnapped.

"There's a guest who is a perfect match for the woman Marcus described." Holly tapped her pastel pink nail with a rhinestone starburst on the tablecloth. "She checked in five days ago. I overheard her talking to a couple on the patio. She was talking about difficult family relationships and her reluctance to come home again."

Marcus bounced in his seat. He pointed a finger at her.

The woman shook her head with pausing. "No names. However, I'm certain I heard talk of old friends."

"Mm-hmmm." Mrs. C murmured without taking her gaze off the pictures of the young royals playing in the match. "Savannah Lester might be making an appearance, eh?"

I nodded as I shifted my gaze to Holly.

"Exactly." The younger woman stabbed her finger at the unblinking Brit. "After reading the alert, I found the woman's identity."

My expression tightened. Had she alerted the woman?

"Not to worry." Holly assured me, evidently reading my concern. "All I had to do was check the credit slips from the boutique at the time of the conversation. There weren't many and I knew two of the four people from past visits. I cross checked the registration information. The woman has an address from DC."

The door in the far corner opened. The servers entered silently, removed the empty settings, and placed two plates before each of us. Two small pieces of moist cakes with gooey frosting sat invitingly on silver etched plates.

With questions on my tongue, I took a bite of what looked like spice cake with fruits and nuts topped with an airy maple frosting. As the dessert melted on my tongue I glanced at Kevin. "Next time we get married, we should do it here."

My hubby smirked. "I'll talk to my financier."

"Your money person will shoot it down." As I licked my fork, my brain wrested control from my tastebuds. "Back to business. What's the name of the guest?"

"I made a copy of an entry she filled out for a drawing." Holly eyes glittered. She delivered the news in, for her, a calm tone. Reaching into a folder on her left, she pulled out a slip of paper and passed it to Marcus. "Since the original was in a public space, there's no claim to confidentiality."

Her words ended on a squeal of delight.

Marcus glanced up from the card. "That's cool, Holly."

I gave her an admiring look. "Have you been studying up on the law?"

"Oh, no." Her dampening tone instantly shot down that idea.

I didn't blame her. School wasn't for me either.

"I asked a lawyer friend." She tossed her head toward the hall. Then she giggled at Mrs. C. "I learned from the best. Why do your own work?"

That's always been my motto. I felt an ember of kinship for the woman.

"Absolutely, luv." Mrs. C agreed with abandon. "People enjoy helping. It makes them feel a part of something."

Marcus gave me a sideways glance through his long, black eyelashes. "Sounds like someone else I know."

I put my arm around his shoulder and gave him a squeeze. "People *love* to be a part of something."

He snorted as he tapped the woman's information card. "Washington, DC."

Holly gave a mew of disappointment accompanied by puppy-dog eyes. "The name and address don't fit, but the description does and she's acting hinky."

My anticipation deflated. The name of the town meant nothing, but it might be fake. "That's not Audrey Houlding's address. What's the name?"

"Paige Helen Bly." Holly and Marcus spoke at the same time.

"A name. Finally!" A nagging voice wondered who put their middle name on a contest entry, but my excitement squashed logic.

Marcus's eyes widened. "This could be Lily's mysterious friend, Paige."

Realization flowed around the table.

The boy child was wound up so tight, he didn't pause for breath before launching into fast paced, blow-by-blow rendition of Amos's missing granddaughter and her friends, Savannah and Audrey's supposed absence.

"Maybe the woman is one of them." Holly's blue eyes went megawatt. "The Mercantile is in the oldest part of town. The building has an old hidey-hole, but why kill Lily for finding that out?"

"It's hard to nail down a motive when the victim is unknown." As my mind whirled, I focused on the threads of the puzzle. "Lily told a lot of people about her find and her plans to use the information for an activity during the festival and the class reunions. The blueprints themselves can't be the reason behind the murder, if the victim is Lily."

Kevin, who'd been following the discussion with Rabi, leaned forward. "Perhaps Lily discovered something else."

Mrs. C watched matched rows of mounted players parade in front of a bustling crowd. Team members waved and saluted as the sunlight lit up the scene. A roar from the crowd filled the air. The older woman saluted with her fork. "And why converge in the basement of the Mercantile?"

"The timing points to Lily announcing her plans." Kevin's expression tensed. "The *locations* on the old documents might be the key."

Marcus's fists pounded the table so hard the tiny crystal salt and pepper shakers danced in place. "Lily uncovered a secret worth killing for."

"That makes as much sense as anything else we've got." I dragged the words out.

The boy had the nerve to roll his eyes at me. "What happened to the papers Lily found?"

"The planning committee should have copies. If not, Amos might be able to recreate the blueprints." That might answer a few of my questions. "I'll check the high school first thing tomorrow. Pictures of Lily's graduating class should hold some answers. The yearbooks aren't online."

No one else had anything more to offer. As usual at the beginning of a case I had more questions than answers. Holly's information didn't directly connect the mystery woman to the case. It might be Audrey or Savannah or Lily for that matter. If so, why the fake name?

"I did a search on the Houlding family after lunch." My quiet statement drew an outraged glare from Marcus, along with a long, low growl. I held up a hand to forestall the outburst. "I waited until Holly could hear it. I didn't want to go through the explanation twice."

The boy shook his head violently. The light reflected off his shiny black hair. "You could have told *me!*"

Holly's squeal and clapping all but drowned out his outraged response. When she grabbed his arm and shook it while muttering, "I'm part of the team. I'm part of the team." Marcus rolled his eyes and surrendered with a smile at the young woman.

It was moments like this when I felt an almost maternal affection for Holly. After a moment, she pressed her lips together and aimed her shining eyes at me.

I made a bet with myself I wouldn't make it through my first statement without interruption. "Audrey Patience Houlding is the company VP. I downloaded a photo. She is the woman from the bakery. I also checked their bottom line."

Kevin's laugh broke across my comment. "Numbers are your friends."

A chorus of groans rose from the table. I do love numbers, and I lost my bet. No interruptions.

"Tell us about the money." Marcus's finger targeted me from an inch away. "Is the Houlding family smuggling drugs?"

"Not as far as I can tell." I'd been pretty bummed to see the numbers balance. "But it would help their cash flow. They've staved off bankruptcy for several years. A developer is interested in their land. Audrey is the lone holdout."

"Motive." My son's eyes grew big. "Paige could be a nickname for Patience."

"Nice catch," I admitted.

"Send me her picture. I have Lily's," Marcus ordered. "I'll text it to the group. We can see if Holly recognizes either of them as the mystery woman."

"Coming your way." I forwarded him the picture of Audrey Houlding. "I forwarded Audrey's photo to Wilson."

A series of dings and buzzes erupted around the table.

Holly opened the attachments. "Neither of these people is the woman at the boutique."

Of course, not. A clear ID would be too easy.

"Did you have an unobstructed view?" Kevin asked in a calm, friendly voice.

I doubt anyone except me noticed the tension in his tone. My nerves tightened.

Holly stopped in mid-nod. Her brow furrowed.

"Hat?" Kevin continued. "Sunglasses? How far away?"

The soft questions built a picture. Holly's confident expression crumpled. "She was wearing a hat and sunglasses both times I saw her. With a scarf wrapped around her hair. You think it was a disguise?"

I frowned. An alias and a disguise. If this wasn't our woman, she was probably hiding from the mob. "It's possible. Kevin knows all the tricks."

Marcus's scrunched up face mirrored my feelings. "Add a wig, she could be anybody. Or anybody could be her."

Rabi steepled his hands. "Why?"

"Lovely." Mrs. C's comment came out of left field. When she sat back, the distant expression vanished. Her body stiffened as she shifted from fantasy to reality. "Someone wants Paige to be seen at the hotel. The other possibility is one or all of the young ladies are playing a game of deception."

"Oh, goody. More complications." I'd been hoping to simplify the case not make it worse. "But who is Paige?"

"They're not the woman." Holly's mouth curled up. Her brow furrowed. "Unless... No. I'm sure. Maybe this one?"

Well, that's testimony a jury would believe. "Audrey Houlding is five-five in her stocking feet. Medium build. Could you tell how tall she was? Was she wearing heels? Flats?"

I added the last part in response to Holly's interested but semi-blank look.

The younger woman grimaced. "She was sitting down both times. She wore wide-legged pants that brushed the floor."

Mrs. C tsked without taking her gaze off the parade of limos and waving crowds. "Taken all together, her attire is rather suspicious."

"Agreed." Kevin rarely rendered judgement on suspects. However, this was his area of expertise. "She covered the bases in disguising herself. Hair. Face. Height."

So far, every new lead only created more questions. "Is Paige travelling alone or did she arrive with someone?"

"Alone." The younger woman answered quickly. She looked relieved to have a definite answer. "She's in a king suite."

"Business or personal?" Surprise laced through Marcus's voice. "'Cuz that's pricey. Who comes to Langsdale on holiday by yourself?"

Kevin gave the boy a thumbs up. "Good point."

Holly pointed a pink tipped nail at the registration card in Marcus's hand. "She checked the box for business on the reservation. However, her room is covered by her personal credit card. Also, she's not connected with any of the groups registered at the hotel this week."'"

Kevin spun a fork around his fingers like a baton. "Getting a fake credit card is no easy task for most people."

I chewed on a rich chocolate bite of cake with a mocha cream cheese frosting topped with toffee pieces. I felt very elegant, feasting on wedding dishes while watching a fancy sporting event. I pointed my fork at Holly.

"This is by far the best team meeting we've ever had." Noting her excited smile, I flicked a glance at Mrs. C. "We're surrounded by weddings and royal events."

The royal family. Marriage. Names. The words set off a ricochet in my brain. Startled, I tried to follow the path, but the trail dissipated. With no idea what my brain was trying to say, I logged the eerie moment in my private files and moved on. "Has Paige met anyone? Does she go out?"

Holly started to speak then servers filed in. Two in front picked up empty dishes with practiced efficiency. The four behind them set down the entrees for the second wedding. They swept off the metal covers with a flourish.

Marcus wrinkled his nose. "What's this?"

"Sea-bass in a pastry shell with grilled scallops in a lemon cream sauce." Holly intoned in a light, cheery tone used by tourist guides and teachers the world over. "Mixed vegetables with dill spiced seasoning will be served with either main course. The other entry is tilapia with grilled pineapple and wild rice with a coconut curry sauce, plus assorted vegetables."

The servers exited as silently as they'd arrived.

"I feel like I'm on a royal visit." And this is probably as close as I'd ever get.

Once the door shut, Holly's business-like mask melted before an inner glow. "Paige stays in her room, hasn't been seen with anyone. She insisted on the ground floor with a patio."

"Those are so boss!" Marcus stabbed a finger at Holly. "When we stayed here, I could walk right outside into the garden or to the pool. It was great. We should come here again."

"We could have monthly meetings here." Holly's dazzling grin and blazing white teeth could have blinded someone in the full sun. She gasped and her eyes widened. "Or I could help with surveillance."

Sure, with her dazzling looks this woman would blend right in. She looked so excited. I couldn't shoot her down. Instead, I waited a full three seconds before I prompted her. "Is there more about the ground floor room?"

"Oh, sure." With no dimming of her smile, Holly continued. "The cleaning crew said the bed is slept in. Wet towels. Clothes and makeup present. Room charges. But she hasn't been seen since Tuesday, five days. Meals are left outside the room."

A gnawing feeling started in the pit of my stomach. Anyone could see how the story would end. Paige disappeared the same day the victim was killed.

Holly continued. "I had the gardener's assistant keep an eye on the patio while he worked on a hedge. I was stunned! You probably know who walked into the room, don't you?"

She pointed at me.

I'd been willing to let her deliver the punchline, but who wouldn't know the answer by now? "A staff member. Paige bribed them to cover for her."

Holly clapped her hands. "The maid even had her hat and sunglasses. I have her waiting to talk to you."

I doubted she'd have any useful answers. The real question was: who and where was Paige Bly?

11

—·—

5 Down; 4 Letters;
Clue: Information not previously known.
Answer: News.

After last night's indulgent wedding suppers with Holly, Monday morning dawned gray and dreary. Ok, not really. Outside, the sun was shining. The heat was unrelenting, and sunglasses were a necessity.

Inside my apartment was doom and gloom. Wearing a scowl, I shut the laptop and pushed it away. The interview with the maid who'd earned three hundred dollars to cover for the missing woman gave me nothing new.

The woman calling herself Paige Bly had worn the same sunglasses and oversized hat Holly had seen her in. She'd added a medical mask to cover the lower half of her face. Straight, pale blonde hair showed beneath the hat.

Audrey Houlding and Lily Gilbert were brunettes in their most recent pictures. Since the high school hadn't gone digital with their yearbooks, Savannah Lester was an unknown. Paige Bly's hair color? Who knows? I couldn't even confirm she was real. No one by that name lived in Oregon or California.

Was Paige involved with the dead woman? *Was* she the dead woman? Were Savannah, Lily, or Audrey using Paige as their alias? Why would any of them plan ahead to sustain the illusion she was at the hotel? The woman evidently planned to return. The room was paid for until Wednesday morning. Two days from now. Would Paige Bly return? "My best guess is either Paige Bly is a real person, or the identity is an escape route from... the uncle."

"That's very interesting, dear." Mrs. C, puttering in the kitchen, tossed the comment over her shoulder. "Aliases. Hidden identities. Our prey is definitely attempting to remain under the radar."

The stills from the security cameras, which Holly provided, showed so little Marcus couldn't use his facial recognition program.

The timing pointed to Lily's disclosure of her plans to use the old blueprints for a scavenger hunt at the festival. But why? The documents were in the public record.

"She hasn't made any mistakes." Kevin, the suspicious type, tapped the photos. "Normal people look around, especially at a resort like the Silver Swan. We were all gawking."

I sat at the kitchen table with Kevin and Marcus. Well, when the boy child was sitting, he was next to Kevin.

The child must have an extra battery he plugs in overnight. He kept popping up and down. First to help Mrs. C who puttered around the stove cooking breakfast. The slippers of the day had the Union Jack wearing a crown. I'd found them at the specialty shop on the main drag that deals with everything an anglophile or a transplanted Brit would love.

Between her humming the British national anthem and Marcus playing with the cats, my third cup of coffee was barely keeping me sane.

Marcus had warned everyone delay would not be tolerated. From his hurry up attitude, anyone would think the local airport was on the verge of disappearing.

Marcus bolted into the room. The cats scrambled after him, clawing at the purple light from his handheld laser. He pointed at me and his father. "You're not talking, are you? Don't discuss the case until Rabi gets here. Don't try to do anything behind my back. I'm watching you."

He spoke in an ominous tone and flashed his fingers from his eyes to us.

Kevin saluted. "Sure you don't need help, Mrs. C?"

The older woman waved a spatula. "I'm fine, luv. You rest."

I struggled to keep my eyes open. Thankfully, Kevin had rendered his judgment before the stricture of silence. A bump and a rattle of shelves sounded from the living room. I gritted my teeth, but there was no crash.

"You can think quietly to yourselves." Marcus's generous relaxation of his rules floated over a few more thuds. "Or talk about other things."

"Thanks." Though my sarcasm was wasted, I raised my coffee cup in gratitude. Resting my chin on my hand, I let my mind wander. I still had to check if Paige Bly or any Paige attended school in Langsdale fifteen years ago.

At the moment, I didn't have the energy. By the time the royal polo game was over and the wedding feasts were finished, I was in a food coma. I was alert enough to remember the Beef Wellington and fruit filled spice cake got the nod for one wedding. The pastry crusted sea bass and toffee cake would be on the menu for the second couple.

Good thing I'd researched the principals yesterday. My brain kept clicking away on my list of to do's. If I waited long enough, Wilson might ID the dead woman. With enough coffee, I might get there first, but I doubted it.

A thought shot across my mind like a comet. I opened my eyes. "Why did the woman want to disappear for a few days?"

I hadn't meant to say anything, but my mouth was moving.

Kevin continued to watch Mrs. C. His eyes flicked toward the living room. "I'll pretend I didn't hear anything."

His lips didn't move. Mine did when one side of my mouth quirked up. "Thanks."

Marcus and the cats weren't in sight. From the pounding on the stairs, they'd run up to the loft. Who was chasing who was hard to say. A knock on the door managed to be heard over the melee.

"I'll get it!" Marcus pounded down the stairs.

I don't know why he bothered. Mrs. C hadn't locked the door behind her and Rabi has a key.

Marcus skidded to a stop and flung the door open. "Hey, Rabi. We haven't talked about the case. I kept an eye on them."

The door closed with a click in mid-sentence. The two of them were halfway across the living room.

"Good man," Rabi said, nodding solemnly.

"Hey, Rabi." Kevin and I spoke simultaneously.

Okay, mine was a mumble, but I raised my mug.

Thankfully, Rabi took that as a sign to grab the coffee pot and top me off. Doing so, he set a box on the table.

My eyes shot open. "Sierra Sweets Pastry."

My mouth salivated at the familiar tan box entwined with brown and green tendrils climbing over silver mountains. I popped open the lid and inhaled the sight of pastries, glazes, and fruit filling.

"Just in time." Mrs. C shuffled over carrying a large glass pie pan filled with a quiche. "Do be a good lad and get the sauce, eh?"

"Sure thing, Mrs. C." Marcus did an end run behind me to grab the metal pitcher with a deep blue exterior.

In a moment, we were seated. Silence ensued as we ate the delicious repast.

"Mmmm." I closed my eyes as I enjoyed a bite of veggie, bacon, and cheesy quiche with hollandaise sauce. I'd already devoured half of a German chocolate Danish. "You are the best, Mrs. C. So are you, Rabi. Such good team members."

"Yeah." Marcus scoffed. "They do all the work and you get to eat."

"Exactly." I shot back, feeling very righteous. "And I didn't see you lift a finger to provide breakfast."

He drew back. His eyes wide. "I kept the cats busy. You're welcome."

I took a bite, trying unsuccessfully to hide a smile. A weight crawling across my legs signaled the appearance of one of his feline siblings. Mr. Pickles, the big male with white paws, stretched himself across my lap. He eyed me with his deep green eyes. "Give it up. I'm not giving you one morsel of my food."

"They deserve a treat." Marcus handed a bite to Rookie, the solid gray female. "Now, we can discuss the case."

I wasn't sure where to begin. Might as well cover the basics. "I dug into the background on the main players. Mrs. C's info was, of course, spot on. Twenty-five years ago, Harvey Lester married Monica Sutton. Her eleven-year-old daughter, Savannah, took the last name Lester. No record of an official adoption. No name for her birth father so far. Any word on him, Mrs. C?"

The older woman paused before answering. "I don't believe they were married or that Sutton was her real name. Monica seemed to be running from him, which proves nothing. The poor dear suspected the postman of evil intent. Savannah spoke of her birth father with affection. The girl knew him, but Monica had peculiar ideas."

"That's one way of putting it." I snorted. "Monica was on several prescriptions to control delusions and paranoia."

Marcus gasped. "That's amazing, TR."

He didn't have to sound *that* shocked.

"I am a card-carrying PI." I spoke in a superior tone, then ruined the moment by laughing.

Kevin met Mrs. C's gaze with a thoughtful look. "You said she kept to herself, rarely helped in the store."

"Aye." The older woman's expression softened. She seemed to look into the distance. After twenty odd years in Langsdale, she had a vast storehouse of knowledge. "She stocked supplies in the basement, submitted the orders. She told tales, involving the Witness Protection Program and hiding from the mob. The government trying to steal her daughter. Ghosts in the walls guarding family gold. Savannah had very little freedom. Harvey and the girl tried to hide Monica's problems. Poor tyke dealt with her mother's hallucinations all her life."

As I nodded in sympathy, Marcus pounded the table. "Do you have more? We have to solve a murder."

So much for empathy. "Savannah left town at eighteen. After that I lose her trail. Eight years ago, Harvey sold the shop and moved away. You received cards from Harvey."

The older woman nodded readily but she had an enigmatic look in her eyes. "Harvey sent Elena and Otis several pictures of the cottage where he lived. They posted them at the store, including Savannah's card saying he'd died. They hosted a remembrance for him, well attended. Lovely evening."

Despite her heartfelt words, an odd tone in her voice raised my antenna. "Did anything strike you as odd?"

"Several items, now that it's under the microscope." Mrs. C's eyes narrowed in thought. "Harvey wasn't in any of the pictures he sent. He was a bit of a ham you see. Always larking about. We all mentioned it at the time. What is the point of photos if he wasn't in them?"

It was a small matter, but it might be a sticking point. Why not send a picture of himself? Unless... "You saw him after he sold the store, correct?"

Mrs. C nodded half-heartedly. "Savannah helped him pack. They were going through Monica's personal items. He lived above the store. He promised to say goodbye, but one day the store was shuttered, and they were both gone."

Marcus's face scrunched up in a frown. "What happened?"

The older woman bit a miniscule nibble off her fork and chewed slowly. "Elena and Otis arrived days later and announced Harvey had collapsed from overwork. Evidently, Savannah notified the new owners that she'd flown Harvey to live with her until he was stronger."

"You don't believe that story." Kevin's steady tone had a question behind it. His steely gaze focused all his attention on the woman. "You never did."

"Savannah was in town at the time." Mrs. C's British accent carried a serious tone. A tightening of her jaw was evidence of her feelings. "She was seen in the store. Why wasn't Harvey hospitalized locally or resting in his apartment?"

"Dun-du-dun." Marcus intoned the dark melody in a slow, deep voice, but his dark eyes were studious. "No one actually saw Harvey leave and Savannah couldn't come up with a picture of him. But why would she kill him?"

"This background makes my next tidbit more ominous." I'd taken several bites while Marcus and Mrs. C were speaking. "I can't find anything under Savannah Lester or Sutton after Harvey left. She would have been about twenty-five. No marriage license or name change, officially."

Rabi cocked his head to one side. The first outward sign he'd been listening.

"Yes," I pointed at him, though he'd said nothing. "Savannah is within the height and weight range of the victim."

"She meets your criteria." Kevin spoke with a confidence that warmed me. Leaning forward, he continued. "She'd be familiar with the store and the neighborhood. She may have connected with her birth father and reverted to her legal name."

"I have no clue how to find that trail." My sharp tone betrayed my frustration. "Lily contacted her about the reunion and festival plans perhaps using an e-mail from high school."

Marcus snapped his fingers. "Anything else?"

"I want it on record how much I did." I pointed to myself with both hands. "And I have more. I confirmed Jared Houlding was a professional poker player of off and on skill. Some months he couldn't pay his rent, then he'd be swimming in money."

Kevin fixed me with an intense stare. "A tournament win would explain his fancy blue car."

"Maybe he couldn't cover a bet." Marcus had his chin resting on his fists, pushing his cheeks up. He looked like a chipmunk. "So, someone pushed him down the stairs and took his fancy car."

I snorted. "We need proof. Keep an open mind or we might overlook a clue."

"Yeah, whatever." The boy gave me a sideways look as he dismissed my caution. A grin danced on his lips.

Rabi's expression stiffened. "Known associates?"

"Nothing solid so far." I had so many leads. Without knowing which one to follow, I had to pursue them all. "He grew up in the neighborhood. Lily and the others were two years older. I plan to follow up with the school and see if I can find his buddy with the famous lawyer name."

Mrs. C chewed slowly. "A thread to tie them together."

I gave the other woman and Rabi a pleading look. "If anyone wants to put out feelers on Jared for possible investors or connections, that would be a huge help."

The two exchanged a look and nodded.

"Maybe we'll get a lead at the airport." Marcus puffed out his chest. "Rabi, Mrs. C, and me are going this morning for my school assignment."

His wide-eyed, innocent expression accompanied by a fake smile were very unnerving. He dropped the pose in a heartbeat. "All we need is one good clip of the middle-aged couple. We can show it around and give it to Wilson for an ID."

I munched on my German chocolate Danish. "I took a run at Paige H. Bly. No matches in Nevada, Washington, California, or Oregon. Odds are it's an alias for either Audrey, Lily, or Savannah."

"Not good." Mrs. C added more sauce to her plate. Her eyes narrowed. "Assuming one of them was hiding, possibly from the couple at the airport, they may have found her."

"That's possible." I pointed my fork at the older woman. "I'll tell Wilson what we learned. If I keep him in the dark, he'll be mad. I would be and I wouldn't share with him."

Marcus snickered as I grabbed my phone. "He can do the legwork for you. Maybe I'll give *him* a junior PI license."

Amidst the laughter and calls of conflict of interest, I dialed the detective and invited him over for updates and breakfast. Turned out, he'd just finished reinterviewing Otis and Elena. He promised to come over in ten minutes.

He made it in five. The food was probably a bigger draw than my promise of information. His long legs thumping up the stairs preceded his entrance. He rapped on the door a few times before testing the knob.

Marcus didn't make any attempt to get to the door before Wilson walked in. He crossed the floor in a few strides. His eyes grew wide at the sight of the pastry box.

"Don't get up." His snide comment was pointless since no one had moved. "I know where the plates are."

I continued eating the delectable breakfast. I may not be able to cook without creating chaos, but I give full credit to those who have the skill. "Wilson, remember, this is quid pro quo."

"Sure." He returned with a plate and utensils. With a round of nods, he sat next to Mrs. C facing Marcus at the other end of the table.

I took his easy agreement as an indication of how little he'd learned. "Dealer's choice."

"I'll go first." He grabbed a glazed croissant from the box, saluting Rabi with the pastry. Though no one had spoken as to their source, Wilson *was* a detective. He knew neither Kevin nor I would pop for the baked goods. "I'm getting pressure to make an arrest. Elena and Otis are the only ones with keys to that room. They claim it's too inconvenient to use, but a source told me Elena mentioned knocking out the wall to connect to the main basement. For that, she would have had to go into the storage room. She found a squatter. They fought and the stranger ends up dead."

Surprise overrode the dread building in my gut. I groaned in disgust. "That can't be *your* scenario, Wilson. The woman was in upscale business suit."

His tight expression showed his displeasure. "I like to have an ID and a decent motive before I arrest someone for murder. Like I said, the upper ranks want this closed, or at least progress. I don't have a name and I have four other cases plus court appearances."

Wilson could fight the pressure to a certain extent, but he needed answers for ammunition. Like him, I had few leads to offer.

A heavy tread on the stairs stopped the rest of his comment.

His head swiveled toward the door then to me. "Open house today?"

I shrugged. A quick scan of the table showed puzzled expressions.

The only other space on this floor was a storeroom in the back which I once used for my now defunct job with an on-line packaging company.

A metal scratching at the door sounded as someone put a key in the lock.

Marcus stiffened. "They have a key."

I scoffed at his whispered alarm. "Who doesn't have a key to this place? I'm surprised they're foolish enough to think the door is locked."

The knob turned. A large man took two steps into the living room. Since the loft has an open floor plan, he stopped when he saw us.

Jimbo, a former college linebacker and a friend of Kevin's from a scam at the college, blinked in surprise. "Hey, why aren't you guys at work and school?"

"It's July." Marcus pointed out. "What are you doing here? You want breakfast? Is Nate with you?"

Jimbo and his partner had been together going on five months. Though some preached taking it slow - that would be me - the pairing had worked well.

The blond man, six-foot-four and weighing in at over two hundred fifty pounds of solid muscle, crossed to the kitchen with surprising speed for his size. "Nate went to San Diego for a visit. His grandfather's turning ninety. You serious about the food?"

"This crowd is very serious about food." Kevin waved him toward the kitchen with a glance at the quickly disappearing quiche.

"Luv, do get the second quiche from the oven." Mrs. C waved at Jimbo as he walked toward the cupboard. "I left it to warm. Can you also manage the pan of extra Hollandaise on the burner?"

"Sure thing." Jimbo stretched in two directions at once to nab a plate, the quiche, and the saucepan in one swirling motion. "I had a bagel an hour ago, but it's fading. This is great timing."

Kevin and Marcus added an extra chair between them.

Jimbo sat and served himself while Mrs. C refilled the covered pitcher. The one time I'd suggested simply putting the pan on the table, Mrs. C's quelling glance had made my faux pas clear. I never suggested that again.

While I searched for a way to bring up Wilson's progress, Jimbo waved his fork at the assembly. "If you all need to discuss that lady getting killed, go ahead. I won't listen."

Wilson snorted. "There's not much anyone on the street doesn't already know."

Jimbo grimaced as he nodded. "Stabbed after they bashed her head in, that's just mean."

I shrugged as the detective looked at me with a resigned expression. The neighborhood was a lot like the small town in Kentucky where I'd grown up. There were few secrets.

"On that note, I'll tell you what we've learned." I pushed my empty plate back. Giving Marcus and Holly full credit, I updated Wilson about the woman at the Silver Swan. Her absence for the last few days drew a sharp look.

When I finished, Marcus leaned forward. "Holly promised to keep an eye on the room. Since the murder hasn't hit the media yet, Paige might come back."

Wilson tapped the pictures we'd given him. "These are no help. Hats and sunglasses every time she leaves the room? No ID on the victim. The Houlding family told local authorities Audrey is out of town negotiating a contract. She's overdue checking in but she told them that might happen. She didn't mention stopping in Langsdale, but obviously she met her friends. I'll run her credit cards."

I leaned back in my chair. "I'm going to the high school this morning to check the yearbooks and get pictures of the principles. Later, I plan to hit up Amos to see what Lily found on the blueprints."

The detective, who was on his feet, snapped his fingers. "I requested a copy of the documents to be sent to the precinct."

My eyes widened in surprise.

Wilson managed to look offended. "You're not the only who chases down neighborhood rumors. I lost the chess game."

"TR did, too. Most people lose against Amos." Marcus comforted the man. "He likes to see how you play. He says it tells a lot about the person."

"Thanks." The thin man's straw-colored hair and long limbs made me think a scarecrow was in the room. The detective turned to Jimbo. "Why did you stop by this morning?"

Though his tone was casual, the smile had vanished.

Sure, interrogate people in my dining room.

Actually, I expected it. Detectives get paid to be suspicious. Add in the fact that people tend to lie and hide information, it stands to reason Wilson rarely left any loose thread lying around.

Jimbo, who was undoubtedly the most innocent soul in the room, including Marcus, blinked his big brown eyes at the detective. "I need to borrow Kev's tools. A pipe broke in the basement of my apartment building. The landlord can't get a plumber until tomorrow. I said I'd look at it."

I lowered my gaze to hide my grimace. The small chance of Jimbo fixing the pipe was in direct proportion to the probability of him making the problem worse. Jimbo did heavy lifting for me and Kevin many times. He's been in charge of small jobs. However, plumbing was a special skill.

"Okay." Jimbo instantly fell off the detective's radar. The tall man towered over Mrs. C. "Thanks for breakfast. It was delicious. Tracy, keep the info coming."

I smiled sweetly. No mention had been made of the gang's visit to the local airport. "Are we keeping Chief Chumley in the loop?"

Wilson groaned. "Don't talk to me about that man."

Over my laughter, the scarecrow walked out the door.

Jimbo looked up from his almost empty plate. "Should I have told Detective Wilson about my lead?"

My brain, starting to gear up, jumped the rails. I stared at the man's guileless face.

"It's not much, but Marcus's e-mail asked for any information." He shrugged his broad shoulders as he looked at Kevin. "I do need the tools. The leak's getting worse."

I pulled my gaze away from Jimbo to eye Marcus. "Is the entire town on your emergency shout out?"

The boy frowned. "We have to spread a wide net to catch a lot of fish, TR."

"I can't argue with results." My son's on-line blast had brought us solid leads. I smiled at Jimbo. "What did you hear?"

"It might be nothing." The man waved a fork at me before turning his attention to his plate. "When the e-mail mentioned Jared Houlding, I remembered a conversation with my neighbor. She watched a poker tournament in a town outside of Vegas. Jared and his friend were at the same table, acting like they were strangers."

Jimbo turned his attention to eating.

I waited for the punchline. A minute passed. I gripped my coffee cup. "Is there more to your lead?"

"They were cheating." Kevin spoke confidently. His fingers tapped the table. "A common technique is working together to squeeze a middle player to higher bids. There are other methods."

My hubby could have gone into greater detail. When the Feilens studied for a scam, mistakes were not tolerated.

The clues in my crossword puzzle rearranged. The pinball board lit up. "It's interesting, but how would it relate to the murder?"

Kevin's fingers beat a rapid rhythm on the table. "They were playing beyond their skill, easy to get in trouble with the wrong people. But unless they cheated the dead woman, I don't see a connection."

Marcus scowled at me before facing Jimbo. "It's a weird coincidence."

I cleaned the last bite of quiche off my fork in a ruminative mood. I stared into space trying to re-sort my clues into a working puzzle. "Put it on the board, but nothing points to Jared or his buddy being involved in this woman's death. Of course, I don't have a name or a motive yet, so maybe it does tie together."

Marcus growled deep in his throat. Then, his expression cleared. "My school project at the airport will get pictures of the aunt and uncle. Then, we can get names. With Rabi and Mrs. C, we'll get the goods."

Instead of my earlier trepidation, impatience filled me to get names for the fake PI and his female companion. I started to stack dishes. Once I had a name, I could figure out which players they were connected to. "I can't wait."

My hubby eyed Rabi. "Our guy still working at the airport?"

Rabi answered with a nod. "His brother in security cleared us. Management loves giving tours. Full access."

Mrs. C, emptying the sauce into a container, stabbed a serving spoon at Rabi. "My contact confirmed the admin was furious at them for arriving under a no-flight warning. Security insisted on names and addresses, but she couldn't access the list. That and the video are the targets."

Rabi gave a sharp nod of approval to the older woman's plan of attack.

"Good show, Mrs. C." I applauded the news with undisguised abandon. At this point, I was all in for their scheme. I needed names more than anything.

Marcus rubbed his hands together. "This is going to be fun."

I staunchly ignored the gloating tone in his voice. I put the pile of dishes in Mrs. C's outstretched hands. "Jimbo, is your basement really leaking?"

The man deposited the quiche on the range. He looked at me in surprise. "That's why I came. I thought of Paul while you guys talked about the case."

"I'll get the tools." Kevin gestured to Jimbo. "We can pick up Ernie on the way. He can't work because of arthritis, but he was a plumber for fifty years. He can talk us through anything."

That settled that issue. "Afterward, we can compare notes."

Marcus crossed his arms over his chest and eyed me with a narrowed gaze. "What are you going to do? A crossword puzzle?"

"Listen, Mr. Attitude." I fisted my hands on my hips in the face of his attack. "I'm going to the high school for pictures and info."

I was still hoping Lily's trail didn't end with the dead woman.

12

—·—

6 Across; 4 Letters;
Clue: Become friendly with someone.
Answer: Buds.

As I opened the door of the two-story building on Farview Road, I had no plan. The pale brick facade filled with windows reminded me of my high school in Kentucky. Also, the Langsdale High School sign was a dead giveaway. Walking across the wide main hall with lockers stretching out on both sides of me, the principal's office stared me in the face.

A fifty-something woman with a dirty blond ponytail sat at the front desk. The nameplate read Adelaide Carson. Her sleepy look changed to a cordial expression as she greeted me. "May I help you?"

"I have a few questions regarding the class reunions planned for September." On impulse, I decided to go the official route and handed her my PI card.

A glance at my ID brought a smile to Adelaide's face and a light to her eyes. She gave me her full attention. "A PI. How exciting. Does it pay a lot?"

I smiled at every worker's constant refrain. "Being a PI is one of my three jobs. You be the judge."

She laughed. "You're on a case? What's this about?"

Your guess is as good as mine, lady. Murder? Fraud? Felony? I refused to admit I didn't have a clue.

"It's confidential," I said in a sad tone. "We're not allowed to discuss our cases. How long have you worked at the high school?"

"Two or three lifetimes, so far." She laughed at her answer. "That's about twenty years in real time."

I laughed along with her. I liked this woman. "That's great for me and my case."

The woman's body seized suddenly. She put a hand over her mouth before pointing at me. "Is this about the dead woman they found at the corner grocer? Are you working with the police?"

Good thing Wilson was keeping the story out of the paper. Besides, who needed the media when the neighborhood had its own network? Although, I saw no reason for the woman to whisper. From what I'd seen, we may have been the only two people in the building.

I scrunched up my face and nodded. Then, I made a show of glancing up and down the hall. "I can't say anything."

"Of course, not," she said with a conspiratorial air. She bit her lip as her eyes brightened.

I glanced at the closed door behind her. "Is anyone else here?"

"They're in a meeting in the main library." She waved a hand to the right. "It's at the end of the hall. They just started. It won't be done for another hour."

"I don't mind." Especially with such a willing soul to talk to. To cement our budding friendship, I ordered coffee delivery from the shop on the corner. Not only did I get a cup of my favorite beverage, I got to write it off on my expense account.

We were both in a mellow mood as we took our first sip.

I sat on the chair she offered. "It's pretty quiet here. Do you get much foot traffic?"

"Not at all." Adelaide scoffed. "The state officials got a burr under their saddle about the desk being covered. I don't mind. It's better than sitting through a meeting."

My grin widened. "I haven't heard people talk about a burr under a saddle since I left Kentucky."

Turns out my new acquaintance grew up on a horse ranch in the sandhills of Nebraska. That sealed our sisterhood.

"You can probably help me." I glanced down the hall. "That way I won't have to wait for the meeting to end."

"What do you need?" Adelaide inched up on her chair. "Is the case about one of our former students?"

"I think so." What could I say that wouldn't give too many details? "Some aspects of the case point to the upcoming class reunions. It would be a big help if I could look at some of your yearbooks. Do you have them on-site?"

Her brow furrowed. "Is that legal?"

My brain reached for arguments to tip her to my side. "The information could be a motive for an active murder investigation. The yearbooks might help solve the case."

"Really?" Adelaide's expression sparked. She looked around the deserted lobby. Her body was tensed for action as she pointed to a door in the corner. "They're in the administrative library. They're a matter of public record. I think. You don't need a court order to look at them, right?"

"I'm sure I don't." Especially since I couldn't get one. Wilson would laugh if I asked him. "Besides, I *am* a detective."

Okay! So, I'm a *private* detective. Let's not quibble. It's a blurry line in the field and I was desperate.

Adelaide eyed me with a hopeful gaze. Like many people, she *so* wanted to be a part of a case.

I leaned closer, creating a conspiratorial aura. "No one will know I've been here. I just need to look at them. No harm. No foul."

And if you want to believe I'll leave quietly if you say no, go right ahead.

Her look sparked from an ember to a fire. With a mischievous grin, Adelaide stood quickly. "Perfect. Let's go."

Oh, goody. We were a team.

A few minutes later, she pulled the ten, fifteen, and twenty class yearbooks for me. Since I hadn't specified which year I was interested in, I asked about the general structure of the planning committee.

"There's one overall committee for the festival. Each of the main classes were asked to create an activity." Adelaide's tone indicated an oft repeated statement. "Some have been more forthcoming than others. One in particular sounds like fun. Lily Gilbert found old maps for the local area and is planning some type of scavenger hunt for fake silver nuggets. She's going to involve the local stores to make it a neighborhood event."

"That'll be fun." Silver nuggets. No mention of gold. I was currently looking through the book from ten years ago. I kept turning pages while I asked about other plans. "When are the final activities due?"

"Two weeks." Adelaide answered readily. "We need time to print up the information and arrange all the details."

I tilted my head for any sound of movement. This place could have been a tomb. I was content talking to my bud, but I wouldn't mind a diversion. "Did you see the old documents she found?"

"No, she didn't bring them with her. I'm looking forward to seeing them."

Would I have to take pictures of random people until I found the ones I wanted? How much information could I give out without risking a leak? For Wilson's sake I couldn't be the source of a disclosure on this case. Swearing people to silence never worked.

When footsteps in the hall announced an arrival, I breathed a sigh of relief.

Adelaide looked over her shoulder. "The workmen are here to work on the gym. The flooring and bleachers are being fixed up for fall. I'll have to leave you. You're okay?"

I waved her away with a smile and sigh of relief. "I'm fine. I'll keep looking."

As soon as she left, I grabbed Lily's year book and flipped to the graduating seniors. A few snaps from my phone camera and I had photos of Lily, Savannah, and Audrey. Back to the beginning of the alphabet to scan for anyone named Paige and... what had Amos said? A famous lawyer's name? That had better be obvious or I was doomed.

My fingers skimmed across the list of names. I wanted to hurry but I couldn't risk overlooking any detail. One Paige under the C's. A quick picture. Into the D's.

Frank Darrow.

My finger moved past the name, but a bell pealed in my mind, deafening me to the real world. Darrow, as in the famous lawyer, Clarence Darrow. Jared's friend. Bingo! My brain did a somersault and stuck the landing. A name and a face.

Another quick picture. I glanced at the door, but it remained closed. No sound. A few more minutes and I was at the end of the senior class. One more girl name Paige. Flipping through the rest of the book, I saw a few pictures of the group at Friday night games. A younger Jared Houlding was present, next to Darrow.

Footsteps on the linoleum outside pulled me back to reality. I swept up the books and shoved them back in place. Pocketing my phone, I faced the door, ready with an innocent story for anyone other than Adelaide.

When the door opened, my new bud was smiling at me. "Did you find anything useful?"

"I have everything I need." I assured her. Questions multiplied in my brain as I spoke. Eager to leave, I walked to the door and past her. As I bid farewell, bells rang in my head.

The door clicked shut behind me.

"Is it one of our students?" Adelaide's hands clutched each other. She wore a worried frown. "Lily was due to update us on her progress. She hasn't missed a deadline until now."

I sympathized with her uncertainty. My brain shoved the questions and clues aside. "I truly don't know who the dead woman is. She hasn't been identified. I'm looking for the answers."

With my brain busy and my body aimed at the door, my feet swiveled toward Adelaide. "Has anyone called about Lily Gilbert? Perhaps her friends know where she is. Were they on the committee with her?"

The woman grunted. "I don't believe any of them were involved in her project."

But they *knew* about it. Amos confirmed that. What did anyone have to fear from this project? If I couldn't come up with a name for the victim and a motive for the murder, Elena and Otis could end up in jail.

Once outside I felt buoyed by my successful venture. Armed with names and pictures, a quick search from my car gave me Frank Darrow's address. I also downloaded pictures from social media for both of the Paiges I'd found. Either one of them might have married and come to town as Paige Bly. Considering the trouble the woman had gone to in order to hide her face, I still believed Paige Bly was an alias. However, I had to cover all bets.

I texted all six photos to Holly: Savannah, Audrey, Lily, both Paiges, and Frank. I didn't have the patience to wait until Marcus could do an age progression. Next, I headed to the Mercantile for another photo array. Several moments later, I faced Elena and Otis in the cubbyhole of an office. From the doorway, I watched them eye the pictures spread out on the desk.

Elena sat down. Otis looked over her shoulder.

"I know Frank." The man said instantly. "He's been in several times, usually with Jared, the guy who died in May."

Elena nodded, glancing toward the shop. She'd fought tooth and nail before leaving the shop to come back here. "I don't like him. Too slick. Always wants something for nothing. Can't hold a job."

Otis snorted. "He's allergic to work. Gambles away everything he touches. He's in deep to the wrong people."

I perked up at the ominous tone. "Is he?"

"Bagatti." Otis whispered the name of one of the biggest bookies in town.

If you didn't have ready cash and you wanted to bet big, Bagatti was the man to go to. Of course, losing might cost you more than money. Frank would be desperate if that bookie was his banker.

"What about the women?" I asked, tucking the information away. "Remember these are high school pictures. They'd be older. Their hair or weight might be different."

Elena tapped one photo. "The survey lady wasn't Lily. She stopped by when she was in town to visit Amos. She talked about a game for the festival, remember?"

Otis smiled for the first time in several minutes. "She plans to make our store a stop for some treasure hunt. She asked if some old hidey hole was still in the storage room. I forgot about that."

That sparked my interest. "Did you show it to her?"

"Of course not. The walls are solid." Elena's scathing tone was matched by her frown. "Once you find the killer Tracy, we can make plans for Lily's game. It'll be good for business. The Fall Festival always brings in a crowd."

I appreciated their confidence in my ability, but I had a lot of questions to answer before I could close this case. "Look at the other pictures. Could any of the women be the Survey Lady?"

That's what I wanted to know.

Elena studied each picture in turn. "The woman had blond hair. Her eyes were bright blue like contact lenses. I only noticed when she adjusted the sunglasses."

"You didn't mention her odd eye color before." My sharp tone betrayed my frustration. Other than Kevin, eyes that color of blue were likely colored contacts. Another disguise.

Elena looked up at me with a sharp expression. "I'm sure I mentioned it."

She pushed Lily's photo away, then one of the Paiges. Her finger hovered over then landed on Savannah Lester's face. "This one. The shape of her chin, narrow."

"You're sure?" My pulse quickened. This put Savannah in town on Tuesday. It also proved she and Audrey both lied about coming to town to meet Lily. Unless Lily had lied to Amos. Either way, Elena's identification didn't prove Savannah was the murdered woman, but she might be the killer.

Elena and Otis exchanged smiles before turning to me with excited expressions.

"Good news, huh?" Otis looked as if the ID solved the case.

"Absolutely." I sounded confident even to myself. It was a major step forward.

A moment later, I plopped down in the driver's seat in my fifteen-year-old Buick and listened to the engine hesitate. Hoping it wasn't an omen I was relieved when the engine turned over on the second try.

Patting my purse, I focused on having found pictures and names. That had been my goal and I achieved it. Now what?

The airport ploy was in full swing and it was too early for Kevin to get away from the handyman job he was giving an estimate on. I had time for one more quick stop. The only solid lead I had was Frank Darrow's address, but if he was desperate for money, would he be laying around where he could be found?

A quick tour of his neighborhood found me idling in front of Bud Olsen's Bar. Sure, it was only ten o'clock on a Monday morning, but Nevada doesn't have blue laws blocking the sale of liquor. Few states do anymore but Nevada never did as far as I know. I turned off the car and sauntered inside.

The place was small, dimly lit and smelled like old beer. I almost gagged, but there were a dozen regulars who evidently didn't mind. Acting on Kevin's advice and my own experience, I did a quick scan without lingering on anyone. Then I chose a small table in a back corner with a view of the room.

A tired waitress took my order for a virgin Bloody Mary.

As I waited, I reviewed what I knew. Audrey Houlding was nowhere to be found in Langsdale. At least she hadn't been found by me. Perhaps she was crashing with a buddy or she'd already left town. That would be the smart thing to do if she was involved with this murder, but desperate people rarely make intelligent decisions.

When the waitress set the thick mug on the table, I held up a twenty and a five for the eight-dollar drink. "Do you ever see Frank Darrow in here?"

She snorted as she took the money. "That man should pay rent. He uses the back booth as an office."

She jerked her head to an empty booth behind me.

Of course, the one booth *not* in my line of sight. This wouldn't happen to Rabi. I sipped the concoction and turned my phone in her direction. "Have you seen this woman with him?"

She studied Audrey's picture before looking at me with a knowing smile. When I coughed up another twenty, she nodded. "Three days ago. She was looking for him. They're due."

Fifteen minutes later, I was tired of my drink, I'd lost ten games of solitaire, and I figured the second twenty had been a mistake. I had to leave soon to meet Kevin.

When a door in the back of the bar creaked open then slammed shut, the waitress shot me a glance.

I mentally apologized for doubting her. Slumping over as if tired or drunk, I leaned my chin on my fist and waited on pins and needles. A pair of quick, hard footsteps sounded behind me.

"What do you think-- "

"Shut up." A man's arrogant whisper cut the women off. "Sit here and keep it down."

The waitress took an order for two Irish coffees and left.

Reversing the view on my camera phone gave me a great view. Frank was six feet with a decent build. His blond hair and hazel eyes gave him a surfer profile. A hard expression detracted from his looks. I took a couple photos of him and Audrey, who'd brought a travel mug into the bar. Then, I started to record the scene.

Audrey leaned forward. Her finger stabbed at the table. "Where is the money you owed Jared? He told me about the tournament you won in April. You stiffed him on the prize money."

"Calm down. You're drawing attention." Frank cautioned in a hard voice, following his own advice. "Jared and I worked that out. We were even when he died."

I almost laughed. Easy enough to say you cleared the slate with a dead man.

Audrey, now more composed, gave him a stink eye. She didn't believe him either, but what could she do? She had to know Frank was in debt. "Jared died before he sent me the money he promised. Then his car vanished. That was worth a hundred grand."

Frank shook his head. "The car's in pieces in Mexico by now. Forget it."

Audrey's anger melted into disappointment, but an ember sparked in her eyes. "What about this gold Lily found? I never believed Savannah's crazy mother before, but if the gold is real, we could both be in the clear."

"Don't be a fool. Lily didn't find or see any gold." Frank spat out the words in a scathing tone. His gaze shifted as he ran a hand through his hair. "Amos is a rambling old man repeating second hand stories."

My body remained slumped but my mind was jumping up and down. Amos had a few years on Mrs. C, but he was as sharp as anyone. Were these two planning to lie to each other about everything? Why was Frank trying so hard to downplay this talk of gold? Had he killed the woman in the basement?

Audrey looked as skeptical as I felt. "Amos is no fool."

Frank scoffed. "It's still old gossip from a drunk. I'm not banking on it."

Audrey's jaw tightened, obviously not buying Frank's attempt to downplay this wild story. "It's worth a try. I found those blueprints same as Lily. The hidey-hole is in that basement. I'll search on my own."

"The police are still watching that store." Frank sneered. "If Savannah thought there was gold to be found, she'd be here."

Audrey's expression hardened. "I can't get hold of Savannah or Lily. One of them could be the dead woman they found in the basement."

The man's attention and gaze snapped to the front entrance as it opened to admit a flash of almost blinding sunlight. His whole body tensed. Only when two fifty-something, bottle blondes walked in did Frank relax.

"Perhaps Savannah did come to town." Audrey splayed her hands on the table. Her narrowed gaze studied him closely. "Who do you think the dead woman is? The description matches Lily. If those two argued about the gold, Savannah might be on the run. Unless she's hanging around town to try for the gold again."

Frank's gaze flicked around the room. Worried about being found or buying time to think of an answer? "Savannah was tough. No way Lily would win a fight with her."

"What do you mean, Savannah *was* tough?" Audrey's shrill voice betrayed her nerves.

"Get off my case." Frank shot daggers at her. "I meant in high school. Savannah always had a leave me alone attitude. She hasn't changed."

Audrey slapped the table. "I knew it. You contacted Savannah. You used the new e-mail you found on my phone. I told you not to."

Frank reared across the table like a lion at an antelope. "What if I did e-mail her to ask for a loan? She's not in witness protection."

Why was Audrey so protective of Savannah's e-mail address? And what did Frank mean by witness protection? Was Savannah using a different name?

Audrey groaned and flicked her hair off her face. "What did Savannah say?"

"She blew me off." Frank turned his head, blocking his face from her view. "Said she was done chasing her mother's delusions."

With a little maneuvering of my camera, I saw his eyes harden with the lie. My heart picked up speed. What if Savannah had come to town in response to *Frank's* demands. What could he threaten her with? To expose her new name? Why would that scare her?

"I wish Savannah was here. She knew where the key was hidden." Audrey continued. "She used it during high school."

I stifled a gasp. A hidden key? It was cliché, but it might be enough to keep Elena and Otis out of jail.

"You can't believe the gold is there. Why are you still in town?" The man's clenched fist smacked the table. "Why are you hounding me?"

"Because you owed Jared money." Audrey hissed. She stabbed the table. Her eyes were full of fury. "And don't give me any more lies about paying him off. I can't go home without ready cash for the bank. I just need to buy time to restructure the company to sell gourmet meals using our seafood."

"That again." Frank growled. With his shoulders against the back of the booth, his wide-eyed gaze held the look of a trapped animal. Audrey wasn't going to leave. "Listen up. I don't have any money for you, for my landlady, or for the bookie I owe."

He paused for a heartbeat, then his expression morphed to a sweet smile. "But I got a deal for you."

Uh-oh, watch out, Audrey.

In the midst of this exchange, I noted neither of them referred to Lily helping them. That wasn't a good sign.

Audrey's body stiffened at his changed demeanor. She retreated with a wary air. "What are you proposing?"

Smart woman.

Frank leaned in. "There's a high-stakes poker game with a couple of easy marks. We both need the cash. Come with me. Dress nice. Distract the other players."

Audrey considered it, then gave a sharp nod. "If you win, we'll split the money."

"Yeah. Sure," he agreed quickly and too enthusiastically.

Good thing he couldn't see the disbelief on my face. He had no intention of giving her his winnings. He'd take the cash and quit this town before she could blink.

Her eyes narrowed. "I'll be there and ready to play. I'm a better poker player than Jared ever was. Why didn't I think of that before?"

Frank straightened, looking relieved. "I'll text you the time and place."

"Listen." Audrey's nails beat a rhythm on the worn table. A flirtatious smile lightened her expression. "The gold is worth trying for. We've got nothing to lose. The cops are done."

"Oh, no." Frank stared at the door. He went pale under his tan. He'd barely uttered the words, when, with a speed beyond that of mortal men, he slipped out of the booth and vanished.

"What the-?" Audrey's stunned reaction was almost comical.

The front door opened, sending a splash of light into the dark interior. A huge figure blocked the door. A smaller, but no less unattractive man, followed him in. Bagatti's muscle. Had to be.

Audrey's disgusted exclamation was interrupted by the waitress delivering the two drinks and demanding nineteen dollars. The younger woman started to refuse then thought better of it. She handed over a twenty with an impatient, "Keep the change."

"Gee, thanks," the waitress spoke in a flat tone. "A whole dollar."

Audrey grabbed her travel mug and gathered herself to stand. Then she eyed the drinks. Within seconds, she'd poured both into her own to go cup.

A teetotaler, not.

She sat for a moment with a pensive gaze. Her head shifted toward the path Frank had taken. Before she could follow Frank out the back, I spun out of my chair and took his place in the booth.

In the face of her frown, I leaned forward. "I'm Tracy Belden. A PI hired to find out who murdered the woman in the basement of the Miner's Mercantile."

Her expression tightened, then, she pulled on a business-like mask. "I don't know anything about that."

I bit back a snide comment and opted for sympathy. "Savannah and Lily are missing. They haven't been seen since the woman died. Odds are one of them is dead."

Her face wilted at my words. She shook her head. "No, they both went home. I know - "

"They're both missing." I rapped the table with my knuckles. "You're the friend Lily had lunch with when she saw Amos. You've been in town longer than either of them, crashing with a high school buddy. You've been hounding Frank for money. You put him on Savannah's trail about the gold, didn't you? Her aunt and uncle are in town looking for her. Did you contact them?"

"No, I - " Her denial was immediate. Audrey gritted her teeth. Her panting breath gave her the look of a trapped animal. "Frank tracked down that story. He found them and asked if it was true. I never believed... I wouldn't..."

"Audrey, calm down. We can fix this." Frank's communication with the Indigos must have triggered their arrival here. Evidently everyone was looking for this mysterious gold. However, the woman was ready to have a heart attack. Pitching my voice calm and low, I leaned back to give her room. "I can help you. I promise."

She met my gaze in a forlorn plea. "I don't know. I don't know."

Without warning, she jumped to her feet, shoved the table into my gut, and ran out the back door.

I pushed the table away and clutched my aching ribs. "This never happens to Kevin. People don't run out on him."

The thought of following her came and went. Not only was I due to meet Kevin, but I didn't need to be caught between Frank and Bagatti's men. Grateful for what progress I'd made, I stuck a ten-dollar bill under my mug and walked out the door.

The sunshine had never felt so good. My spirits rose at the thought of giving Wilson the recording. That should be enough to buy him time to find the real murderer.

Buried gold as a motive was laughable, but the players in this whirlpool of a case obviously believed in the hidden treasure. Savannah's mother had evidently known the truth. All I had to do was decipher the addled thoughts of a delusional paranoid woman who'd been dead for over ten years.

13

— • —

10 Down; 5 Letters;
Clue: Sudden fear or anxiety.
Answer: Panic.

Once in the car, giddy from the break in the case, I pounded the steering wheel in excitement. When my phone buzzed with a text. I was surprised to see Kevin had sent the message.

His words were more puzzling: *I'm done investigating the case. Big news! Want a ride to the airport?"*

Emojis of a guy doing cartwheels followed.

With my curiosity mounting, I typed back: *Sure. Whazzup?*

I got back a laughing emoji with tears and an emoji with a hand over its mouth. I threw my phone in my purse. "That man knows how to get my goat. What did he find out?"

Fifteen minutes later the Great White Beast was purring down the highway headed to the small airport on the outskirts of Langsdale.

I eyed my best buddy of ten years and my exasperating hubby with a frustrated frown. "Give me a hint."

"I'll just have to repeat myself." His tone was annoyingly calm. His smug smile was maddening.

"I'll tell you what I found out." I promised in a wheedling tone. "Huge news!"

Kevin shrugged. "Okay, tell me."

I shook my fists at him while growling deep in my throat. My phone rang as I searched for a comeback. Breaking off my response, I glanced at the readout. "Why would Mrs. C be calling? That wasn't the plan."

With trepidation building, I answered the phone. "Hello?"

A cacophony of high-pitched screams and a deep voice yelling commands assaulted my ear. I put the phone on speaker and shared an astonished look with my hubby. The Caddy took off like a rocket on the road.

"Hello?" I yelled. "What's going on?"

"I'm going, darlin'." Mrs. C's high-pitched, Kentucky accented wail overrode everyone else. "Y'all don't worry about me. Carry on. Be brave."

The tension in my shoulders relaxed. Kevin smiled but the car still slipped in and out of traffic.

"Is this Tracy Belden?" A panicked guy screamed. "Your grandmother collapsed. She won't let us call 9-1-1. Is she having a heart attack?"

"Nana!" Marcus's horror-stricken voice cut across the conversation. "Nana, it'll be okay. Just breathe like the doctor told you. Give it three, four minutes, you'll be fine. Hurry! Please!"

Having given the timeline, his voice broke on the final words. A sob sounded.

My free hand covered my mouth to contain my laughter.

"Don't call 9-1-1." Kevin grabbed my wrist and brought the phone to his mouth. "That will only make her worse."

"We don't want that." The guy's voice rose an octave.

"We're five minutes away." Kevin imbued the words with a steady calming tone. "Have everyone stay with her and our son. That will calm them both down."

"Of course. We won't leave them." The other man's hurried words tripped over each other. "Get here! Hurry!"

"Three minutes." Kevin promised before signing off.

I made sure the call disconnected before I burst out laughing. I barely had enough time to recover before Kevin pulled up to the side door marked Security Office.

I burst through the door with my hand on my heart. Mrs. C sat in a wheelchair. Her drooping head leaned against her hand. Kevin followed me in and stood at my side.

A sad looking Marcus patted the older woman's back. "It's okay, Nana. You're fine. It could have happened to anyone."

"Oh, duc- darlin'." Catching herself, Mrs. C added a moan. "I'm so embarrassed. You were having such a good time."

The boy child straightened. He aimed an apologetic look at three people standing close by. "We were done anyway and everyone was so helpful. I'll be sure to include your quick emergency response in my report."

I rushed forward and hovered over Mrs. C. "As long as you're okay, that's all that matters."

"We're very grateful." Kevin walked up to the staff. My hubby instantly captured the attention of the two women and the man. "I'll be certain to inform your superiors about your excellent response and caring manner."

While Kevin's charm obscured their vision, Marcus grabbed the handles of the wheelchair. "We should go."

I and the two rogues slipped out virtually unseen.

Rabi's car was parked near the nineteen-sixty-seven pearly white Cadillac. The lean man made a show of helping Mrs. C into the backseat.

I glanced over my shoulder. "We need an alternative to the airport diner. I think we've worn out our welcome here."

Marcus popped the wheelchair up on its back wheels and aimed it toward the door. "Stella's. We took a vote."

Kevin was still inside.

"You guys have the tapes? The download can't be traced, can it?" Though I was thrilled to have the security feed, I felt obligated to be the sane one.

"TR." Marcus groaned and rolled his eyes. "Don't be such a wuss or I won't take you on any future expeditions."

"Hey, I'm the adult." I pointed out. "You're the child."

"We know the scam," Marcus crowed. He waved me to silence. "We have the feed from the airport and the bank. You can thank Rabi for that part."

I looked at Rabi. "A friend of a friend?"

Rabi shrugged. "Former Marine. See him at the VFW."

"That's so cool, hunh?" Marcus's excited expression was the direct antithesis of Rabi's matter-of-fact attitude.

Five minutes later, our two-car parade took off. Marcus had urged Rabi to get ahead of Kevin. I settled back with a sigh and looked back at Mrs. C. "What went wrong?"

"We'd have been fine if the regional supervisor hadn't dropped in without warning." Her admonishing tone left no doubt who was in the wrong. "The nerve of some people. *We* had an appointment."

I nodded, not trying to hide a smile.

The next instant, Mrs. C's chuckle filled the air. "Oh, ducks, I've had a wonderful day. I haven't faked a heart attack for many a year, eh? Good to know I've still got the knack."

"You're not alone." I chuckled, relieved it was over. "Kevin was investigating on his own. Didn't tell anyone."

"'struth?" Mrs. C's astonished look was all to be hoped for. She nudged Kevin's shoulder. "Branching out, are ye?"

I stabbed my finger at him. "He won't tell me what he found out."

"I'm not repeating myself." His smug look counteracted his disclaimer.

Progress on the case took backset to lunch, which arrived on a tray. Each burger was wrapped in a diaper of parchment paper. The method not only cut down on the mess as the burgers oozed cheese and a variety of toppings. The restaurant didn't have to deal with plates.

"Mmmm." Marcus's appreciative noise came around a mouthful of melted peanut butter, mayo, and Swiss cheese. He swallowed before adding, "Raw onions are the way to go."

I preferred the grilled onions and cheddar cheese. My brain wanted to discuss Kevin's news and nail down what the tape revealed, but my stomach and mouth outvoted my brain.

Once the table was cleaned and the vote came down to heading home to discuss the case, I put my foot down. "I am not waiting! I have pictures and names and news. Everyone is giving updates now. Especially you."

Kevin raised a brow at my demanding tone, but his grin broke through. "I finished early so I stopped at a casino and found an old acquaintance. He confirmed Jared and Frank were cheating at poker. Low key. No one was on to them that he knew of, but word was getting around. Without Jared, Frank's in deep."

Rabi leaned back in his chair. "Lots of enemies."

"Speaking of Frank Darrow." I told them what I'd learned at the high school, including Lily missing deadlines. Then, I dropped my bombshells. "Frank and Audrey are both desperate for the gold they believe is in the Mercantile. That and the hidden key should clear Otis and Elena."

Frowning, Marcus cocked his head to one side. "Is Jared being a crook tied to the dead lady?"

"Not directly," I admitted. "But it's a coincidence I can't ignore."

"Jared squandered Frank's share of a big poker pot on a car." Kevin kept his voice low, tapping his fingers on the table.

Marcus pointed at Kevin. "When Jared wound up at the bottom of the stairs, Frank got ahold of the car keys. Then, he sold the car to pay part of his debts. But how he did he get it out of the garage without being seen?"

"I've got the goods on it, haven't I?" Mrs. C looked pleased with herself. "My book club heard tell of an old Corvette in the same garage stashed under a tarp to avoid repossession. The bank was tipped off and found the vehicle."

She paused for dramatic effect.

"Some folks say the tow truck left at dawn." The older woman held up a finger. "Others swear it drove away mid-morning. Different truck. Same color tarp."

"No one realized one was Jared's blue sportscar." Marcus laughed. "That's so cool."

"One mystery solved." My gaze narrowed as I put the clues in a new puzzle. "Bagatti has the resources to repaint the car and come up with a fake title and a new VIN."

Kevin's hand hit the back of my chair in a steady rhythm. When I looked at him, he cocked his head to one side. "How does that tie to our murdered woman?"

"The first domino, perhaps." My brain was still rewriting clues in my crossword puzzle. "Adelaide and Elena both said Lily's plan involved fake silver nuggets. The first time I spoke with Amos after I found the body, he said she was going to hide fool's gold. Why is he the only one who mentioned gold?"

Kevin raised a brow. "Trip to the park to talk to Amos?"

Ten minutes later, I marched toward the stone tables with Marcus at my side. The boy was better at sticking than Velcro.

Amos sat in his usual place. His longtime friends, Nattie, a white woman with leathery skin, and Tomas, a small dark-haired man with Hispanic and Native American blood, took up two of the other chairs. They watched me and Marcus approach with silent gazes.

I sat in the empty chair. Marcus stood by my shoulder. "I have nothing to report. I need info."

"Intel." Marcus corrected softly.

Amos reached into his shirt pocket for a sheath of rolled up paper. "I copied what Lily showed me, near as I could remember."

He pushed the pages to me across the stone surface.

I flattened them out, holding the sides with my fingers.

"Wow!" Marcus breathed the work in my ear. "Amos, these are cool! You drew these by hand?"

I shared the boy's sentiments. The detail on the pencil sketched diagrams was amazingly clear. The streets and buildings looked true to scale. I couldn't have done this well with professional equipment.

Main Street, which ran through the center of our neighborhood, was clearly marked. The present location of several shops was easy to discern. I traced the positions with my finger. "This is the Mercantile. Desert Rose Dough. The old bank. The Emporium Hotel was originally a saloon."

"These orange circles." Marcus reached over my shoulder to point to the map. "Are those the hidey-holes for the mined ore?"

Amos nodded. "That's what Lily found on the original blueprints. She had copies of it all."

I studied the picture, sorting out my thoughts before I looked at the old man. "What did Lily say about her plans for the festival?"

Amos repeated what he'd said the first time. He added a bit of detail. His expression grew light when he spoke of his granddaughter's enthusiasm. His smile became wistful. "She had such plans."

Nattie reached over and touched his hand when Amos fell silent. "She was all aglow about making-up treasure bags for people to find. She was going to stash candy and fake silver nuggets in the stores for people to discover."

"Silver nuggets?" Marcus asked.

All three of the others nodded.

Then Amos stilled. A frown formed on his brow. Leaning back, he met my gaze and stroked a long finger across his jaw. "After she left town, she called me. Her tone was different. Serious. Asked me if I'd ever heard of gold stashes in town. Any rumors or stories."

He watched me through a narrowed gaze. "That's what you're fishing for."

I nodded. "You mentioned fool's gold the first time we spoke. Everyone else said Lily intended to plant fake silver nuggets. Why did you connect gold to Lily's story?"

Amos's brow furrowed. "I told her a story about gold. She laughed. "Not silver?" she teased. I said no. Five years ago, Otis needed wiring done. A retired electrician I referred told me about finding a gold coin in the basement. He claimed the coin fell out of a crack in the wall, then the crack disappeared. He couldn't open it again."

I frowned. "Did he tell Otis and Elena? Did you see this coin?"

Amos snorted with laughter then he shook his head. "I never saw a thing. He was drunk when he told me and he was drunk two days later when he ran his car off the road."

Marcus eyed me with a serious expression. "Did Lily act different when you mentioned the gold?"

Amos's face was relaxed as he thought. "No, she was laughing and taking notes about props for the treasure hunt. She mentioned fake silver on the first visit."

I seized on his statement. "When she called you back, did she mention the scavenger hunt in relation to the gold?"

Amos shook his head. "Not once. She was on a different track that day. What changed?"

"I think her friends remembered a wild tale of their own. Looks like they all went hunting for buried treasure." And it ended in greed and murder.

14

— · —

21 Across; 3 Letters;
Clue: A complex system of interconnected threads.
Answer: Web.

L ate Monday afternoon found Marcus, Kevin, and I sitting around
our kitchen table. Marcus had printed out clear headshots of the
older couple from the security tapes. The pilot was well-known and had
flown out the next day. Wayne and Beth Brown, however, had given a
fake address. The names were certainly fake as well.

"These are perfect." I tapped the pictures as I smiled at Marcus. "I'll
have Sammy and Elena confirm this is the man they saw."

"They will. He fits the description." Marcus's small hand patted me
on the shoulder as he leaned in for a better view. "What next? How does
it fit together?"

That was the question of the day. I couldn't fault the boy for his
impatience, except I had no answers.

Kevin had spent several minutes staring at Amos's rendering of the
century old maps. "Any news from Wilson on the victim's ID?"

"Nothing. Audrey must be crashing with Frank. No luck on Savannah. I'm still trying to trace Lily." I rested my chin on my hand. "I've

moved to Fresno on the assumption she met her friend like she told her co-worker. Zilch, so far."

Which strengthened the argument that she was in the morgue or on the lam having killed Savannah, if Savannah was the woman in the basement.

Kevin scanned my scattered hand written notes. "Lily was excited because the old-time maps showed our neighborhood with the original structures."

Marcus hanging on every word, nodded ferociously. He crowded next to Kevin and stabbed at the drawing. "That's the Miner's Mercantile. You can see walls of the original foundation, even the basement. The building is way old."

My hubby's calm demeanor contrasted with the boy's excitement. "Lily shared her find with all her friends."

Kevin held out a hand in a gesture for calm. "This is the corner where the store sits. Main street. Side street. This is the alley. Here's the original foundation. This is the dividing wall between the main basement and the storage area."

Marcus leaned in close. "What does that say? Those scribbles inside the wall?"

Kevin leaned in closer. "Ag, the chemical symbol for silver, and a pickax. That's one of the caches on the map. There are several marked in these buildings."

"People hid their silver so it wouldn't get stolen." The boy child jumped as if he'd been struck by lightning. "Frank and Audrey are looking for gold, not silver."

Kevin's fingers tapped the table. "Monica Sutton talked about ghosts in the walls guarding a hidden cache of gold."

"That's what she said." I couldn't hide my skepticism. If Kevin had sprouted a second head, I wouldn't have been more surprised. "Who would believe a story like that from a delusional woman and a drunk?"

"People are killed every day for a pocket full of lies." Kevin's voice harkened back not only to the region's history, but to his own. "Selling Jared's car brought Frank breathing space, but he owes the wrong people."

"Nobody likes a cheater." Marcus's tone matched Kevin's. "Talk to Three-fingered Louis."

Well, sure, the name alone made his point. "Okay, Frank has little to lose by checking for hidden gold."

Marcus scrunched his face up in a puzzled frown. "If no one found the money and they don't have the key, how did that lady get murdered?"

Kevin gave up his study of the map. He sat back with a skeptical look. "Her bruises prove she fought her killer, but there were no signs of a search."

"This doesn't track." I leaned on his shoulder, ready for some downtime. My brain was tired of looking for connections. "The video of Audrey and Frank saying there was a hidden key might buy Wilson time, but it doesn't prove anything. What are Rabi and Mrs. C up to? Do we have plans for dinner?"

My whiny tone matched my sudden depletion of energy. The adrenaline of the hit with the yearbooks followed by the airport escape had left my brain in a whirl.

Kevin slammed the laptop shut with a sudden move. "They both have plans for the evening."

That perked me up. I could live vicariously through them. "What's going on?"

Marcus nudged my arm. His eyes sparked with a secret. "Rabi's taking Tasha to the Miner's ball downtown. All the snooty people with money will be there. Tasha got tickets through her job."

"I forgot that was tonight." The annual outcry to move the event to a weekend had failed as usual. Tradition had this particular date for when the biggest silver strike in the region had been discovered. The only concession to protests was to start the dinner at five o'clock, so the dance wouldn't go so late. Honestly, the majority of attendees didn't have real jobs anyway. Except people like Tasha, who took the next day off.

The gold and silver decorations at the ball were renowned for their avantgarde designs. Local stations broadcast the arrivals; Langsdale's version of a night at the Oscars.

"Ooohh! Evening gowns and tuxes." I was suitably impressed. "I can't wait to hear the details."

"Rabi had a tux." Marcus's awed tone made this fact sound more unlikely than the invitation itself.

Kevin nodded. "Rabi is a man of many disguises and talents."

Marcus looked at the unflappable Kevin then eyed me.

"I'm surprised." I was. But Rabi never went into detail about his past. He'd said more than once that only today counted.

Marcus, evidently content that I'd had no idea of Rabi's wardrobe, settled into his chair. "Mrs. C went to an afternoon tea. A bunch of people who watched that British and Australian polo wanted to talk about it. They're having sandwiches and scones and petite cakes."

"Petite? As in short cakes?" I frowned, puzzled. "What is that?"

The boy held up one hand with his fingers spread. "Four-layer cakes. They cut 'em into teeny, little pieces."

"Oh, petit-fours." Not that I had any experience with the finer arts of baking or English teas.

"That's what I said." The boy told me in an exasperated tone.

"Pay attention, Belden." Kevin rolled his eyes. Silent laughter showed behind his sarcastic expression.

"They're having like twenty kinds of tea." Shock, awe, and outrage mixed in Marcus's tone and expression. Evidently that was too many varieties in his opinion. "Weird names. They were all excited."

"Who'd have thought?" I asked. "Teas at a tea party. What will those British people think of next?"

"The bottom line is," Marcus spoke over my muttered comments. "We're on our own for supper. I vote we stay home. What about pizza? You're on a case. We can eat big."

The thought was tempting, but it wouldn't do my reputation any good if I gave in easily. I pretended to consider the idea.

"Negotiations between you two take too long." Kevin stepped in. "I'm hungry. B&T's latest client is adding on a breezeway which will double the cost of the job. B&T will pop for pizza. The PI money is safe."

Amid Marcus's groans, my applause, and Kevin's laughter, I grabbed my phone.

Food refreshes the soul, and the brain cells. An hour-and-a-half later, with a belly full of salad, breadsticks, and pizza with cream cheese and Korean barbecue sauce, I found a second wind. I also had the place to myself, except for the cats. The felines had taken up stations on opposite corners of the sectional. They looked like matching bookends.

Kevin and Marcus opted for a trip around the block. Actually, they were driving through the neighborhood. A quick, innocent revisiting the scene of the crime. They planned to chat up the interested parties. Marcus's words. They'd been gone for over an hour.

I was pretty sure their route would take them to the local ice cream stand. I turned my energies to delving into every person, place, or tangent mentioned since I'd found, and worse, smelled the body.

I still hoped for an injured or hiding Lily in the expanded Fresno area. Despite what I told Marcus, my expectation of success was not high. My frustration at my and the police's lack of progress at identifying the victim was an open sore. Although, she'd only been found just over forty-eight hours ago.

At the moment, my eyes ached and my neck was sore. A completed puzzle from the Exotic Places Crossword Puzzle book that started it all lay at my side. I laid my head on the soft, plush sofa cushions. A moment later a paw stepped on my hand. That weight was followed by the more substantial body of... I peeked through one open eyelid... Rookie. The cat proceeded to walk across the laptop, thankfully closed, and draped herself across my lap.

I stroked the silky fur as her scratchy tongue licked my arm. We had a restful, two, maybe three minutes. I can't be sure because when the door banged open, I woke from my doze.

Marcus stared at me, scowling. "Did you fall asleep?"

"No," I retorted in the face of his accusation. "I'm being held hostage by a feline. Besides, I've had a hard day."

"Guess who we found wandering the streets?" Marcus strode forward. "A dazed and confused detective. We took pity on him."

"I believe the dazed part," I said with a laugh.

Wilson, standing behind the child, favored him with a skeptical look. "What version of reality do you exist in?"

"His own." Kevin brought up the rear and shut the door. "You should know that by now."

The detective pointed at each of my guys. "They were crossing my trail. Talking to suspects and witnesses."

"What world do you live in?" My hubby favored the other man with a confused look. "We went for a drive and visited our neighbors."

His tone held the perfect amount of confused innocence to sell the story.

My attention moved from one male to the next while petting Rookie who rubbed her head against my arm. I faced Wilson with shocked look. "How can you accuse either of these poor, tortured innocents of duplicity?"

In answer, the detective loomed over me. "I'll tell you who I'm accusing... you. You're supposed to cooperate, Tracy. I could lock you out of this investigation."

Unsure which lead he'd discovered, I snorted at his threat. "I'm a card-carrying PI. I can talk to anyone I want."

The lanky, scarecrow like detective shook a finger at me. "I've kept you in the loop. I risked my job."

I rolled my eyes at his martyred tone. "You haven't risked anything. You know as well as I do that if either of us solves this case or I provide intel that leads to an arrest, neither the media, the mayor, or your wrapped-too-tight chief is going to care who found what. You'll get the credit."

"It's true." Marcus returned from his quest in the kitchen. He leaned on the back of the sectional watching me and Wilson trade barbs as if we were in a play. He had a bowl of grapes and tossed them into his mouth like popcorn. "She doesn't care about fame, only money."

I put up my hands. "Tell your friends, tell your co-workers, especially, tell your boss. Besides, I tried to keep you in the loop. I left you a message at the station. Your cell phone disconnected without taking me to voice mail."

The detective bared his teeth and growled, looking like a very angry scarecrow. "Stupid thing's broken. I don't know what happened."

Marcus, having just thrown two grapes in his mouth, took a second to shift them to his cheeks. He looked like a chipmunk with wide eyes. "Want me to take a look at it? No charge."

Wilson sighed. The wind left his sails. He looked at me.

I tilted my head toward the boy child. "I'd take him up on it. I usually have to pay."

The detective raked a hand through his straw-like hair. "It's the best offer I've had all day."

Marcus climbed over the back of the sectional, ignoring my frown, set his bowl on the table, and reached for the phone.

Kevin walked in from the kitchen with a tray of cookies in one hand and a glass holding a pale brown drink in the other. "Who wants some of Mrs. C's cookies and an Arnold Palmer?"

Marcus, typing on Wilson's phone, frowned. "What's an Arnold Palmer?"

Wilson clapped his hands so loud the sound reverberated off the walls. Grinning, he reached for the plate and the glass. "I love bribes that can be eaten. So easy to dispose of the evidence."

Kevin chuckled as the detective took the treats and spun on his heels to sit on the sofa to my left. My hubby walked around the sectional and sat on my right side. "The drink is half lemonade, half iced tea."

I sighed as Kevin sat next to me and put an arm around my shoulders.

"Yuck." Our son stuck out his tongue. He frowned at the phone. A trilling sound of a birdcall sounded from Wilson's cell. Marcus frowned. "What's that?"

The answer came from the recesses of my memory. "The call of a bob-white. *The Mystery at Bob-White Cave* starring Trixie Belden. Were you trying to call me, Wilson?"

"That's probably what broke my phone." He shook a cookie at me.

Marcus frowned. "What did you do to this poor thing?"

Wilson with half a cookie in his mouth, shrugged. "I'm innocent until proven guilty."

I slid the laptop out from under Rookie and tossed it to the end of the sectional. "Anyone learn anything new?"

"Uh-unh." Wilson swallowed in time to turn on me. "You have to report first. My sources tell me you've been some very busy bees today."

As cases go, I'd hit on several points of interest. "Here's what happened."

The next several minutes were taken up with a replay of finding the pictures at the high-school, the theory that Jared used Frank's half of a poker pot to buy his fancy car. I followed up with Mrs. C's news about how the missing car disappeared. As my grand finale, I showed him the video of Audrey and Frank on my phone. "I sent you the photos and this video. It's locked in your phone."

"Amos said Otis and Elena didn't change the locks." Marcus spoke without looking away from the phone. "Savannah's old key would work."

Wilson looked suitably impressed with the video. "A hidden key will buy me time. But that video isn't a confession of anything."

"Still no ID on the victim?" Kevin's sympathetic tone diffused some of the heat.

The detective threw his pen down. "TV detectives would have had her name and address in ten minutes. Lily's dentist retired, threw away his records, and is on a three month cruise. Savannah's dentist from high school no longer has her records. I don't have a facial recognition genie. I have an ME who says the time and conditions in the basement advanced the decay of the body."

"He won't commit to anything?" Marcus frowned at the phone. "You need a new ME."

I shared the general sense of frustration. For the record I updated Wilson on my unsuccessful search for Lily. His lack of appreciation matched Marcus's.

"No sign of Lily. No leads on Savannah. One of them is in the morgue." Wilson rubbed a hand over his face. "No judge will give me a search warrant based on this video."

I felt brave enough to venture one more comment. "Are you planning to speak with Frank Darrow?"

Wilson's elbows were balanced on his knees. "I'll stop by his place, put out feelers, but if he's trying to ditch Bagatti, finding Darrow won't be easy. Why don't you track down Frank Darrow?"

"I plan to tomorrow," I admitted. "He didn't answer his phone. But his landlady said he's been coming and going. Can't hurt to try my luck."

Wilson leaned against the cushions. "Be my guest."

"I've never gone this long without knowing who the victim is." I stared at Wilson as if I could force the issue. "I still think Paige Bly is an alias, probably Savannah's."

"Paige might be Lily's alias. She figured out how to find the alleged gold. She and her partner snuck in, came up empty, and the partner killed her." The detective snagged the pictures of the older couple. "I'm not going to ask how you acquired these. I'll run them past Elena. Sammy, too. Fake names. Fakes address. Where does that get me?"

"You'll ID them." I'd never seen the man so downhearted and I had nothing to offer him. "We can start again tomorrow."

Wilson snorted. "I have to finish tonight. Local teens found a body behind some trashcans this afternoon. I'll probably close that case before I find out who killed the woman in the basement."

That pretty much summed up the feeling of the moment. However, the detective's judgement couldn't drown out my inner voice.

As tenuous as the connection seemed, Lily's circle of friends and the murder victim were linked. I was certain they would lead me to the killer. I just didn't know how.

15

— • —

11 Across; 5 Letters;
Clue: A false identity.
Answer: Alias.

"I have two leads to eliminate on Lily Gilbert." I stood by the kitchen table, having just started the dishwasher with Tuesday's breakfast dishes. To further my argument, I held up two fingers.

Mrs. C was wiping off the counter.

Rabi stood in the doorway.

Marcus, having asked for the plan for today, eyed me with a pitying look. "Good for you, TR."

His false enthusiasm was plain. This from a boy child who'd spent the last ten minutes torturing Rabi to give him details of last night's fancy evening that the man didn't care about. Marcus seemed intrigued at the chance to glimpse a world he'd never seen.

Dropping his false smile, the boy pointed at Kevin. "You're up, Kev."

Kevin continued pouring coffee into his travel mug. "I hate to bring reality crashing into an investigation, but I have a job. The supplies are in, the guys are ready, and the painting begins today. Rabi's on point."

"For the record," I held up a hand, wanting to contribute something worthwhile. "I updated the books for the B&T company last night. I have accomplished something solid this week."

"You've turned up quite a bit." Mrs. C came around and gave me a quick squeeze. "The clues will tumble into place and the solution will be in front of you. I've no doubt atall."

"Thanks for the vote of confidence." I needed a boost. Seeing my son's confident expression, I turned on him. "What about you? What are your plans?"

The boy puffed out his chest. "I'm helping Kevin and Rabi on the job."

"Yeah," I shot back. "I'm sure you'll be a huge help."

"Always." Rabi's serious tone counteracted my teasing tone.

"Fine," I said, "but what have you done so far?"

Marcus pointed at his chest before striking a dramatic pose. "I emptied the litter boxes and swept the hall. That which we call a cat, by any other name would smell as sweet. I've done my part."

With words of congratulations on my lips, my mind froze. Any other name. Any other name. The words reverberated in my brain, sweeping back and forth again and again like pillars of sand dancing across the dunes in a desert storm.

"Another name," I muttered, desperate to grab the pieces of the puzzle swirling in my brain. I stared at the wall for several seconds before pouncing on my son. "What did you say?"

The others stared at me with puzzled looks.

Marcus's brow furrowed. "I've done my part."

With my insides balanced on a razor's edge, I shook my head. "Before that."

The boy tensed at my sharp tone. His gaze narrowed. "That which we call a cat? It's from *Romeo and Juliet*."

"Without the cat," Kevin clarified.

"Another name." I held onto the phrase echoing in my mind, determined to find the clue hiding in the shadows. "Another name."

A bell rang in my brain last night when Mrs. C spoke of wedding feasts. I pointed at her. "A lot of women change their names when they get married."

The older woman stared back. "Aye, luv, they do."

Kevin raised both brows. "Odd tangent."

Rabi watched silently.

I froze like a deer caught in a bright light. "Holly was talking about Paige Bly. Paige *Helen* Bly. Nobody puts their middle name on a raffle ticket."

No one answered me. Possibly because I sounded crazy.

"Where's the laptop?" I grabbed it from Marcus who'd picked it up from the shelf. I threw open the top and signed on. Barely able to control my trembling fingers, I typed in a query. "The nickname for Helen is..."

My voice trailed off as I typed.

"Nellie as in Nellie Bly." Marcus watched over my shoulder. His voice rang out in triumph. He was silent as I typed another inquiry before he read from the screen. "Nellie Bly was the first, female investigative reporter. She pulled all kinds of stunts. I did a book a report on her. That wasn't her real name. Oh!"

"Yes." I pointed at him without taking my eyes off the screen. "Nellie Bly's real name was Elizabeth Jane Cochran."

"Is that the real name for the older woman, Beth Brown?" Mrs. C asked.

"Nope." I opened another screen. "One way Savannah Lester could disappear so completely after she left Langsdale at eighteen or whenever she left would be..."

I gestured to Kevin, who at one point, had a dozen names.

"She had another name. Her legal name." He answered obligingly. "She was thumbing her nose at everyone. Proving she was smarter. It's tempting in a con. It can also be deadly."

"Ahhh, she found her birth father." Mrs. C caught on. "Savannah's mother hid her from everyone, including the father she loved."

I explained my epiphany as I searched further. "Lester was Harvey's name. Sutton was her mother's alias. I never found her birth father's name. However, Paige Helen Bly leads to Nellie Bly whose birth name was Cochran. Could Savannah be so arrogant as to use an alias which points to her own birth name of Paige Cochran? If she is, she's on social media."

It took me several minutes, and I had to try multiple variations, but...

"Got her!" I threw up my hands in triumph. Victory had never felt so sweet. I pointed at the screen. "I know that face. Savannah Sutton Lester is Paige Cochran. She didn't have a middle initial listed in the yearbook. Everyone called her Savannah."

The looks of astonishment on the others was more than gratifying. I exhaled a long breath.

"No way!" Marcus's voice sounded next to my ear. He looked over my shoulder. "Survey Lady is Savannah Lester. S.L."

I stabbed my finger at the screen. "That's an older version of the face in the school yearbook. Nothing showed her middle name or initial."

"Hmmmph." Mrs. C responded with a thoughtful air. "Perhaps she'd no need of an alias until later."

"Interesting thought." A few clicks on Paige Cochran's profile brought up her work history. I felt the smile on my lips and exchanged a glance with Marcus.

The boy pointed at Savannah's employer. "She's a VP at a company coordinating train schedules in Washington state. A gray train engine is the logo."

Kevin eyed the other man. "That's a nine, ten-hour drive. Less if you hurry."

"She may have been communicating with Lily and Audrey with an old e-mail address from high school. Lily told her something that scared Savannah enough to leave work and drive to Langsdale." My euphoria vanished before a wave of cold, hard logic. "If she's using the name Paige Bly, she's been in town for days."

"Hiding." Kevin emphasized. "Under an alias."

Marcus folded his arms over his chest. "Do you think she left or is she in the morgue?"

My gaze narrowed. "She might have met Lily without anyone knowing. Frank Darrow is my only lead. I'm going to find that man if I have to chase through every corner of Langsdale, starting with his apartment."

Unless he and Audrey had already left town. I looked up in time to see Kevin and Rabi exchange looks. "I'll keep in touch. I promise."

"Marcus and I can start the job with the others." Kevin spoke first. "You're not chasing a pair of potential murderers alone."

From Rabi's determined expression, he'd reached that conclusion himself. The lean man nodded solemnly. Then his mouth quirked up. "Darrow might need protection."

16

—·—

17 Down; 5 Letters;

Clue: A winding course.

Answer: Twist.

Getting into a secure building is, unfortunately, not that difficult. The first option is to ring the buttons and claim to be delivering food until someone buzzes you in. The second choice is to follow an occupant in when they open the door. It helps if your hands are full of packages.

The two guys Rabi and I followed into Darrow's building wore shorts and sweat-soaked tee-shirts. They never noticed us. I wondered if a woman would have been more cautious.

I was preoccupied at the idea that they'd been jogging in this heat. I was also glad we'd driven in Rabi's car. His air-conditioning works better than my fifteen-year-old Buick.

The two men veered toward the mail room. I pointed Rabi toward the elevators. A moment later we walked down a deserted hall to Darrow's room.

"If he's hiding out, he won't check-in with his landlady." I explained my reasoning to Rabi or perhaps I was just thinking out loud. "I'd be long gone if I were him, but I'm not desperate, or stupid."

Darrow's apartment was at the end of a short side hall. I listened but heard no sound inside. As I raised my fist to knock, my gaze fell on the knob.

The detective shows where the door was unlocked flashed through my mind. For no reason I could explain, my hand reached for the knob. I forced my fingers to halt just shy of the metal. With a look at Rabi, I used my tee-shirt to turn the knob.

Shock ran through me when it opened. Surprised, my fingers slipped free. My whole body froze as the door swings on its hinges.

A rush of cold air brushed my hand. My jaw dropped, but I barely registered Rabi stepping in from of me.

He pushed the door using the back of his hand.

A cold blast of air flowed around his tall, lean frame to slap me in the face. I inhaled as I crowded forward. "Mr. Darrow? Frank Darrow?"

My spidey sense tingled. Alarms blared in my head. An odd smell registered when I inhaled. I touched Rabi's shoulder to stop him, not that he'd advanced far. "I have a bad feeling about this. Let me check. I have a license."

Rabi's inhale was followed by a frown. "Trouble."

I couldn't argue with his judgment. I didn't doubt his conclusion. My gut said the same thing. None of that is why I slipped past him and hurried into the apartment. I had to see for myself.

I'd all but anointed Frank Darrow as the killer. The end of my case was in sight. I could harangue him about meeting Lily and Savannah, alias Paige, behind Audrey's back. I could throw in the crazy rumors of hidden riches. He'd either break – okay, probably not, the guy was a shyster – or, more likely, I'd call Wilson and the detective could get the answers. Either way my job would be done.

But not if Darrow was dead.

The narrow corridor was akin to an ice tunnel. I rubbed the goose-bumps on my arms. The utensils on the floor of the small kitchen gave me pause. Piles of dirty dishes and soiled rags in the sink proved a single guy lived here.

Though, for the record, Kevin's apartment had always been spotless and I knew gals who evidently didn't own a broom, a dishcloth, or a vacuum and wouldn't have used them if they possessed them. The observations came and went as I reached the end of the short hall.

My body stopped inches into the main room. I wrapped my arms around myself, expecting to see my breath any minute. I'd also expected to see another body. Thankfully, there wasn't one. However, overturned end tables, a broken lamp, and scattered debris confirmed a fight had taken place. Then I noticed the congealed puddle of blood which looked like it was frozen solid.

Coupled with the sight and smell, I identified the metallic tang on my tongue as blood. "Is that enough blood to prove death?

Rabi hovered by my side. He shook his head. "Nope. Wounded."

"No forced entry." I noted him lifting his cell phone. Pushing his hand down, I pulled out my phone and dialed 9-1-1. "Evidently Audrey and Frank had a difference of opinion. But which one was wounded or killed?"

My mind whirred, putting clues with answers to see what solution fit the puzzle. I concentrated on speaking with the dispatcher, giving her the address. My next call was to Wilson.

I'll spare you the screaming, the yelling, the demands. Finally, I simply out yelled him. "Of course, I'm outside the apartment. I wouldn't con-taminate a crime scene."

Hanging up, I took a last, slow look around the room. As a gift to my boy child, I took several pictures of the blood stain, the living room, and the kitchen. After e-mailing them to myself, I deleted the photos.

Happy with my civil disobedience, I turned and scurried down the hall. "We should wait in the main hall."

Rabi, standing three feet from the door, simply watched me run by him. Then, he walked out behind me. For the record, we were waiting patiently outside the door when the uniformed officers arrived.

Moments later, Wilson strode passed without stopping. He backtracked instantly and pointed at me. "Have you told anyone about this?"

"No." I'd debated about texting the others. The news would have sent Marcus into orbit. Kevin didn't need the agitation. When Wilson's expression tightened, I held out both hands. "No texts. No calls. Either of us. Honestly."

"Don't." The detective's one word command carried a stern warning. When I gave the scout's salute, he rolled his eyes. "You were a never a scout. Don't go anywhere."

When he left this time, he didn't look back. I gave a uniform twenty bucks and a request for two cups of coffee if anyone went on a coffee run. All I got in return was a blank look. As various techs and officers came, Rabi and I waited. One with stolid patience. One of us fretted and stewed.

Go figure.

Tapping my phone against my chin, I stared at the blank wall. My mind picked through every clue and empty square in my puzzle. When epiphany hit, my whole body jerked.

"The older couple were looking for their long-lost niece. But they didn't know the names she and her mother used in Langsdale. And why did they use an alias? Ah-hah! Did *they* know about the rumors of gold?" I shook my finger at the man next to me. "Are you a betting man?"

Rabi greeted my hurried whisper with a slightly raised brow. "No."

Ignoring his disclaimer, I popped open a social media site on my phone. "I'll bet you a dime to a donut I can find Beth or Wayne Brown in Paige Cochran's social media connections. Over and under is seven minutes."

Rabi didn't react to my prattle.

I glanced hurriedly at the door. No sign on Wilson. While numbers are my friends, social media isn't. However, I can fumble my way around. Marcus could have found results quicker.

You can tell him I said that.

However, I got there eventually. I had to go back through her birth father's history which showed a picture of his little girl and her mother. That led me to Monica Sutton's family. I caught my breath at seeing the faces from the airport security tape. The yell that rose in my throat was held back by force of will, and the fear of attracting Wilson's attention.

Inside the apartment, Wilson could be heard calling what sounded like another detective asking about the arrival time of a CSI specialist.

"CSI person is busy," I assured my completely indifferent confederate. I downloaded pictures from social media. I had their real names, guessing filled in several blank squares.

"Here and here." I showed Rabi pictures of the aunt and uncle. He grunted, but otherwise showed no visible interest. I know he saw them. I held my phone in front of his face. "Angie and Phillip Indigo. One of them, probably Angie, is a sibling to Monica Sutton, Savannah's mother."

The answers in one corner of my puzzle sprang into being. I snapped my fingers. "If the gold was real and Monica knew about it, her sibling would know, too. When Savannah helped Harvey pack, she might have found the gold."

I was so involved with the past I didn't notice the uniform rookie until he stopped in front of me. The young, black guy balanced six cups on a cardboard carrier made for four.

The aroma of coffee infused new life in my veins. I shoved my phone in my purse and pushed off the wall. I grinned at him with shining eyes. "Thanks, Reynolds."

I'd noted his name when I gave him the money. Something I'd learned from watching my parents. Call people by their names, see them as individuals, not placeholders. I took a long, careful drink of the steaming hot liquid. My palm slapped the wall. I fought not to groan. "The elixir of life."

It may have been my imagination but I'm pretty sure Rabi scooted a few inches away from me at that point. Reynolds also looked at me funny as he moved away.

"This stuff goes straight to my brain." After another sip, I got back on track with Savannah's movements. "After Harvey sold the shop, Savannah became Paige Cochran. Mrs. C said the name Savannah Sutton was a fake. The girl knew and liked her birth father. She reverted to her birth name, but why hide? To forget the past or run from it?"

I put myself in her mind set. Deep in thought, I paused with the cup at my lips. "Eight years ago, she returned to help Harvey go through her mother's belongings. That's when she found the gold. She sold it. Did Harvey object?"

My mind played out the scene. "They fought and she killed him. No one saw him leave. Is Harvey still in that basement? Is that what Savannah's hiding?"

That scenario locked a lot of answers in place. But not the one that mattered. Which missing woman had been killed?

Wilson yelled, demanding to know why the specialist was late.

"I'm coming." A voice answered from the direction of the elevator. A thickset, dark-haired white man scurried around the corner with a black case in hand. "Wilson, I'm here."

The CSI specialist had arrived.

I put my head down and looked at my phone. Hopefully, he'd walk right past me. Wilson wasn't a quiet person. This was my chance to get the inside scoop on Darrow's murder. Had he died before or after last night's poker game? My money was on Darrow murdering the woman, then being killed by Audrey.

The guy hustled up the hall. My head was pointed down but I watched the man's progress. Huffing and in a hurry, his gaze flicked to his left, swept past the lean man to my right and landed... on me.

Honestly? Rabi was six foot tall. When he wants, he's one of the most intimidating people I've ever met. The CSI lead didn't register Rabi was even there. His eyes didn't hesitate until he pointed at me. "Who's she?"

I acted like I was in another dimension and didn't hear him.

A uniformed police officer stepped out of the apartment and urged him forward. "Detective Wilson has questions on the bloodstain. He's getting very impatient."

"Fine." Pulling away, the man hurried into the apartment.

I released my breath and put on a big smile. "Thanks, Reynolds."

The young guy gave me a wink and walked to the end of the hall.

"Sure, now someone notices me. That's not fair." I ranted at Rabi. "You have to teach me that."

The man's dark eyes slid my way with a skeptical look. "It's a gift."

I snickered and traced my puzzle clues. "Where was I? Oh, yeah, packing up Monica Sutton's belongings. The ripples spread from that event. But if there was gold, where did it come from?"

While my fingers did some rambling, I listened with half-an-ear to the discussion floating down the narrow hall. Wilson's impatient questions mixed with the CSI guy's surprisingly deep-toned comeback. No conclusions could be drawn since the exam hadn't begun yet.

Putting my brain on alert to follow the conversation, I dove into Savannah's history. It's amazing what you can find on social media. For the record, Angie was Monica's sister. Their ancestors came from South Africa a few generations back. They still had relatives there who visited the family several times. Delving into sensational cases from that country after so long was a bit more work, but I had years of experience.

"Oh, my word." Shock propelled the words out of my mouth. I met Rabi's gaze. "Missing Krugerrands. One hundred newly minted nineteen-sixty-seven coins disappeared from the mint over fifty years ago. Two days later, the story was retracted. An error in counting was blamed. A cover-up? I'll bet Monica Sutton's relative had the stolen gold coins. When a delusional Monica Sutton ran away with her daughter, she stole the gold as well."

Though his expression didn't change, a spark kindled in his eyes. "The ghost guarding the gold."

Even paranoid people have enemies. I'd read that in a book. Evidently, even delusional people tell the truth. Monica Sutton's tales of gold were based on fact.

"Buried treasure." I collapsed against the wall. "Marcus will never let me hear the end of this."

"Don't shush me." The tech's yowl echoed from inside the apartment. "It's like an ice-box in here. That messes with the time of the attack. My best guess is between Monday at eleven to Tuesday at two a.m. I can tell you more after the tests. That's all I'll say."

The thud of approaching footsteps and Wilson's barked commands spurred me to action. I shoved my phone in my purse and zipped it shut. Looking for something to do with my hands, I realized my coffee cup was gone.

Rabi, holding two cups, held one out to me. He must have taken it when I was deep into my search.

"Thanks." I took a drink of the still hot brew. The stuff at the station didn't measure up and that's where we were headed. I met Rabi's gaze. "Act casual."

The stoic man, who hadn't moved and had barely spoken since we'd arrive, gave me a flat stare. "I'll try."

As Wilson's footsteps sounded in the hall, I realized Savannah's aunt and uncle had a motive for murder as well. Would either of them have known enough to track down Frank's address? If not, had Audrey or Frank been stabbed? And which of them were still alive?

17

—·—

14 Across; 3 Letters;
Clue: Make a mistake.
Answer: Err.

"You've had an easier day than I did." I leaned my head on my palm. By Tuesday evening the sun had baked Langsdale to a crisp. Fortunately, Kevin and I were seated at an outside patio in the shade of a local coffee shop.

Supper had come and gone. A meeting had come and gone wherein Rabi and I relayed, with seemingly endless side comments from Marcus and Mrs. C, what we'd learned.

Sometime between then and early Tuesday morning, per CSI's best guess, someone had been stabbed in Frank Darrow's apartment. No results on the blood type so far, so the victim was unknown. Dead or alive was also an open question. No blood trail had been found outside the apartment.

The body might have been moved. Impossible for Audrey if Frank were the victim. Not impossible for Bagatti, but why would the bookie hide the body? Frank could have and likely would have disposed of Audrey's body.

Watching people come and go, I softened my comment with a smile. "You only put in eight hours of hard work while watching a twelve-year-old boy. Pffft."

Kevin raised his raspberry lemonade. "If you'd quit finding bodies, you wouldn't have your own interview chair at the police station. Marcus is jealous."

"Next time I'll let him talk to Wilson." I pushed away my empty bowl. We both knew I'd do no such thing, but it would have been interesting. "Wilson was thrilled to have pictures and IDs on Phillip and Angie Indigo."

"Did Phillip catch Savannah?" Kevin sounded like a narrator on a true crime show. "The aunt and uncle know about the gold. That gives them motive, but who has the gold? Did Frank kill the dead woman and steal the gold? Then the Indigos killed Frank."

Since my mug was empty, I growled at him and stole a sip of his lemonade. "That's your payment for taunting me. I don't even know who the dead woman is yet."

"What are you thinking?" He spoke in a soft tone.

"I'm fortifying myself." I rolled the mixture around on my tongue. I had to swallow hard to get it down my throat. "I have to update Amos."

Suddenly, the table was full of our missing members. Marcus slid into the chair opposite me. Mrs. C perched on hers. Rabi sat between them. They'd left several minutes ago to get the scoop from the patrons.

Marcus's expression was somber. "What are you going to tell Amos? You don't have any leads on Lily."

"That's what I'm going to tell him." I swirled my mug, not sure I could get another sip down.

"No trail at all, luv?" Mrs. C asked in a business-like tone.

"Nothing. No withdrawals from her bank account. Her credit cards haven't been used in over a week. Her phone is missing, and the police say it can't be tracked." I appreciated focusing on the logic of the problem. "She could have met Audrey, Savannah, or even Frank in Fresno and returned with them to Langsdale."

And been killed. I added silently. The clothes matched the victim. I took a breath. "She might have returned to Langsdale alone and hid out at Frank's place."

And murdered Savannah. I threw that into my mental pot for good measure. I wasn't sure which scenario was worse.

"Either way," I admitted. "I've come up blank on finding her. I have two longshot contacts who haven't returned my calls. A morgue in a Fresno suburb and a smalltown hospital even farther away. I sent them both Lily's photo days ago. Neither is a good bet."

Marcus's black eyes drooped. "That sucks."

"Yes, it does," I agreed. This wasn't the only time I'd found a missing person deceased. It probably wouldn't be the last, but it was the first time the client had been an acquaintance, a friend. And delivering the news never got easier. "Comes with the job."

"The important thing is..." I paused, looking for a way to break the downer mood. Reaching across the table, I put my hands over his. "Are we up to date on the reports for Crawford?"

Marcus pulled his hands away. "What's this *we* stuff? You got fleas?"

Grandpa Belden's favorite saying. Laughter rang around the table.

"You should file those reports." I admonished with a smile.

"They're done." My son shot back with a snotty attitude.

We all rose and headed for the door.

Kevin trailed behind with me. "Want me to come with you?"

I shook my head. "An audience doesn't help in this situation."

He squeezed my hand and brushed a kiss on my cheek.

I waved good-bye to the others and headed for my Buick. I'd made an excuse to drive separately, anticipating this end. I'd held onto a slim bough of hope long enough. Further delays weren't fair to Amos.

Several moments later, I walked across grass covered with the dappled shade of the trees. While the temperature still hovered in the nineties, the branches blocked the fading rays of the sun.

I hadn't called ahead, unwilling to add to the old man's tension. I'd deliberately parked at his back, so he wouldn't have to watch me approach step-by-step. I didn't know how late he stayed in the park, but when you're anticipating the worst, apartment walls have a way of closing in on you.

The chess pieces were set up on the board for a fresh game, but I had no intention of playing. My footsteps crunched on the gravel as I walked up to him.

"Hey, Tracy." Amos's soft greeting carried on the still air.

I scanned the almost deserted area. The children had gone home for supper. The tourists had drifted to livelier spots. Nattie and Tomas, long-time friends of Amos, sat on a nearby bench watching me closely.

I sat down on Amos's left side and dove in without pause. "I haven't found Lily."

Though the man didn't move, his muscles clenched as my words landed like a body blow. His tired gaze met mine with a weary expression that had seen too many deaths and buried too many loved ones.

"I searched a good portion of California and Nevada. Went up the coast to Canada. All around Fresno." I sighed, but there was no way to lighten my next words. "Detective Wilson said the facial recognition program should have a decent match by tomorrow."

"Thanks." The old man spoke in a hoarse whisper. He swallowed hard. "I know you tried. You can't change what is, babe. We got to roll with the punches."

Despite his philosophical words, his shoulders bowed, and he put his head in his hand.

Nattie and Tomas had made their way over. The woman, standing to his right, put her arms around Amos as the other man sat down and gripped his friend's arm. Tears rolled down their faces.

I met their gazes in silent sympathy. There was nothing more to say. The ring of my phone shattered the moment, though Amos didn't react. I glanced at the readout. The small hospital outside of Fresno. My last desperate reach. Unsure whether I should answer, knowing it would bury the last hope, I swiped across and said hello.

The woman on the line identified herself as Nurse Blake. "I'm sorry it took so long, Ms. Belden. I'm responding to your query regarding our coma patient, Maria Castanza. She was identified at the scene of the accident by a friend."

The shadows darkened at her words. "Okay. Thank you for calling back."

"As I said, the woman was identified at the time." The nurse rattled on with an almost annoying tone. "However, she hadn't responded to anything since coming out of the medically induced coma due to bleeding on the brain. Since we received your photo, we tried addressing her as Lily. She's made amazing progress in the past few hours."

My body felt as if someone had knifed me in the heart. The woman's voice sounded in my ear for a moment before I could regain control. I didn't dare glance at Amos or the others. False hope now would be like losing Lily again.

"Ma'am, are you certain?" I didn't dare say more without giving away the gist of the conversation. With my heart going double time in my chest, I was almost too scared to hope. "What's the prognosis?"

"She's expected to make a full recovery." The nurse assured me. "She was struck by a car Monday night. The driver didn't stop. Fortunately, a bachelorette party of nurses saw the whole thing. They called 9-1-1 and administered CPR. By the time the ambulance and police arrived a friend identified her as Maria Castanza. She had a punctured lung, several broken ribs, but the bleeding on the brain has been resolved. The prognosis is excellent."

I heard her tapping on a keyboard. "The staff, the legal department, and the administration have signed off on the new identification. Our patient is Lily Gilbert. She's responding. She keeps calling for someone named Amy? Or Amon, maybe?"

I caught my breath. Putting my hand over my mouth, I could barely breathe. My hand clasped Amos's arm. I met his wondering, fearful gaze and fought to find my voice. "Amos is who she's asking for. Her grandfather, Amos Gilbert."

The shock on Amos's face morphed to a desperate joy as his hand squeezed my arm with a fierce strength. Nattie screamed and clasped her hands to her chest before flinging her arms around Amos. Tomas slapped the other man's hands.

Now, everyone was crying for a different reason. Tears of joy. I almost couldn't breathe. I'd looked for Lily for days, but I hadn't honestly thought to find her alive. I've never been so glad to be wrong.

Nattie looked around, swinging her head from side-to-side. She drew in a breath, ready to shout the happy news to the neighborhood.

Fear jolted me to action. I pulled the phone away from my mouth and snapped my fingers at Nattie.

"No!" I whispered in a fierce tone. I shook my finger at all three of them, subduing the jubilation only slightly as they hugged each other. "Quiet!"

Turning my attention to Nurse Blake, I marshalled my thoughts. "Listen, carefully. Do not change her name in your files. Call Security and have them post someone at her door twenty-four-seven. She's a witness in an open murder investigation in Langsdale, Nevada."

"Oh." The response was faint, but her surprise was palpable.

"I'm going to give you the name and number of the homicide detective on the case." I grabbed my notebook to write down the contact information for Amos even as I told the nurse the steps the hospital needed to take. "He'll call you very soon. Has anyone called about or visited this patient?"

I had to wonder why the driver hadn't finished the job. The bridal party's quick response must have interfered with the driver's plans.

"Phone calls will be hard to trace." The nurse answered slowly. "But she's been in ICU since her arrival. Visitors would have to log in at the nurse's station and show ID."

"Thank, goodness." I muttered under my breath. "Don't upgrade her status. As far as anyone knows, she's still in a coma, unresponsive. Her only relative is Amos Gilbert. Don't let anyone else visit her."

Tomas nudged Amos's arm. "We can drive down tomorrow."

After a quick glance, Amos kept his gaze on me.

I shook my head regretfully. "Talk to Wilson first."

Amos nodded. He let out a shaky breath, hardly daring to believe. "I can wait. I'll call her."

I gave him a thumbs up and focused on the nurse. "Call security right now. Get someone on her door. No one except medical personnel in or out. Detective Wilson will contact you."

I was already moving on to my next step when Amos's hand tightened on my forearm. I met his tear-filled gaze with a smile and a lighter heart. "I'm so glad Lily's alive."

"I owe you." Amos had never spoken of payment since I'd folded Lily's case into Elena and Otis's. "Bruno down at Cascio's owes me. He said he'd cover up to ten people with all the trimmings. I owe you a lot more, but the meal is yours. I'll tell him you're going to cash in the slip."

Elation momentarily blocked out the case. Cascio's was an old-time Italian steakhouse that went back decades. I couldn't remember the last time I'd eaten there, certainly not on my own dime. I'd have to choose the right moment to play this card.

As I walked away from the happy trio behind me, my brain reverted to the unanswered question. Which of her friends had the strongest motive to kill Lily?

18

— • —

15 Across; 6 Letters;
Clue: A hidden reason to act.
Answer: Motive.

"The emergency meeting of the Belden Tanner Agency is now in session." Marcus stood in Mrs. C's living room with his arms raised to the ceiling. The cats sat at his feet watching him like a preacher at a pulpit. Though the whiteboards with crime scene photos and lists of suspects detracted from that image.

However, the victim now had a name: Savannah Lester, aka Paige Cochran. Wilson was still going through the motions, but I was convinced and this was my meeting, well Marcus's meeting.

I stared at my son and his new affectation. When Rookie sauntered up to the sofa where I sat next to Kevin, I pulled the cat onto my lap. "Rookie, your human brother is getting delusions of grandeur."

The child in question dropped his arms and aimed a smirk at me. "You get lots of stars, TR! I thought Lily was dead for sure."

"La, we all did, luv." Mrs. C who'd insisted on hosting the meeting, had been puttering around her kitchen. "Kudos to your mother for digging in the trenches."

Rabi rose and took a tray from the older woman's hands.

Kevin's admiring gaze turned serious. "Why did you keep digging?"

I'd been curious about that myself. What had driven me to search what seemed to be dead-end, pardon the pun, trails? "Something didn't fit. It nagged at me."

"What?" Marcus plopped down on one of the overstuffed chairs. Though he spoke to me, his eyes followed the tray's journey to the coffee table. His eyes grew big at the sight of six small fruit tarts and a bowl of homemade whipped cream.

"Seriously?" My mouth was already salivating, but I tried to be the voice of reason. "We've done nothing but eat this week."

Confirming the information with the nurse, taking leave of Amos, then calling Wilson and relating the news had taken a while. Then, I'd texted the gang and we decided to get together.

Marcus waved a hand at the treats. "They're full of fruit, TR."

Kevin shifted forward on the sofa. "Marcus and I can split yours if you don't want it."

"It was just an observation." I'd like to see them try to take my fruit tart.

Mrs. C set a stack of dessert plates down and put a tart on each. She looked around the circle. "Whipped cream for everyone, eh?"

"Absolutely." I set the cat on the cushion beside me and took the tart, covered with a generous helping of cream. "Sorry, cat, you're on your own."

"Why did you keep looking?" Marcus's sharp tone was accompanied by his fork tapping his plate. "The hair was like Lily's. Height and weight matched."

I mulled over the questions as I swallowed. "My brain wouldn't give up without proof the victim was Lily. All of the answers in the puzzle have to fit together. If one answer is wrong, it throws off everything else. I had to get it right."

The boy child fixed me with an eagle eye. "Why pound her face? That's mean. Was it just 'cuz of the fight?

"I think so." I forked off a bite of the tart.

My son, who'd just shoved a huge bite into his mouth, inhaled and looked ready to speak.

I nailed him with my best Mom look, daring him to talk with a mouth full of food.

He half-smiled and chewed with an abundance of motion. After he swallowed, his smile widened. "What now?"

I scraped the remnants of the tart off my plate as I considered the status of the case. "The Fresno Police Department are guarding Lily's hospital room twenty-four-seven. Her name hasn't been updated. As far as anyone knows, she's near death. But Amos, Nattie, and Tomas are driving to see her."

A bubbly relief feeling filled me at the happy ending for the Amos and Lily.

Kevin watched me closely. "Do you think the killer will go after Lily?"

"No, I don't." I'd looked at the new circumstances from several angles. I heaved a sigh. "I need the hit-and-run report. Any luck, Mrs. C?"

"I'm gutted, ducks." The woman's frown multiplied her wrinkles. "I never made it to California. I do love the American south. New Orleans is a special favorite. Grand times. Oh, the Mardi Gras I attended. I could tell you stories…"

"No doubt." I spoke quickly as her voice trailed off. I could only imagine the content of her Mardi Gras adventures. I nodded in the face of her rapturous, but unhelpful, response. "Good to know if we ever go south."

Marcus watched me with a smug expression.

"What are you grinning at?" I asked.

"We have the report." The boy child announced.

"Really?" I looked at Rabi. The man had surprised me on one of my previous cases. "A military contact?"

Rabi nodded in my direction.

Puzzled, I turned to see Kevin holding out two pieces of paper. I sputtered, trying to find the right words. "You? Who do *you* know?"

He drew himself up and pretended to be affronted. "I know lots of people. California was my main hunting ground. I was undercover, MI-6, eh?"

His perfect British accent could have come from Mrs. C.

I snickered behind my hand, along with the others. How could I have forgotten? More than one of Kevin's twelve identities had been based in California. "Who's your contact?"

He put his finger next to his nose in the universal signal of a con. Then, he laughed. "Read the report, Belden."

For a former con artist, the man was annoyingly discreet. I'd never get any information out of him. My gaze flashed over the name of the parties involved and the location before starting on the accident report.

"Now, we've got the west coast and the south covered," Marcus crowed.

A few moments later, I came back from Fresno, California to Mrs. C's quiet living room. Still putting questions with answers, I looked at the curious expressions. "Did you all read this?"

"No!" Marcus pounded the table with both hands. "He printed it off right before you came in. He wouldn't let anyone read it."

Marcus's accusation was accompanied by a fierce glare at his father, who remained completely unperturbed.

Kevin lifted one shoulder in a negligent shrug. "Belden fits the pieces together. Besides, why should we do all the work? Time for her to earn her money."

Our son's expression switched to a joyful righteousness. "Yeah! So, what happened?"

I shook the papers in my hand. "Nine o'clock at night. A dark area between streetlights. Witnesses say the injured woman, Lily, was crossing the street when a car accelerated out of nowhere and headed right for her. Lily went flying, and the car disappeared. People ran out of a nearby bar. Moments later, a woman came running up, screaming for Maria."

Mrs. C chuckled. "Cryin' and weepin' for her friend. Throws herself on the body. Long hair covers her face, eh? Grand, just grand. Always adds to the confusion."

Marcus threw back his head and laughed. "It's like you were there, Mrs. C."

"I have been, ducks." Mrs. C snorted.

"You're spot on." I assured her. "The mystery woman ID'd the victim as Maria Castanza. The EMT's originally pronounced her dead at the scene. Witnesses thought she had a purse but one wasn't recovered."

Kevin nodded with a knowing smile. "It left on the shoulder of the mystery woman."

"No doubt." I snapped the report with my finger. "The EMTs got Lily's heart going in the ambulance. She's been in ICU ever since. Wilson said the hospital got a couple of calls, but Lily wasn't expected to come out of the coma."

"The mystery woman had to be Savannah Lester. She tried to kill Lily then returned to Langsdale." I mentally returned to the scene of the crime.

"Perhaps her uncle or her aunt killed her." My gaze rose from the paper. I stared at Mrs. C's faded rugs while picturing the murder. "They knew she was in town. One of them could have forced her into the basement."

"Greed will turn many a soul down a dark path." Kevin's words sounded like a quote, but I couldn't place the source. When I raised a brow, he met my gaze. "Grandma Feilen."

"I should have known," I said. No one knew the power greed had over the hearts of people better than the matriarch of a grifting family. She was a tough old bird. As far as I knew, the woman hadn't spoken to her once favorite grandson in the ten years since he'd left the clan.

Marcus clicked his tongue. "Never get between someone and their payout."

Words of wisdom from a former street urchin.

"Savannah's murder most likely happened while searching for the gold or the gold was there and her partner killed her and left the body there." I flopped against the sofa. The accident report fell to my lap. "Who attacked who in Darrow's apartment?"

Mrs. C had picked up her knitting at some point. She clicked the silver needles together. "A falling out among thieves I reckon. He won big at that poker game and neither ever intended to share the goods, did they? One or 'tother was stabbed and left for dead. The one fled. Later, the victim woke up and fled as well."

The dramatic narration ended with a flourish.

I felt like applauding. "Not a bad scenario."

"BOLO?" Rabi's single word brought the conversation back to the heart of the case in his usual succinct style.

"Wilson put out a BOLO for the older couple as soon as I gave him their names," I confirmed. "He contacted the local authorities where they live. Airports, trains. No sign of them so far. The police are also looking for Audrey and Frank."

Marcus swept his hands through the air. He'd been adding details to the omni-present whiteboards. "If they want the gold, they're in town."

True. However, Phillip and Angie Indigo weren't my problem. "Either way, the dead woman has been identified. When Otis called to ask when he could stop paying, I told him today was the last day."

Kevin eyed me with enigmatic expression. "You're done."

Marcus's eyes grew wide. He looked at me. "No!"

"I cleared Elena and Otis and I found Lily. That's what I was hired to do." I struggled to keep my tone strong as Kevin gave me a knowing smile.

"We can't be done!" Our son looked around wildly, then his face lit up. He pointed at me. "You haven't finished your crossword puzzle, have you?"

Despite his strong tone, his expression betrayed his uncertainty.

My confident pose collapsed.

"I haven't." I buried my head in my hands. "I have unanswered questions. I have empty squares. I have to finish my puzzle, but I can't work for free. It's against the rules."

Mrs. C stared at me with a confused expression. "Who made that rule?"

Kevin chuckled as he pointed at me. "She did."

I met Marcus's gaze, who shared my misery, complete with a pouty lip.

"I'll hire you." Rabi's low tone interrupted my sorrowful moment. "I'll never sleep."

"Unless you know who killed Darrow?" I turned to his perfect, deadpan expression, knowing he wouldn't lose a wink of sleep at the unanswered questions. "I share your pain."

Kevin snapped his fingers. "I'll split the cost. We can pay you off with a road trip to San Francisco before school starts."

"Yes!" Marcus's stomped on the floor and raised a fist in the air. "Mrs. C, we're going to 'frisco."

The older woman clasped her hands to her chest. "Fisherman's Wharf. The ferry rides."

"Alcatraz." My son screamed. "We're going to the big house."

My head spun around to face my better half. "Whoa! We can't afford that."

My hubby shrugged. "We're splitting the bill and I know a place we could stay in San Francisco. Besides, what's the point of having a toehold in the lower middleclass if we can't go into debt? It's the American way."

He had a point. And my fiscal half pointed out that since we'd married, Kevin and I were only paying one rent. The B&T business, while not stellar, was steady. Not only would this give me an excuse to finish the case, I loved San Francisco. I bit my lip, meeting the expectant gazes of Marcus and Mrs. C. "Road trip."

Moments later, when the yelling died down, the older woman resumed her knitting. "Until then, what's to do on the case, eh?"

"I'll have to sleep on that." I slumped as reality slapped me in the face. What could I do that Wilson and the police couldn't? We didn't have a line on any of the suspects. "I'm still not sure the missing gold is real or if the love of money alone lit the fuse on this chain of violence."

19

——·——

9 Across; 5 Letters;
Clue: A set of principles governing activity.
Answer: Rules.

A ringing phone sounded as a translucent plane landed on a sandy beach. Frowning, I scanned the incoming waves. There shouldn't be a phone on the beach.

I jarred awake as my brain realized the ringing wasn't in my dream. Blinking the dreamworld out of my eyes, I grabbed my cell phone. Blurry numbers showed the time was four-thirty in the morning. Kevin's arm tightened as I balanced on one elbow.

"Hello?" I croaked out the word through a dry throat. I glanced over my shoulder into Kevin's gaze. The rat looked wide awake.

"Do any of your clients own a clock?" He smirked, knowing the early morning was worse for me.

I snorted as I listened for a voice over the phone. All I heard was heavy breathing. I wasn't sure if it was me or the caller. "Hello?"

A sharp, faint intake of breath sounded. "Tracy?"

I pressed the phone against my ear. Did I know this voice? "This is Tracy. Who is this?"

"He's here." Panic added a desperate note to the shaky voice. "You have to come."

"Who's there? Elena?" Fear brought my upright. "Is it the Indigos? Are you in danger? I'll call 9-1-1."

Kevin's warmth left my side. A rustle sounded behind me.

By the time I looked, he was dialing.

"No!" The command was instant and compelling.

Frowning, I put out a hand to stop Kevin from hitting send. I could only shrug at his questioning expression. "Elena. Are you in danger? I can call Detective Wilson. Who's with you?"

"No one." Her voice was so low I had to strain to hear. "You have to come. Now. Please, don't call the police. Promise me."

That's when she started crying, intermixing sobs with pleas. In the end, I surrendered. "Okay. Fine. I'll be there in five minutes. As long as you're not in danger I won't call."

Until after I arrive. Disconnecting the call, I jumped out of bed. As I reached for my clothes, I saw Kevin hang up his phone.

"Did you call 9-1-1?" My heart leapt, hoping for a yes.

"Better." Kevin promised. "Rabi's meeting us."

I breathed a sigh of relief. Shoving my feet into my shoes, I looked back with my hand on the door. "Do you think she killed Indigo?"

Dread filled me. I did *not* need another body on this case. Especially since Elena and Otis should be off the hook for the original murder. Although, a dead Phillip Indigo would wrap up the loose ends.

I opened the door and peeked into the quiet, dark living room.

"What are you doing?" Kevin's warm breath fanned my cheek.

"No sign of Marcus." I was honestly surprised. The last time a client called me at oh-dark-thirty, the boy child had been on the other side of the bedroom door before I had time to get dressed.

"Tch." Kevin reached over my head to open the door. "Go. We can ask Mrs. C to come up and sleep on the couch."

A moment later, I shut the door on the Caddy. "You think Marcus is asleep in his bed?"

Kevin rolled his eyes. "Yes, I do."

"You act like that's a given," I retorted. "Don't blame me if your son and his over-age partner beat us to the crime scene."

"You received a phone call from a hysterical client. Again." Kevin shot back. "There is no crime scene."

"So far." He spoke with more certainty than I felt. The way this case was going, I felt there was bound to be another crime scene before it was over. Thankfully, the only person who awaited us at the Miner's Mercantile was Rabi. The man stood in the shadows in the alley. His form was barely discernable except for a glint of moonlight in the darkness.

Kevin had parked on the side street. There was no sign of Rabi's car. He must have left it on the other side of the alley.

I searched every niche and shadow as we walked to the back of the store. My gaze was drawn to the stairs leading to the storeroom. There was no sign of Elena. I held out my hands in a silent question.

Rabi met us a few feet from the main basement. Using two rigid fingers, he pointed to his ear, then to the main basement in the middle of the rear wall.

I barely had time to shift my attention when Elena's dark form launched itself at me and grabbed me in a rib-cracking hold. Overcoming my shock and thudding heart, I braced myself for the impact.

"You came." Elena's fingers dug into my back as she whispered her mantra. "You came. You came."

We were evidently ignoring Kevin and Rabi standing like sentinels to either side.

When I tried to step back, she came with me. I had to grab her shoulders, set my feet, and use some umph to break her hold and push her back. "Elena, take a breath. You're safe."

She nodded, but it took a few gulping sobs for her to calm down. Finally, she used her already damp tee-shirt to wipe her tears and her runny nose.

I'm not overly fastidious, but I grimaced when I looked at the damp spot she'd left on my shirt. Marshalling my thoughts, I put my hands on Elena's shoulders. "What are you doing down here?"

She exhaled slowly. "The detective called."

I'd expected more, but her tone sounded final. So, I prompted her. "Detective Wilson? About the case?"

Elena nodded. "He told Otis he and you found information that would hopefully lead to an arrest of another person."

I'd actually found the clues, but I nodded encouragement.

Another deep breath eased the tension in the woman's frame. "I was so relieved. I decided to make a fresh start and inventory the supplies in the basement. The order has to be submitted weeks in advance to allow for shipping."

Talking about the routine calmed her down.

"I started at the front and went through the shelves one-by-one." She made a circular motion with her hand. Her eyes widened. "All the way to the back."

Her whole body locked up from one heartbeat to the next. I stepped close and put an arm around her shoulders. "You got to the far shelf without a problem?"

She nodded like an out-of-control bobblehead. "I knocked a can behind the set of shelves along the back wall. I was pulling the shelves out when I saw paint peeling along a straight line on the wall. I've never moved those shelves. I had no reason to look that close. Before Saturday,

I wouldn't have questioned it, but I've wondered since you found her why that woman was in our basement. Who's targeting us?"

I couldn't blame her. The Mercantile as the scene of the crime had gnawed at me for days.

Her hands clutched each other. "I grabbed the crowbar from the toolbox and pried the shelves away from the wall."

I waited, but she clammed up and shook her head. "Okay, I'll check it out. You stay here with - "

She grabbed the hand I raised to point at Rabi in a death grip. Pardon the pun.

Why the woman thought she'd be safer with me in a dark basement rather than with Rabi and Kevin, I couldn't fathom, but I obviously wasn't getting rid of her.

"We'll all go." Kevin's mellow voice flowed over me like warm honey, calming my nerves. He spun the flashlight he'd brought from the glove compartment. "Me first."

Actually, the main basement was well lit. The shelves in this part were stocked and dust free. As I followed Kevin, Amos's drawing superimposed itself on the room.

I touched Kevin's shoulder. "That hidden section was in the back corner, wasn't it?"

"Yep." Kevin's tone carried an enigmatic note. He slowed and stopped at the last set of shelves. He met my gaze as he faced the corner.

I hurried to his side.

Elena planted herself against the end of the shelves and closed her eyes. "I'll wait here."

Rabi stepped behind me and Kevin as my husband aimed the flashlight at the corner.

Elena's determined attack had broken a few of the middle shelves and pried them away from the wall. Some of the plaster had cracked and broken. Chunks of plaster and dust littered the floor. The crowbar was stuck in the wreckage of what might have been a hinged door, right next to the skeletal arm that now hung loose from the wall. A torn, ragged shirt displayed a few ribs.

"He's here." I muttered Elena's hysterical comment. Raising my hand, I pointed at the exposed bones. "Is that..."

"Real." Rabi answered without hesitation.

Don't ask me how he knew, but who was I to argue with an expert?

As Kevin panned the flashlight, a metallic glint bounced back at us. He held out a hand to stop us as he walked forward. Halting a couple of feet away, he aimed the light at the shiny objects.

He leaned close, studying them intently.

They could only be one thing. "Are those the gold coins?"

"Krugerrands." He straightened and looked at me. "Fake."

Shock swept through me. How could he tell so quickly and without touching them? But again, who was I to argue with an expert?

"I may have to start a whole new crossword puzzle for this," I murmured. And if I ever got my hand loose from Elena, I had to call Wilson and tell him, "We just found Harvey Lester."

***

"Why. Didn't. You. Wake. Me. Up?" Marcus smacked the kitchen table with both hands at each word.

Thankfully, I had a cup of coffee in my hand. I was trying to mainline the boost of caffeine into my body. After dealing with Wilson and waking Otis, not to mention a good portion of the neighborhood, Kevin, Rabi, and I made it home around seven o'clock.

I inhaled the steam from the dark roast coffee with my eyes barely open. "I should still be in bed. As Mrs. C would say, I'm knackered."

"You found a body without me." Marcus's outrage continued unabated. "This may be the last chance we have to find a body in a wall."

Kevin stared at the boy. "Hopefully, it *is* the last time, but Rabi took more crime scene photos than the CSI team."

The boy child glared at me. "At least someone thought of me."

"Yeah. Yeah. Yeah." I muttered.

Mrs. C poured tea from the pot into her china cup with its matching saucer. The smile on her lips matched the avid interest in her eyes. Then her expression melted into sympathy. "Tch, poor Harvey never left town. The Christmas cards were naught but a well-tailored lie. Excellent cover though."

Her tone changed to reluctant admiration.

I raised my cup in a salute to Savannah Lester's deception.

Rabi, filling his own cup, thankfully took my act as a sign to top off my coffee, too.

Smiling in gratitude, I continued. "The greeting cards signed with Harvey's name left a perfect trail. People never doubted that he'd left town and died elsewhere."

"Like Lily." Kevin gestured with his half-eaten croissant breakfast sandwich. He'd insisted on buying a dozen to calm the masses.

The maneuver hadn't worked on Marcus who glowered over his second sandwich.

"Don't think food will get you off the hook." The boy shook his stuffed croissant at me. "You didn't even take pictures."

I frowned at the child. Elena had refused to loosen her white-knuckled grip on my hand. If I hadn't had Wilson on speed-dial, he would have been the last to know. Rabi ended up calling 9-1-1. I grimaced under the weight of Marcus's accusing stare.

The boy eyed Rabi, who rewarded him with a nod. After they fist bumped, Marcus shared a smile with Kevin. "Why are you looking like that?"

Kevin flipped his fingers and send a coin rolling across the table aimed at Marcus.

My brain barely registered the burnished hue before Marcus yelped and scooped up the golden treasure.

"What is that?" Shock swept through me like an icy blast. "That's one of the fake Krugerrands. You can't do that!"

I hadn't seen him touch the coins scattered on the broken shelf.

Marcus clutched the coin tightly. His body gyrated in every direction at once and his grin would have put the Cheshire Cat to shame. "Real buried treasure!"

I was never going to get his golden hoard away from him, but still... "You can't take evidence from a crime scene."

"I *can*." Completely unrepentant, Kevin corrected me in the face of obvious evidence that he *had* taken the coin. "There were only four at the scene. They came from a ripped pocket in the shirt. One less won't affect Wilson's case."

Everything he said was true. Perhaps I felt a weird kind of ownership of the scene since it was my case. Maybe I'd been working too closely with Wilson. I glared at the love of my life. "I'm the most law-abiding person at this table."

Kevin stared at me for a moment, then he snorted, trying to bury a laugh. "Okay."

Mrs. C tittered as well. "The bar is not high in that regard, luv."

She had me there. My outrage evaporated. I watched Marcus examine his treasure with Rabi. My gaze narrowed. I faced Kevin. "How did you know the coin was fake before you picked it up?"

My hubby eyed the Krugerrand with a meditative expression. "Something about the sheen plus the small number of coins. Sometimes, you just know."

Like when I'm working on a puzzle. The solution just comes to me.

Kevin took a last bite of his breakfast, still eyeing the coin. "The gold coating is real. Weight is flawless. Imprint's perfect. Someone who worked at the mint made these."

"That's why the story was retracted. Some count on a machine was off, but no real coins were missing." I mused without taking my gaze off the fake. "How much is that worth?"

Kevin snorted. "Not worth the trouble of melting it down for the gold coating."

Marcus, who'd been listening intently, looked at us. "Monica Sutton's relatives live in South Africa. One of them must have pressed the fake coins somehow."

"There's no cache of coins inside the wall, just the four from his pocket before it fell apart. Savannah must have forgotten Harvey had them on him." Kevin spoke with amused undertones.

Light reflected off the coin Marcus had set spinning.

I imagined the thought process of someone seeing a hundred gold, glittering coins for the first time. "Who would recognize it as a fake?"

Kevin met my gaze with a knowing look. "A coin expert familiar with Krugerrands would know after an examination."

My pulse quickened. "What about a greedy fool on the internet?"

My hubby smiled and shook his head. "No way."

"What could you, well, what could an average person sell the fakes for at the time of Harvey's death?" I pressed.

"Twenty-five-hundred dollars, each." He gave the estimate with little hesitation. "Assuming they passed it off as a first nineteen-sixty-seven minting and marked it down to ensure the sale."

"A hundred coins?" Marcus's eyes widened. "That's a quarter of a million dollars!"

"Minus five." I corrected. "The electrician found one and Harvey had four in his pocket. When Savannah killed him, she must have overlooked the coins he'd taken to the bank to get assessed."

"Panic." Rabi's cool tone was an antithesis of the word.

The boy's gaze shifted to the coin in his hand. He eyed it with a speculative gaze. Then, he clasped it to his chest and gave Kevin an adoring look. "I wouldn't sell mine for anything."

"Ninety-five coins." My mind took off, following the trail of the missing coins. "Monica Sutton organized the supplies in the basement. She must have hidden the coins down there for... some deluded reason. Perhaps she knew they were fake or she was saving them for a rainy day."

Mrs. C poured herself a new cup of tea. She slowly stirred a sugar cube into the steaming liquid. "Ironic. After Monica hid the coins, she prattled to the children about the treasure."

Kevin tapped a quick rhythm on the table. "Which Savannah, weary of a lifetime of hallucinations, told Audrey, Frank, and Lily to ignore."

I took a long drink of coffee, emptying half the cup. The caffeine sizzled through my synapses. "Until Harvey sold the store. Savannah returned and went through every box in the basement. That's when she found the coins. Not in the wall, in a box in the far corner. Somehow Harvey discovered they were fake."

Mrs. C stared into her tea. "Harvey would never have taken part in selling fraudulent coins as real ones."

Her voice contained a sad certainty.

I paused in thought, conscious of her feelings. When I took a breath to continue, the ring of my cell phone skittered along my nerves.

"Wilson." Marcus pointed at me as he made his guess.

I glanced at the readout and frowned. "Hey, Holly. What's up?"

Though Marcus had kept her updated, I felt a bit guilty at not calling the younger woman.

"Tracy, you'll never believe what happened."

Holly's whisper sent tension through every muscle in my body. What is it with me and whispering women today? Swallowing a sigh, I put a hand to my head. "What is it, Holly?"

Marcus waved both arms over his head. He was half on the table and already pointing at my cell. He looked ready to wrest the phone out of my grasp.

Kevin put out a hand to stop the boy.

"I'm putting you on speaker, Holly." I tapped the button and waved the phone at my son, who climbed back in his chair. "The gang's all here."

"Hey. Hi, guys. How's it going?" Her perky tone had done a hundred-and-eighty-degree shift from the melodramatic greeting. "This is so exciting."

"Holly?" I fought to keep my tone calm. "Why did you call?"

"Someone entered Paige Bly's room." The dramatic tension was back. "About twenty minutes ago. I was tied up on a zoom call with a wedding couple in Europe. I just got away and saw the notice on my phone. After the team meeting, I put a command on the room's keypad to send me an alert if anyone entered."

I frowned. "Could it be a maid or-"

"No." Holly's tone was confident. "I told them not to enter the room for any reason and not to talk about my instructions. I threatened them with the police."

Her voice carried an underlying glee for her daring.

Who could... If Paige's killer knew about her hotel room, they might have taken the key card from her. I looked around the table and realized I was on my feet.

Marcus made a circle with his hand then pantomimed a steering wheel.

I opened my mouth, then pivoted from my planned response. I didn't have the time to argue with the boy or the others. "Holly, could the person who entered the room have left through the patio without you knowing?"

"No way," she assured me. "I rigged both readers to alert me if either door was opened. I'll know if they leave. Are the Scoobies coming?"

I could practically hear her jumping in place. "We'll be there as soon as we can. Call me if you see any movement."

20

—·—

20 Across; 6 Letters;
Clue: Furtive; Underhanded.
Answer: Sneaky.

As arranged on the ride over, we met Holly at a side entrance of the Silver Swan. As soon as she spotted the Great White Beast, the bubbly blonde put her hands over her mouth and stomped her feet. With the stilettos she wore, I'd have broken both ankles. Give her castanets and she could have been dancing.

As I walked up to her, she flung out her phone and waved it at me.

"No movement." She leaned forward and delivered the news in a stage whisper that carried over half the parking lot.

Used to her effervescence by now, I gritted my teeth and nodded. "Good to know."

A moment later, she ushered us all into a small side room. Chairs and tables were stacked against the wall.

As we formed a circle around Holly, she drew herself up ramrod straight like a soldier at attention. "No change since the door opened thirty minutes ago. There are no cameras in the area. I didn't want to risk involving the staff or tipping off our suspect."

"Good decisions." Impressed, I patted her on the back trying to hide my surprise at her actions. "How many exits are there from that room?"

Holly counted off on her fingers. "The patio door to the garden which leads to the parking lot. The hall outside the door leads to the entrance you just came in. I copied my key if you need to get in the room."

A fission of concern crept up my spine.

"However," the younger woman held up her ID card, "I locked the connecting door. No one can get in this hall except me."

Marcus nudged her arm. "Way to go, Holly!"

A murmur of congratulations swept our small circle.

Holly, basking in the praise, continued. "The other end of the hall goes to the main lobby."

"Okay." I considered the options. "By the way, did you call Detective Wilson?"

"No." Holly turned her big, blue eyes on me. "Did you?"

I didn't answer. I avoided looking at Kevin. We'd discussed the subject on the drive over. I'd laid out my reasons for not calling the man immediately. Kevin had called my list a bunch of self-serving rationalizations because I wanted to be on-scene first.

I refused to justify his accusation. However, faced with a possible confrontation, there was no other choice. "I didn't call the police. I wanted to confirm someone was in the room. However, I think you..."

Holly's smile doubled in wattage.

I pivoted to face Kevin and his know-it-all expression. "You should call Wilson. I'll wander through the garden outside of Paige Bly's room to see if there's any movement."

Marcus sucked in a breath big enough for major explosion.

I pointed at him. "You and Mrs. C can take up station in the lobby. Be on the lookout for our suspects."

The boy doubled up his fists and looked at the older woman. "We'll be on the front lines, Mrs. C."

"Oh, that's grand, that is." The older woman cooed. "I love the divans in the lobby. We can people watch, possibly order a treat to pass the time."

"Order high tea if you have the time." I was already having second thoughts about this deployment. I eyed Rabi. "Rabi can watch the door in the hall in case whoever's in the room leaves that way. Give him the key you made, just in case."

Which would ensure the suspect would never make it to the lobby.

The lean man acknowledged my plan with a knowing nod.

"Holly, you –"

The blond woman's expression turned serious. "I should meet the police at the front entrance and direct them to the room."

"Perfect." Anticipation built inside of me as the final answers came in sight. As soon as the thought formed, my back brain came to life. It nudged me, clearly annoyed, as my puzzle flashed in my mind's eye.

An unsettled feeling filled me. Something didn't add up. I'd missed a connection. The last few answers in my grid refused to fill in. Frowning, I shoved my reservations to the side.

Kevin gestured to me with his phone. "I'll back Tracy up."

"Great." Fine with me. I wouldn't win that argument anyway. "Show us the way, Holly, then everyone get in position."

A few moments later, I strolled down a winding path bordered by native plants, bushes, and trees. The blazing sun heated the back of my shirt to a smoldering inferno. The room didn't have a direct view of the path I was on. I'd tried to no avail to see inside the room but the shades were drawn.

Kevin had taken up position at the corner of the building to keep me in sight.

Wilson had not been happy to hear we were on site.

I selfishly laughed behind my hand while an unflappable Kevin updated the detective. My hubby promised we would take no action.

I didn't intend to confront anyone. I didn't expect the older couple to leave the room before the police arrived. They didn't know *we* knew about Paige Bly's alias and this room.

I couldn't figure out why Angie and Phillip Indigo came to the hotel. Holly assured me nothing had been left in the room. So, why not bolt out of town when they had the chance?

I went back to the beginning of the puzzle. While I flicked at the leaves on the overhanging branches, I replayed the interviews, then reviewed what I'd read.

Timeline. Players. Crimes. Motives.

The motive had to tie back to the coins. Fakes, and long gone. Sold after Harvey died. Savannah had lied. I stopped in place and gasped as the lower grid of my crossword puzzle reordered itself.

"*That's* where we all went wrong." Like a crossword puzzle, one wrong word would lead you astray. Only when you had the correct answer did the others fall in place. Partially hidden by a flowering bush, I heard a French door slide open. The sound came from the direction of Paige's room. Surprised, I stilled.

I hurried to the next turn for a better view. Sure enough, our quarry was bolting. I glanced over my shoulder at Kevin, then hurried forward. I couldn't afford to miss my chance.

I stopped in the middle of the paved walk. The man facing me stopped abruptly "Forget it, Frank. You're not going anywhere."

The man's whole body jerked as he stopped. His mouth tightened. The lip of the baseball cap and over-sized sunglasses hid a large portion of his face. He threw back his head and looked down his nose at me. "Get out of my way."

Peasant. He didn't say it, but his imperious manner made his attitude clear. My annoyance rose as I faced off with him. Putting my hands on my hips, I moved to the center of the sidewalk. "Your ruse is over. The police are on their way."

"What the..." His face went slack. His mouth gaped open. He pulled off the glasses and glared at me. "You're that local PI Elena and Otis hired. I have nothing to do with that murder."

"I think you do." I crossed my arms over my chest.

His expression shifted to a mocking grin. "Tell it to the cops. I have a plane to catch. Move aside."

His disdainful tone shot my outrage meter to the red zone.

I put out my arm, palm out and hit him in the chest, then danced out of his reach. I was surprised when he winced and halted. "It was you from the beginning. Savannah betrayed Lily, but you killed Savannah. All for gold coins that were sold long ago."

Though his expression betrayed nothing, his body stiffened. He pressed his hand to his left side, holding himself stiffly.

I watched him closely, remembering the blood in his apartment. Why would a man like Frank let me push him around? "You're hurt, aren't you, Frank? It's your blood on the carpet in your apartment."

His fists clenched. "Shut up."

"What's the fun in that?" I taunted him. "You must have won big at poker last night. Or was it Audrey's winnings? Two desperate people. Both needing money. What happened? You weren't willing to share?"

His body stiffened. His glare was hot enough to cut me in two.

I didn't give him time to speak. I pointed to his chest. "She got the better of you. Did she leave you for dead last night?"

"I'm done." Frank drew himself up straighter. "If the police want to question me, they can find me. This story is crazy. I'm leaving. Get out of my way."

"Or what?" Attitude, I'd learned early on, takes you a long way in a confrontation.

The guy looked surprised at my refusal.

"Nothing went like any of you thought it would once Lily found the old blueprints." Now I had his attention. "She pictured the scavenger hunt as a lark. She e-mailed the old gang to plan for the reunion."

Frank stared at me. His shoulders rose and fell as he took a deep breath.

I fisted my hands on my hips. "Amos's story about a gold coin being found set off a ripple effect. Her e-mails about hidey-holes and hidden money drew in Audrey and Savannah, though for different reasons. You heard the talk on the street about treasure. Everyone was hounding you. Audrey was already in town and in your face. You were desperate enough to believe anything."

The man gave a slight laugh. "Lily didn't talk to me about her plans."

"Of course not." I nodded in pseudo-sympathy. "But Audrey let something slip about Savannah's birth name. She told me so herself."

He opened his mouth to respond, then thought better of it and simply shook his head.

"I'll tell you what I think happened." I squared off against the man, giving myself a little more room as I did so. "You researched Savannah's maternal relatives, just like I did. And you discovered Monica really was connected to a gold mine of sorts. You e-mailed Savannah and demanded she meet you."

He'd been watching me steadily, keeping his distance rather than push past me. Suddenly, he waved his arm as if to sweep away my words. "You can't pin Savannah's death on me. You just said Lily and Audrey knew the truth. They could have met with her and fought over the gold."

His lapse had snapped the trap shut. I shook my head. "How do you know Savannah's dead?"

Confusion covered his features. "That's what everyone's talking about; the murdered woman in the Miner's Mercantile."

"How do you know the victim isn't Lily?" I asked.

"What kind of a detective are you?" he sneered. "Lily went home to San Diego."

His rough tone carried a note of absolute certainty, but I had the trump card. "Lily's been missing for days. She was last seen about the time the woman was killed. The dead woman's identity hasn't been confirmed."

At least not by the police. I'm convinced Savannah Lester is the murder victim.

Frank swayed to one side as sweat broke out on his upper lip. His expression tightened as I spoke. "I didn't hurt Lily."

"No, Savannah did." His face went slack at my words. "Savannah lured Lily to Fresno and ran her down to stop her scheme involving those hidey-holes. Then, Savannah returned to Langsdale. She questioned Elena to make sure they weren't planning to upgrade the basement room. That night she used the hidden key to let you into the storage room. That's when you killed her."

Frank raised his fists. He stepped toward me with a dark, menacing expression.

"How did you know about Savannah's room here?" I stepped back, staying out of his reach. "When you killed Savannah, you took her bag. Is that where you found her hotel key? Did Savannah tell you she left a stash in the safe?"

His eyes looked from side-to-side, perhaps looking for the police.

I was beginning to wonder where Wilson was myself. If he was so eager to be here, what was taking so long?

I pressed my advantage. "The one thing none of you realized was that Savannah couldn't let anyone poke around that basement. That's where she'd already found the gold. That's where she argued with her stepfather, and that's where she buried Harvey Lester years ago when she killed him."

As my points hit home, his eyes widened. Rather than backdown, his expression turned cold and hard. "That's what she was hiding. When I threatened to tell the cops her new name, she said she'd find the gold for me. She didn't want it. When we got inside that basement room, she laughed at me. She said the coins were long gone and a loser like me didn't deserve gold. I thought I was home free and suddenly, there was nothing. She kept laughing."

He pushed forward, hissing the words at me. "She told me to get out of her way. She was leaving. I had my switchblade in my hand. I couldn't let her go. I couldn't let her be seen in town. Audrey would know it was me."

"So you beat her beyond recognition." I braced myself and partially raised my hands to my side. Only knowing Kevin was close by kept the fear at bay.

A movement showed Rabi outside the French doors.

Frank was beyond noticing anything. "Savannah lied to all of us. She betrayed her friends."

"So did you." I pointed out.

His expression darkened as he gathered himself to attack. He didn't have time to move before Kevin waded in.

He punched Frank in the side then pushed the wincing man backward. Two uniform police officers leapt in as well. They each took one arm and wrestled the man away cursing.

Kevin eyed me with a flat start. "What happened to 'I'm not going to confront anyone'?"

Before answering, I gave my white knight a big kiss. Then, I stepped back. Speaking to both Kevin and Wilson who stood behind him with a stern expression, I pointed at the now handcuffed man. "He started it."

21

— · —

16 Across; 4 Letters;
Clue: Finished; Completed.
Answer: Over.

I settled my elbows on the cheap wooden table at the police station. Raising the chipped coffee mug, I smiled at Kevin, who sat at the head of the table to my right.

He gave me a sideways glance accompanied by a soft smile. "I'm not the person you need to butter up."

I snorted. "I'm not trying to butter anyone up."

His smile grew to a grin. "I've noticed."

I stared at the steaming cup of coffee. After being awoken at four-thirty and finding a skeleton in a wall, I was grateful for the caffeine. What I really wanted was to go home and collapse on my couch. However, I'd been outvoted.

By Marcus, Mrs. C, Holly, and most importantly, by Wilson who said the decision wasn't up for a vote. Kevin and Rabi remained neutral.

So, having given our statements, Kevin and I sat in the small breakroom. The others had scattered. Holly had been offered help by a gaggle of officers. Mrs. C invited herself to the records rooms. Marcus had dragged Rabi off to heaven knows where.

"This is so cool." Marcus's dramatic entrance startled me out of my reverie. He ran up the side of the table toward Kevin. Pulling out a chair with a screech across the floor, he clambered into it. "They fingerprinted me."

Kevin raised a brow. "Haven't they done that several times in the last few years?"

Rabi, who'd been in the doorway, stepped back and waved Holly and Mrs. C forward before entering.

Holly was wiping black ink off of her fingers with a wet wipe. "That was interesting. I've never been fingerprinted before."

Mrs. C, shuffling in her cat head slippers, smiled benignly. "I asked one of the bobbies if he'd be a dear and bring in a spot of tea."

I sipped my coffee, not surprised the older woman wouldn't address the topic of fingerprints. No doubt hers were on records somewhere. "Did Wilson say we could leave yet?"

"No." Marcus underlined his emphatic answer by smacking the table. "Not without a full explanation. When did you realize Frank Darrow was behind the whole scheme? Who did the old couple kill?"

Weary from the adrenaline crash, I realized I might as well explain now rather than later. "I didn't know Frank was at the heart of the plot until a moment before I saw him. Angie and Phillip Indigo didn't kill anyone, including Harvey."

"You sure, ducks?" A note of disappointment crept in Mrs. C's question. "The way they snuck into town doesn't sit right."

Holly sat next to Marcus with her hands folded on the table. She looked like a pupil at school. "I'd love to hear the entire solution, beginning to end."

A soft rustle at the door announced Wilson's arrival. He leaned against the door jamb. "I'd like to hear it, too."

I snorted in the face of his annoying attitude. "I'm sure you have the answers already."

"I do," he said with a total assurance. "Including confirmation that the dead woman is Savannah Lester, aka Paige Cochran. Her dental records finally arrived. But I'd like to hear your version. By the way, the local police confirmed the Indigos are home."

Marcus frowned. "Already?"

"Timing is everything." I quoted. "That's what messed me up on this whole case. I couldn't account for the Indigos being in town."

Wilson came farther into the room. "I can fill in those blanks. Frank was stupid enough to call them and ask about Monica's family history in South Africa. That set off all kinds of alarms. The family's been looking for Monica and the gold since she and her daughter disappeared with the coins twenty-five years ago."

"Ah-hah!" Marcus slapped the table. "The unknown factor."

The detective continued. "Angie and Phillip both work in IT. Tracing Frank's location from his phone number and his e-mail was easy work for the Indigos. They came thinking Savannah still lived here. Someone pointed them to the Mercantile, but they couldn't make any progress. Once word got out that a woman was murdered, they cut their losses and went home."

"I knew they weren't working together," I retorted. "Phillip Indigo was looking for Savannah. She couldn't have been the person who alerted them to the potential problem."

Kevin put out a hand. "Start at the beginning. Who found the gold coins and when?"

I took a long drink of the hot coffee to gather my thoughts. "When Harvey sold the store, Savannah returned to sort through her mother's belongings. That's when she found the coins hidden in the main basement. The only thing that makes sense is she told Harvey and offered to share."

Mrs. C frowned in thought. "Poor Harvey tried to do the right thing."

I nodded in sympathy. "He took five coins to the bank to authenticate them and learned they were fake and practically worthless. Maybe he wanted to destroy them, but Savannah felt entitled to a payoff."

"That's when they fought." Marcus clenched his fists on the table. "She killed him and stuffed him in the hidey-hole. She left town, sold the coins, and pocketed the money."

"Savannah was on easy street." Wilson took up the story. "Until Lily e-mailed the old gang about her plans to use the hidden caches for the reunion. Audrey was in town with her teeth in Frank like a terrier with a bone. She wouldn't leave. She let it slip about the gold coin the electrician found, Monica's tall tales, and Savannah's real name."

I eyed my coffee, but the cup was barely warm. I like my coffee scalding hot. "He has a gambler's soul. He was willing to bet on anything, and he was the only one desperate enough to research Monica's family history."

"And he struck gold." Marcus burst into laughter at his own wit. "What about Audrey? Did she stab Frank?"

"She admitted stabbing him when I called her." Wilson ran a hand through his straw-colored hair, looking more relaxed now that he was on firmer ground. "She won big at poker. She was willing to share, but Frank wanted it all. He had to get out of town. He pulled the same knife he used to kill Savannah, but this time Audrey got the upper hand. When she stabbed him, he fell and hit his head."

"She just left him there?" I asked, wondering if Audrey would be in trouble.

"She panicked." Wilson sounded sympathetic. "She turned down the AC, thinking he was dead. When she saw he was breathing, she grabbed the money and the knife and ran. Once she was away, she called 9-1-1 and reported an injury."

"No way." Marcus frowned at the detective. "The cops would have found him long before TR got there."

"If Audrey had given them the correct address." Wilson smirked. "She mixed up the north and south directions and she didn't answer when they called to confirm the info."

"What will happen to her?" Kevin's tone was casual, but I could see the sympathy in his eyes. "Who gets the money?"

"I talked to the DA." Wilson couldn't keep his smile hidden. "Considering Frank killed Savannah, Audrey's got a strong case for self-defense. As to the money, she won fair and square. It's hers."

"That seems almost too easy." Audrey was getting off kind of light, but perhaps she'd earned it. She'd lost her brother. "At least, she'll be able to save her company."

Mrs. C looked up from her knitting. "So, it was Savannah who decoyed Lily to Fresno and almost killed her. Then, she rushed back and took Frank to the wrong side of the basement. When they argued, Savannah lost the fight."

Holly threw up her hands. "I'm confused. Who rented the room?"

"Savannah did. She used the Paige Bly alias and planned to slip out of town after killing Frank." Wilson inserted the update. "With the room paid for, she hoped if anyone was onto her, they'd be watching the room."

"She had her bases covered as you Yanks say." Mrs. C's admiration burst forth.

"Between Savannah and Audrey's mix of lies and disguises, they had all of us looking in the wrong direction." I pointed at the two youngest people at the table. "If not for Marcus's e-mail blast and Holly ferreting out Audrey's hiding place, I wouldn't have been able to solve the case."

"No!" Holly's exclamation was followed by a loud clap as she hit the table with both hands. "You would never have quit till you finished your puzzle. No way!"

"Thanks for the vote of confidence, but everyone did their part." I paused to consider my next words. Tension built as I forced myself to take the plunge. "In appreciation... I'm springing for supper for everyone."

Gasps filled the room. Marcus's shriek over-rode all the others. He flopped against his chair with a hand over his heart. "Give me some warning! I could have had a heart attack."

I leaned forward and frowned at the boy. "Do you want me to leave you behind?"

"What about me?" Wilson strode to the table and flung his arms out. "I did my part in this case."

His claim was interrupted by a bob-white whistle. Frowning, he grabbed his phone. Wilson swiped the screen, then smiled. He turned the screen toward the rest of us. "It's a picture of Amos and Lily."

"Yay!" A sigh of relief escaped me at hearing of their happy ending.

Marcus pointed at the detective. "You can be our apprentice. I'll put you on the e-mail blast."

Wilson laughed. "Just don't tell my boss. 'Cuz I'm going to this dinner. We all know this is never happening again."

Kevin eyed me with a know-it-all expression as he clapped. "We have to invite Crawford and Roxie. They'll want to see this in person."

I tried to defend myself, but the chorus of agreement and applause drowned me out. No one needed to know that Amos and Bruno were covering the check for this. With this crowd, I probably wouldn't get away with my scheme, but I was certainly going to try!

Click here and check out Tracy Belden's first case! https://www.am azon.com/dp/B097Q7CWP2

Or take a look at the entire series: https://mybook.to/8vhMXp

GREETINGS TO EVERYONE WHO MADE IT THIS FAR!!

Part of me is surprised every time I stop and think that my books are published. It's so great to know that people are reading and enjoying them. Having spent my life reading books, I'm amazed that I've created a world full of characters who didn't exist before.

I always enjoy writing about Tracy and the gang, especially this time when they worked a case in their own neighborhood. It was fun to see characters from earlier cases – Jimbo, Crawford, and of course, Holly – drop by to offer clues or do their part to solve the case.

Watching the twists and turns of plot unravel as I write surprises me as much as the story surprises you. And, yes, I am planning to set the next book in San Francisco, just don't ask me what's going to happen.

If you enjoyed the book, please leave a review at your favorite bookseller, on Amazon, or on Goodreads. Tell your friends or your family.

Find me on Facebook: Louise Foster, Author

https://www.facebook.com/Louise-Foster-Author-1075177175081 96/?modal=admin_todo_tour

I also love to hear from readers: Louise.louisefoster@gmail.com

Thank you for giving me your time to read this book and your support by buying it. I don't take either for granted.

I hope you enjoy Tracy's next case as well,

Louise

MEET THE AUTHOR

Louise Foster is the author of the Crossword Puzzle Cozy Mystery series. She didn't pursue a writing career until well out of college. However, a lifelong love of reading and solving puzzles proved to be good training when the writing bug bit. While she enjoys reading many different types of books, from thrillers to fantasy to science fiction, mysteries have always intrigued her.

Working on jigsaw puzzles as well as crossword puzzles with her family has also been a constant part of her life. A habit that carries through to today.

In the Crossword Puzzle Mystery Series, her love of writing and solving puzzles came together. Hopefully, you'll love the quirky characters and their high-spirited adventures as much she enjoyed writing them.

In gratitude

Publishing can be a long journey. It was for me. I never would have seen my first book brought to life without the help of a number of people I've met along the way. To name only a few:

The members of RAH (Romance Authors of the Heartland) for their knowledge and patience regarding everything involving the craft of writing to the business of publishing, especially Chery Griffin who pushed me off the cliff into indie publishing and Cindy Kirk for the many hours of critiquing my stories.

Steven Novak for my wonderful covers.

Mary Therese Huffy, my editor, for her endless patience and sharp eyes when I go off track.

A special thanks to my readers!! Thank you for your support.